THE QUIET

THE QUIET

BARNABY MARTIN

MACMILLAN

First published 2025 by Macmillan
an imprint of Pan Macmillan
The Smithson, 6 Briset Street, London EC1M 5NR
EU representative: Macmillan Publishers Ireland Ltd, 1st Floor,
The Liffey Trust Centre, 117–126 Sheriff Street Upper,
Dublin 1, D01 YC43
Associated companies throughout the world
www.panmacmillan.com

ISBN 978-1-0350-5148-9 HB
ISBN 978-1-0350-5149-6 TPB

1 3 5 7 9 8 6 4 2

A CIP catalogue record for this book is available from the British Library.

Typeset in Fairfield LT Std by Palimpsest Book Production Ltd, Falkirk, Stirlingshire
Printed and bound by CPI Group (UK) Ltd, Croydon, CR0 4YY

Visit www.panmacmillan.com to read more about all our books
and to buy them. You will also find features, author interviews and
news of any author events, and you can sign up for e-newsletters
so that you're always first to hear about our new releases.

'Man with all his noble qualities, with sympathy which feels for the most debased, with benevolence which extends not only to other men but to the humblest living creature, with his god-like intellect which has penetrated into the movements and constitution of the solar system – with all these exalted powers – Man still bears in his bodily frame the indelible stamp of his lowly origin.'

Charles Darwin, *The Descent of Man, and Selection in Relation to Sex*, 1871

PROLOGUE

'Where is the child?' the man says coldly.

He takes a step into the flat.

'Are they in the bedroom?

'No, there's no one here,' I say, in a half-voice, paralysed. 'There's no one . . .'

The man strides forward, opens the bedroom door, and looks in.

'Come on, son.'

Son. He's not your son.

He goes inside and pulls Isaac out by his arm. Isaac screams.

'No, please,' I say desperately. I try to take Isaac's hand, but the man pushes me to the floor. Isaac is crying softly, reaching out with his free arm, his eyes red and small. The man stares at me.

'Under the Atavism Act of 2043, your son is being adopted.' His tone is officious, short. He's reciting a script. 'Accordingly, he will undergo genetic testing at your local centre, and if he passes, he will be taken into the care of the State. If not, he will be returned to you. Do you understand?'

'No, I don't. I don't.' My heart is cracking. 'Please don't take him. I'm . . . I'm Dr Hannah Newnham. Do you know that name?'

PART ONE

PART ONE

CHAPTER ONE

I turn over and look at Isaac. He's sleeping on his back, so soundly despite the heat and light. I don't know how he does it. Even after years of sleeping in the day and working at night, I'm still not used to it.

For the next few hours, I travel in and out of consciousness, waking each time with sweat dripping down my legs and head, letting sleep find me when it can.

I'm alone, suspended in a world of infinite stars and black sky, all compressed, just space and still water.

I open my eyes with the alarm. Isaac is already up. He's left his CD player and headphones behind, sitting in the small indent in the mattress left by his body. I fold his sheet over and re-align his pillow. They need washing; the smell is deep-rooted. I'll do it later if I can get some soap.

I hear him in the kitchen, humming to himself, and I stop at the bedroom door and listen for a while. His voice is sweet and thin, like air passing through straw, and he's singing a tune I haven't heard before. One of his own melodies. It's fragile, like the nursery rhymes I used to sing with Theo when we were young, but more angular. Isaac looks at me when I enter, but he keeps humming, holding on to the last notes of his song. I bring his drawings on the kitchen table into a rough pile, put them to one side and make him breakfast. Some of the bread isn't mouldy, and we have a small chunk of butter left over from last week.

'I'll try to get you something nice,' I sign. 'Some fresh food.'

His hum gets louder and opens up into a bright *ah* sound.

'Remember, to yourself,' I say.

'To myself,' he signs back, and he stops singing, out loud at least.

We make our way down the stairs, past graffiti, empty cans thrown into corners, a bald man I don't recognise. The turn-over in this place is rapid. I glance behind me, and notice he's wearing a UV suit, similar to those worn by the police, but he disappears around the corner before I can see if there's any writing on the back. Isaac pulls me forward and I'm hit by the acrid smell of fresh paint. Some new tags have appeared, one in bright green letters with liquid still running down the edge of a newly formed *t*. I don't know what most of the words mean – new gang names, or just kids making things up.

A column of hot air rushes up the stairwell, and with it a deep, resonating sound. Isaac breaks free of my hand and skips down the next few steps, running towards the noise. He reaches a balcony looking out over the river and starts jumping up to try to hear the sound more clearly. I catch up to him. 'Okay, headphones on'. I take his CD player out of my bag, put fresh batteries in, place the headphones around his head, and press play. He disappears into the music.

Jarvis is sitting at his desk when we reach the bottom of the stairs, his head down, writing. When he sees us, he smiles, and starts jogging towards Isaac, raising his hand when he reaches him. He looks tired. Isaac is staring at the spinning CD in his player. I gently press his shoulder, tip my head towards Jarvis, and Isaac reaches up to complete the high-five. A little ritual turning over.

'Hi, Isaac,' Jarvis says, signing the words with his speech.

'Hello, Jarvis.' I respond on Isaac's behalf. The high-five is enough for him and he begins to pull at a loose thread on his hoody.

'Busy day?'

'No more than usual.'

Jarvis turns and walks back to his desk.

'Two patrols have been past, disturbances from Flats 5 and 21 again. A gunshot just after midday. Couldn't place it. You're the first person I've spoken to since handover.'

'I saw someone new upstairs. Do you know who he is?'

'What does he look like?'

'Bald, middle-aged, that's all I caught. He had a UV suit on.'

'No, sorry. I've not been told anything yet,' he says. 'Might be official.'

Isaac looks into Jarvis's office, then back to me, as if waiting to be told what to do next.

'We'd better go,' I say to Jarvis. A look of disappointment flashes across his face.

'Sorry.'

'Don't worry,' he says. 'I understand.'

Isaac starts poking his big toe through a growing hole in his shoe. I raise his chin with my hand and take his eyes into mine.

'Okay?' I sign, and he nods back at me. I look up at Jarvis. 'Will we see you in the morning?'

'Yep,' he replies. 'The new night porter likes to leave early.'

'Okay,' I say. 'Have a good night.'

'You too.'

The Southern Bank is quiet this evening. By the river, a few homeless people sleep on benches or on the ground, a group of teenagers in hoods have taken over a skatepark, commuters walk towards the South Station. I stand still for a while, holding Isaac's hand, and look over to the northern side of the river. The setting sun brightens the edges of the dark buildings on the embankment, like they're being lit from the inside. I wait for the light to recede, but before it can Isaac nudges my side with his elbow. I look down and smile, and we move on.

We walk west, following the river, and turn off towards the station. Commuters appear from all directions. Most people are moving quickly, but a few are stationary: standing in the doorways of boarded-up shops, sitting on the steps, leaning their backs against railings and statues, all of them looking up to the sky. You can hear the Soundfield so clearly tonight. It's the humidity. The air is thick and hot, and the dull Hum from the Field is racing through it. It's easier to tune out the noise when it's just a distant drone, something that lives in a separate world, tens of kilometres above our heads, but today it's impossible to ignore. Some people have earplugs in, those who can't bear the sound, but it doesn't bother me that much. I'm used to it, and the earplugs don't stop the vibrations anyway. But I still won't look up like others, not yet. I'll just listen. Isaac has now tilted his head to the sky and has started humming along with the Field. A B-flat, I think, two octaves higher than the drone. To him, the Soundfield is beautiful. He doesn't know what the world was like before it arrived, so he doesn't fear or hate it. He loves it, and so I try to imagine what he's seeing. The first stars in the night, the dissolving sun, a shimmering field of dust and dark.

Isaac gets distracted by the preacher standing at the entrance to the South Station, and I have to pull him past her. She's half-shouting, half-singing, something about priests and trumpets, performing her lines as if she's in a play, and I can still hear her as we pass through the barriers into a world of glass and metal. This is the city I know – busy and anonymous. I look towards our spot. It's clear, but there's a police officer standing just next to it. I'll need to turn my back to him. Isaac knows what to do and runs ahead, letting go of my hand. He turns towards me when I emerge out of the crowd. I crouch down and take his CD player out of the front pocket of his hoody. Battery level looks good, the headphones are attached, the CD spinning. I can't remember what music I put in yesterday, but hopefully he'll have enough for the rest of the journey. I return the headphones to his ears, put his hood up around the cups, and push the player back into his pocket. I put my head against his head and close my eyes. I find his smell behind the days of dirt. The volume is too loud. 'A little lower,' I sign, and he reaches into his pocket to turn the wheel on the side of the player.

'Ready?' I say.

'Ready,' he signs back.

We stop at the sharp edge of a block of commuters flanked by a line of armed police officers reaching round to the left. The message from the two huge screens is read by a man today, and the novelty makes it harder to ignore. Notices about armed guards and unattended items, things we used to hear before the world collapsed, along with some new-world announcements. *The Atavism Programme is our future: your child could be a part of that future.* It's read as if it means nothing, but it means everything to me.

We filter into the crowd, joining a stream of people heading underground. Down below, the Hum of the Soundfield has gone, along with noise from the screens and tannoy, but it's louder than anywhere up top. I feel the weight of hundreds of people around me. The metallic air makes it difficult to breathe. A train arrives. It's full, but a man in a string vest tries to force himself into a carriage. The people inside start shouting and push him back onto the platform. He tries again. A hand forces him out, and he falls to the floor. He picks himself up and feels the back of his head. I see blood on his fingers. The next train is nearly empty. We find two seats, Isaac opposite me, and I have to concentrate hard to stop myself from gagging with the smell of vomit. But Isaac doesn't seem to notice. His feet are jiggling.

'Hold still,' I sign, and he nods back.

I get out my notes for today's lecture and start looking over them. Reams of thumbed paper, slightly stained by coffee. I don't really need to do this but it's comforting, and I need something to distract me from the smell. '*Verbal dyspraxia . . .*', '*. . . genome sequencing*', '*. . . the KE family*', '*. . . transcription factors*', '*. . . the language gene*'.

'Do you know what makes you *you*?' I hear Dad's voice in my head. I was five, maybe six – a decade before the Soundfield arrived.

'Well, Hannah, it's your DNA. Deoxyribose nucleic acid,' he said, drawing two interlocking helical strands on a piece of paper. 'DNA makes up our genes, and genes are the things which make us *unique*.' He smiled at me. 'The structure of DNA was discovered by two scientists called Watson and Crick. After they had found this special shape,' – he pointed at his drawing – 'they ran into a pub in Cambridge and shouted that they had "unlocked the secret of life". Science is what makes the world come *alive*, Hannah. Never forget that.'

This is the only complete memory I have of him, and I'm not even sure it's real. But that phrase – *unlocked the secret of life* – stayed with me even after he left. I would sometimes lie in bed and imagine I was like those men, making discoveries, unlocking the secrets of the world. What Dad didn't tell me was that Watson and Crick's discovery couldn't have happened without the work of another scientist, Rosalind Franklin. He must have known about Franklin, but he chose to leave her out. I don't why he did that. I would have liked the story better with her in it.

CHAPTER TWO

I let go of Isaac's hand as we travel up the escalator. He stands one step above me, stretching his arm out to reach the handrail, rhythmically tapping his fingers to his music. As we get closer to the surface, the Soundfield's Hum slowly reappears. The tunnel traps the sound, making the screws and loose metal of the escalator shake. The noise vibrates in me, like it's trying to break me, but in the lulls between the peaks, there's almost nothing of the Field. It's not silent, but it's quiet enough that I can hear the escalator, people talking, bags rustling, and I can imagine a world where the Soundfield doesn't exist.

I'm not concentrating, and trip over at the top of the escalator. I find my balance, take Isaac by the hand, and lead him out of the station, into the night and warm air. A police convoy goes past at speed – three armoured trucks, one with a dozen men sitting in two rows in the back. I drop my head to hide my face. The officers' clothes and guns are painted in amber by the streetlights, like a filter has been thrown over the scene.

We walk down a long street then turn a corner. At the end of the road, I see two men standing next to a small sentry box, one of them carrying an assault rifle. The letters *Tertiary Education Unit 14* sit on the wall of the large building behind them, lit by harsh white light. We join a short queue leading to the entrance. I drop down to Isaac's level, remove his headphones from underneath his hood and put his CD player in my bag.

'Okay?' I sign, and he nods hesitantly. We shuffle forward.

'Passes, please.' I recognise the guard's voice – he's been with us for a few weeks now. I hand over our ID cards and he scans them with a small machine in his hand. The screen reflects in his visor. I see our mirrored names, our fake names.

'Morning, Dr Williams,' he says, 'and Isaac. Go on through.'

The doors slam shut behind us as we enter the building, and I notice the smell of damp has faded since yesterday. We pass through a pair of large double doors with the words *Departments of Astrophysics, Molecular Biology and Genetics* written above, and turn right to sign in. No other lecturers have arrived yet. I record my arrival time on the screen and make my way down the corridor towards my office, letting go of Isaac's hand so he can walk ahead of me. He feels safe here; so do I. There's a row of lockers on the left, some still held closed with rusted padlocks; a glass presentation case on the other wall, now empty apart from a small silver trophy, knocked onto its side and collecting dust. The ceiling sits low in the corridor – low enough that you could reach it with a good jump – and the lights flicker erratically. I imagine this place filled with colour and light and young children. My school wasn't unlike this one. Our building was grey, and every surface felt cheap, but there was life in it. I learnt things there that changed the way I thought about the world, and so it was my home for a while. This place can feel like that sometimes.

I pass Lecture Halls One, Two and Four, and make my way down to the far end of the corridor to my office. The room opposite mine is being cleared for a new professor, but there's no one in it yet and there are no other offices beyond mine. It's a dead end. I have this area to myself, set back from the two corridors branching off to the other lecture halls.

Isaac runs to the corner of the room and jumps into the swivel chair, spinning himself around a few times. I put my bag down, take out my notes and place them on the desk. The room is falling apart – there are exposed wires hanging from the ceiling, a large crack in the window which seems to be getting bigger, and a heavy whiteboard that's coming off the wall – but I don't mind. It's mine, and Isaac's. Our broken world.

I scan the bookcase and pick out a textbook on botany and turn to the pages on plant structure and put it in front of him. He stops spinning in the chair, regains his balance, and grabs the heavy book with both hands, pulling it towards himself. He starts passing his index finger over the words and stops at a diagram of the reproductive parts of a flower.

'That's how a flower makes more of itself,' I say, moving my flattened left hand in an up-and-down motion against my right hand to show the sign for *reproduction*. Isaac repeats it back to me.

'Reproduction, that's it.'

He turns back to the book and starts humming quietly as he flips through the pages, but I don't stop him singing this time. He won't be heard all the way down here.

I leave Isaac and head to Lecture Hall Three. I think I'm teaching there first.

'Hannah, can I have a word?'

Dr Manners is walking towards me. He dresses like someone playing the part of a professor in a film – round glasses and a woollen cardigan.

'Morning, Peter. Can it wait? I'm about to teach.' He stands too close and I can smell the cigarettes on his breath.

'It won't take long. We need someone to cover David's class in the morning. He's off again. It's only one lecture – on the *FOXP2* . . .'

'No, I'm sorry. I can't.' I interrupt him. 'I've got to look after Isaac, and I'm going to see my mum after I've finished teaching. Why don't you ask Alice?'

'She's on at the same time. At any rate, she's covered more than anyone else.'

'I'm sorry. No one else can take care of Isaac.' I walk away, trying not to catch his eye.

'Hannah . . .' he says firmly.

I don't look back. I can imagine his face; I don't need to see it.

I'm halfway into the lecture hall before my mind comes back to the present. The students have already gone quiet, as they always do when a teacher enters. It's a little unnerving, although I'm just the cue, not the reason for their silence. I reach the lectern at the front and take in the room. Lecture Hall Three is a hybrid thing: two old square classrooms over two floors knocked into one, with tiered seating retrofitted onto the back. The metal structure seems to pull at the walls, like it might collapse in on itself one day.

'Good evening, everyone.' My eyes catch the camera in the far-right corner and the guard standing just beneath it. He's watching the students. I guess about twenty missing today. Still, the room feels full enough. I turn my back to the class and write three words in chalk on the board as I begin my lecture.

'We've learnt more about the neurological basis of move-ment, sight, or anything associated with the brain, by seeing what happens when something goes *wrong* than in any other context.' I put down the chalk and look at the words I've just written.

'Take the well-known example of Phineas Gage.' I turn to face the room. 'Gage was a nineteenth-century railroad foreman who had a horrific accident whilst working on the construction of a new railway in Cavendish, Vermont in September 1848. At the time of the incident, he was preparing a blasting hole, which involved boring a deep hole into a rock, placing some explosive powder and a fuse at the bottom, and then packing it with sand or clay using a tamping iron – a large metal rod that, in Gage's case, was about a metre long and three centimetres in diameter. At around half-past four in the afternoon, Gage was finishing his preparations, when he was distracted by something behind him. He turned around, and unintentionally put his head over the blasting hole. The tamping rod sparked against the rock, the explosive powder ignited, and the rod fired out towards Gage. At the time his mouth was open – he was about to speak – and so the rod passed through his mouth, into his brain, past his left eye, then out through the frontal bone, fracturing his skull. The tamping rod landed eighty feet away, taking with it a large part of Gage's frontal lobe. Astonishingly, he survived the accident and lived a relatively normal life afterwards. But something had changed in him.

'Before September 1848, Phineas Gage was a personable, intelligent and kind foreman who was respected by his colleagues. But after the accident, he became angry much more quickly. He swore, he was impatient, and was unable to make or stick to plans. We know now that the frontal lobe is responsible for things like decision making and future planning. And as we saw with Gage, damage to this part of the brain can cause radical changes in someone's personality, to the point where they become unrecognisable to the people around them. Gage was still an emotional person after the accident. But the emotions he expressed were, to his friends, *wrong*.'

I pause to sip some water and to mark out this section from the next.

'And this is where the *KE family* comes into the story. Sixteen members of the same family shared a developmental speech disorder, a condition which, similar to Gage's frontal lobe lesion, offered us rare and invaluable insights into how the brain works. Insights which led to the discovery of a hidden gene, and which laid the foundations for our work on the Soundfield today.'

I pick up the piece of chalk in front of me and turn to the blackboard, looking at the three words written in large capital letters.

THE ATAVISM LECTURES.

'Okay, let's begin.'

CHAPTER THREE

I often think about the first time I gave a lecture, before I joined the TEU, before my research ended. I stumbled through my words and didn't have them memorised, but the feeling I got from telling my story and having people listen was like nothing I'd experienced before. Fear and hope. Now, I have my scripts learnt and my pacing is honed, but I still get that feeling now, even if I am being watched. I catch myself looking at the camera three times today: once when I improvise a line, another when the guard changes over, and a final time when a student leaves without explanation. When it happens, I force myself to look back into the room, at the students' faces or their clothes. It helps, for a moment, to focus on nothing instead of everything. There's a girl in the front row with holes in the bottom of her shoes and a small tattoo on her ankle. Behind her sits a boy in an orange top, stained with something that looks like mud on its side.

On the back row on the far left is a young man wearing camouflage trousers, leaning on a leather satchel to write. Next to him is a girl, almost asleep. The students don't seem to notice the cameras or the guards, or the weapons they carry. If you grow up in a world surrounded by ice, everything feels numb.

'Thanks everyone,' I say. 'That's all for today.'

The students start making their way down the risers, which creak under their weight. I organise my notes, bringing them together into a neat pile. As I leave, I catch the eye of the girl with the tattoo on her ankle. I give a half-smile and she returns it. Her face is optimistic and beautiful, like the way a picture looks in your mind before you draw it. I used to date someone like her just after the Soundfield appeared. Mia, she was called. I had only dated boys before her, but I was trying things out. That's what you do when you think the world is ending: you become everything you haven't been before. In reality, though, the world doesn't end in a point, but a curve.

Isaac has piled several books on my desk since I left him. He's still got the botany one out, but he's now found one on human evolution, along with a few musical study scores. He's looking through an orchestral piece, something from the twenty-first century, but I can't tell the composer. I rest my chin on his head, and peer over the music. He's humming the bass line, two octaves up. A passacaglia, I think. The double basses are repeating their line, but it's transposed up a semitone each time. When the viola comes in, I hum it in time with Isaac's part, and for a few bars of music, we sing in the same register, moving in and out of each other's lines, clashing and resolving, like waves beating against rocks. We finish the phrase, and I lift my head. Isaac turns and looks up at me, smiling.

'Hungry?' I sign. He nods and I reach for my bag and get out some crackers.

'To yourself,' I sign.

'To myself,' he signs back. He grabs the desk and pulls himself forward, silently returning to the music, sprinkling crumbs onto the woodwind parts as he reads.

The rest of the night's talks go as expected – two new groups beginning the Atavism Lectures, and one second-year class finishing off a series on bipedalism. There aren't shutters on the windows – there's no one in the building during the day – so I can see the night's blackness from my office and the lecture halls. When I was at school, I used to track the passing of the day by the light – cold, and sharp in the morning, at its brightest at lunch, then warm and hazy when school was about to end. Now I can't tell what time it is. It all seems dark to me.

I've adjusted to working at night over the years, out of habit more than anything, but it still doesn't feel right. My friend at university – this was back when we called them universities, and not TEUs – used to make drawings of us working in the dark: a portrait of someone sitting alone in a lab; a group of us eating a meal in the early hours of the morning. We had just switched, ahead of most of the country, and we were still working out how we felt about it. One day, she drew a picture of a faceless woman standing outside in the light, reaching her hand out in front of her to shield her eyes from the sun. She saw me looking at it.

'It's not done yet,' she said.

'What is it?' I replied.

'I'm trying to work out what it would be like to be out in the day again,' she said. 'I don't know, it's just an idea at the moment.'

I said it was good, then went back to my room and thought about the drawing for the next few hours whilst pretending to do some reading.

I imagined a future where we tried to adapt to the environmental changes, to live in a world of rising temperatures and toxic levels of ultra-violet radiation. I thought about how we might spend years artificially selecting for melanin production, allowing only those who could survive in the light to reproduce, first in secret, then on a global scale. I heard the protests and arguments, and calls for it to stop, but after the noise died out, I imagined those who'd survived, our descendants, stepping into the sun, shielding their eyes, walking across a burnt land to a new home.

I asked her for the drawing later, but she said she'd thrown it away.

'I couldn't get it right,' she said.

*

I pack my bag as Isaac continues to read. He's got through most of his score tonight, following every part line by line, putting it all together in his mind. He looks lost when I put it back on the shelf. 'Tomorrow,' I sign, and he nods back at me. I glance at the front cover so I can remember what he's been looking at – a piece called *In Seven Days*.

We make our way to the exit to sign out and I hear voices coming from Lecture Hall Two a little way down the corridor. The room has just been converted into a temporary staff area, with a few plastic chairs around the edge, a couple of folding tables and old coffee machine at the side. I haven't got time to go in, I've got to get to Mum, but I can't help turning my head as I pass. A group are talking in heavy tones, standing in a tight circle. Alice comes out of the room, sees me and smiles apathetically. I wonder if she's covering David's lecture.

'Alice?' She turns around. 'What's happening?'

She looks back towards the exit, as if she's deciding whether or to not to abandon the conversation before it's begun.

'It's David, why he's not in today. His son, Arth, has been adopted.' She says this with little emotion and starts walking away.

'Do you know how it happened?' I say.

She turns her head back to me and looks at Isaac. She sighs, and her expression softens.

'You know how it is,' she says in a low voice, 'it comes out of nowhere. They were buying supplies, I think, David and Ellie, and Arth wandered off. They only noticed a few minutes later, but by then he'd already been taken. David spoke to one of them. They gave him some bullshit about how much their son might contribute to the Programme. Ellie couldn't stop crying. I don't know how they're going to cope . . .'

'Will he come back if he doesn't pass the tests?'

Alice touches her belly without thinking. I'd forgotten. I shouldn't have said anything. She sees me looking and pulls her hand away like a child who's been caught stealing.

'I'm sorry,' I say quickly.

'It's fine,' she replies, shaking her head gently. 'They don't know if Arth will come back. No one ever knows.'

I've only met Ellie once, when she came to collect David a few months ago. Arth was with her. He looked about the same age as Isaac. She seemed nice, and Arth was sweet.

'Thank you for telling me,' I say.

Alice gives a half-formed smile and walks off, but before she goes into her office, I see her return her hand to her belly. A deliberate thought this time, not a reflex. I feel sick imagining how she's feeling. I think they take the baby's blood before they cut the cord.

I take Isaac to one side, under the shadow of a row of tall lockers, and pull his CD player out of my bag. He takes his headphones, threads the wire under his hoody and places the cups over his ears, and I press play.

'Time to go home,' I sign.

As we retrace our steps from last evening, I can feel the buildings cooling, breathing for a moment before they're set alight by the day. The return journey is always easier, somehow. I'm sweaty and tired, and my mouth tastes metallic from talking, but I've lost the weight of the work, and have had a few more hours with my son. When we get to the South Station, the preacher has moved away from our entrance, but I can still hear her. She must be in the tunnel on the west side. Isaac lowers his headphones, looks in the direction of the sound, then back to me, with hope in his eyes.

'This evening,' I say as we head towards the river, 'I'm sure she'll be here then.'

The water is still and dark and I stop for a moment by the embankment wall. I think of David and Ellie and their son, and I make myself feel cold. I haven't actually felt cold in years, but I can think of a time when I was cold, and I can remember what it was like. I can put myself back in that feeling.

When we were young, Theo and I used to go skating on the lake when it had frozen over. It was one of the only things we did together, and I looked forward to it every year. He would help me put on my boots, tying my laces in double knots. I would hold on to his hand tightly to keep me upright. We would skate for hours at a time. But eventually, the winters were too warm for the water to freeze completely, even before the Soundfield heated everything up, and by the time I was fourteen the lake had stopped freezing altogether.

The last year we went out, when I was nine, the water looked solid, but the ice was really only thick enough to skate at the edges. I was getting good by then, so made my way out by myself, pushing away from the beach. I don't remember much of what happened next, but I remember the deep cracking sound and the cold hitting me. I remember the feeling escaping from my arms and legs. I remember trying to call out but no sound appearing. I remember the way it set my skin on fire and forced the air from my lungs.

Isaac is on his toes, trying to look out over the wall. I lift him up and put him down next to me. His feet dangle over the rocks and water below. The Soundfield's Hum comes into my mind, and I realise I've been blocking it out all night. I've learnt to do it over the years. But it feels more present here, next to the river, like it's being funnelled towards us by the water and stone. Isaac squeezes my arm.

'Are you alright?' I sign, but before he can reply, he looks up and the Hum disappears, like it's been turned off in the sky. What's left is an empty quiet. I close my eyes and hold my breath, waiting for someone to give it back to me. Musical lines like wordless voices appear from the stillness, bending outwards like a fractal pattern. The voices rise until they come together on a single note, their harmonics stacking into a column of burning sound, reaching up to the edge of the sky. It turns quickly into a new note, leaving an echo of the last pitch behind it, then slides up to a final cry. It gets louder, quickly, but then stops just as fast, falling back into the silence. After a moment, the Hum returns, and I check on Isaac. His eyes are wide open, looking at the stars. He's breathing heavily. His face is alight.

CHAPTER FOUR

Isaac catches sight of Jarvis through the glass front door of Mandalay House before I do. He runs ahead, and tries to push the door open, making a small noise with the effort. I reach him, we push together, and I smile as I make him believe he's done all the work.

Jarvis glances up from his desk.

'Morning, Hannah.'

He notes down our time of arrival in the book in front of him.

'Do you want to sign in for the day?' he says, but before I can reply, Isaac has disappeared into Jarvis's office.

'How was your night?' Jarvis says, abandoning his last question.

'It was fine,' I reply, and I try to think of anything else to say, but nothing comes to my mind. Jarvis turns his head towards his room, and I look as well. Isaac is sitting on the worn leather sofa and has started playing with a pack of cards, arranging them by colour. He'll shuffle them soon, then re-start.

'I see Isaac has settled himself in,' Jarvis says.

'He knows the routine better than me. Did you sleep okay?'

'Better than most.'

I think about what it would be like to sleep at night again, and it makes me tired.

'Are you visiting your mum this morning?' he asks. He didn't forget his first question. It was just on hold.

'Yes, if that's alright. I'll only be an hour. She doesn't need much.' I bring my bag up to the desk and start looking for ration vouchers.

'Do you want some of these, for your time?' I show him my hand, and he looks surprised. 'It's just you've done this so many times, I feel I should give you something.'

'You don't need to pay me.'

'It's not payment, it's just some food rations. I've got some spare.'

'I know that's a lie.'

I gaze at him and he smiles kindly.

'It's okay,' he says. 'I like looking after him. It's the only company I really get in the week.' He laughs, and I push the vouchers back into my bag. He's right. I need them for Mum and Isaac, and last for me. I go to check on Isaac. His CD player is low on battery, so I find two new ones and slot them in. Only four left. I'll need to get some more. I put in another disc – Scriabin piano music this time – and say goodbye, kissing Isaac on the forehead.

I head back out into the corridor. Jarvis has his head down, writing. I see my name, and Isaac's.

'Thank you for doing this, Jarvis.'

He looks up.

'It's okay,' he replies softly.

This is the only time during the week that I'm not with Isaac. I'm walking empty. It's like when you take something off that you've worn for years, a watch or a ring, and you don't just feel light, you feel out of balance. Your muscles move as if you're still holding the thing, like your mind can't accept that it's not there. Your arm is heavy with no weight on it. That's how I feel without him.

I head back to the river and turn right towards Holland Market. In the distance, I can see its extremities; an ugly, industrial building with a large tower rising from its centre. I think it was some sort of art gallery before the Field, but everything has lost its old purpose now, turned into markets, or shelters, or taken over by the government. When I arrive, I walk through an opening at the base of the vast tower and move into a cavernous, mostly empty hall. Half of it is locked in shadow. Above, three rows of heavy glass panels – some shattered, most covered in dirt – let in hazy columns of moonlight.

It's busy this morning. There are people everywhere. I begin my rounds, starting with the stalls on the right-hand side. I get some soup and canned meat for Mum, and bread, crackers and other cans for me and Isaac. Batteries have gone up in price again. I get enough for three weeks, leaving only twelve vouchers for the rest of the month. I'm thinning. I'm hungry all the time, but I have no choice.

I head out of the market and onto New Bridge, now cast in shadow by the tower behind me. Across the bridge, I turn right, following the curve of the river. After a while, Mum's block of flats comes into view, arching awkwardly above the skyline. There's a small crowd outside the front of the building. I stop. It's a group of men, all wearing the same dark coats, with the same vertical line shaved into the back of their heads. One of them batters a fist on the window of a ground-floor flat and peers inside. He says something and the men laugh raucously. I hide behind the edge of the building next to me. The man by the window picks up a stone and throws it through the glass. 'Are you in there?' he shouts through the hole. He spits on the wall of the flat as the group disperses.

When they're gone, I head to the front door and look in through the broken window. I see an old man sweeping up shards of glass. A cat is perched on the dresser next to him, stretching. The man looks at me, stops brushing, and smiles weakly.

I head inside and run upstairs to the third floor. 'Mum, it's me,' I say as I enter. No answer. I pick up a pile of leaflets and notices lying on the hallway floor. 'Mum?' I call. I hear a noise from the living room. She's here. I look at the papers in my hand. Two notices from the police and one from the porter reminding people to lock their doors during the day – ration cards are getting more expensive; people are getting desperate. I turn right into the kitchen, put the leaflets down on the table and start unpacking the food. I still need to deal with the fridge; I can smell it already.

'Has the fridge been working at all, Mum?' Still no answer. I open the door. The stench is unbearable. It's obviously not been on for days. There are some potatoes covered in a thick green layer, and two pieces of yellowing chicken. Triple rations, wasted. Why did I bring her to this place? I close the fridge, trapping the smell for now, and head down the corridor into the living room. Mum is sitting in her armchair, looking out of the window, a cup of untouched tea and a shortbread biscuit on the table next to her.

'Hi, Mum.' She turns to look at me.

'Hello, Hannah.' I can't tell if she's happy to see me.

'Why didn't you answer? Could you hear me?'

'Yes, but I'm not going to shout.'

'You know the fridge isn't working?' She doesn't answer and looks out of the window again. 'Have you told the porter? Mum?' No reply. 'It's okay,' I say. 'I'll deal with it. I've got some food for you.'

'No canned meat, Hannah. It tastes like dog food.'

'It's fine, Mum.' I go to take her tea.

'Leave that. I haven't finished.'

She must be in pain today.

'That's alright,' I say, 'I'll stay for a bit, keep you company.'

I hear something from the street. More shouting. The voice from earlier. I go to the window and look down. The men in black coats are staring out over the river. One is pissing through the railings.

'Hooligans,' Mum says. 'It's getting worse. The police don't do anything.'

'I know, Mum.'

I sit down on the hard sofa and wait for the shouting to stop. When it does, I look back at Mum and the room. Every surface is covered with things – decorative containers, vases, books, photos, a silver magnifying glass, a framed newspaper clipping from before I was born. Elias and I carried the boxes up the stairs for her, but Mum wanted to unpack them herself. I know why. I would have asked her to throw most of it away. Most of it, but not all of it. On the small table on my right is a picture of Theo and me surrounded by sharp grass and sand. I look young, three or four maybe.

'We were at the beach on the Eastern shore when I took that,' Mum says, seeing me looking at the photo. 'Miles of sand and trees. You loved it there.'

'I don't remember it being taken.'

'Theo would.' She looks away from me. 'Such a clever boy,' she says quietly, like she doesn't want me to hear. In the picture, I'm sitting on the edge of a dune, looking beyond the camera, and Theo is pulling some sharp grass out of the ground, kicking up sand. He always liked to break things, but he rarely put them back together again.

'Was Dad with us on that holiday?' I say, and she shifts in her chair, as if she's trying to turn away from me. I shouldn't have asked. 'Have you had any food today?' No answer again. 'Mum?'

'No, but I don't want any of your canned stuff.'

I wonder if she ever eats, or just throws away the things I buy her, or lets them rot in the fridge. She looks so small, like scrunched-up paper. I get up to pass the biscuit to her. She shakes her head and continues to look out of the window. It's impossible not to be reminded of Theo when I come here. Most of the wall in front of me has been given over to his things: a photo of him at his passing-out ceremony, a copy of the letter from when he was mentioned in dispatches, his first uniform sitting neatly on a small table in the corner. Mum did this all herself. I didn't even know she had half of this stuff.

Mum picks up her tea and takes a sip. She winces. It's obviously gone cold, but she won't let me make her a new one. Her sleeve falls down her arm as she drinks, exposing her naked skin where a bandage should be. I haven't seen the lesion for a while. It's much worse than I remember. The skin is black. I turn my head to look out the window. In the corner of my eye, I see Mum pull her sleeve down over the dead skin.

'I'll make us something to eat,' I say.

Before she can object, I've left the room. I put a can of beef chunks into the microwave and boil some potatoes on the hob. In the cupboard next to the stove, I find two mismatched plates and some dirty cutlery which I wash in cold water.

'Here, Mum,' I say, putting the plate on the table next to her.

'No, I'm not hungry,' she says.

'You should have something.'

I sit back on the sofa and start eating, hoping she'll follow my lead.

'How's work?' She's trying to avoid the food. I don't think she really wants to know.

'Fine, thank you. Lots of new students.'

'Oh . . . that's good.'

She picks up her fork and pokes at the pieces of meat, pushing them around the plate like a five-year-old might do. She cuts a small potato in two and brings it to her mouth.

'Isaac is okay, by the way.'

'Shame I can't talk to him,' she says, chewing.

'You can, Mum. You just don't try.'

'How is he learning anything?'

'I'm teaching him. Between my lectures. His reading's improving, and he's adding new signs most days.'

'But he's not going to school.'

'You know why he can't go to school, Mum. He has to be with me.'

'If every parent were like you, then no one would go to school.'

I don't know what to say to this. I wish she could hear him sing, or see him read music, but I don't often bring him here. I don't want him to see her when she's like this.

'When you were young, if a child had problems, there were people to deal with that,' she says. 'Why can't you find someone to help? Theo would have helped. You can't be doing this all the time. You need someone, Hannah. What about Elias?'

'Mum . . .'

'But he was so kind. He could help.'

'You know why he can't.'

'You could explain . . .'

'Please,' I say sharply. She looks away from me, frowning, then sighs.

'It's hard,' she says. 'I know it is. With everything . . .'

She looks out of the window and I look with her. The sun is beginning to rise. I think of when Elias and I left Mum after we'd moved her in. Elias hugged her goodbye and she started crying. He glanced at me and tried to gently pull away, but she wouldn't let him go. Elias closed his eyes and held her for a while. That was the last time they saw each other.

Mum squeezes her left arm.

'Has Tess been coming to see you?' I ask gently.

'Now and then.'

'She's meant to come twice a week. When was she last here?'

'I don't know. Wednesday, maybe. She did my bandage and it fell off.'

'Have you still got it?'

She waves at the table with Theo's uniform on top. The top drawer is full of sewing needles, and some old samples of curtain fabric. The bandage has been forced in, and it gets caught on something sharp as I try to take it out. It's crisp with dry blood and smells metallic.

'Do you have another one?'

'No, Tess took them. She said she'd bring more.'

'Is there anyone else who can help you if I'm not here? What about your neighbour? Joyce?'

'She's doesn't come out anymore . . . she gets migraines from the Field.'

'We could try another nurse?'

'No, stop fussing.'

I lift her sleeve, pass her hand through the hole of the bandage, and cover her upper arm, tightening it more than I think is comfortable. I don't want it to come off.

'Are you in pain?'

She nods.

'I'll bring some painkillers. Try to eat something. It'll help.' I kiss her on the forehead and for the next fifteen minutes, we eat together without a saying a word. Mum takes some bites of a few pieces of beef and eats a couple of small potatoes, but she can't manage any more than that. Instead of talking, we watch the sun begin to rise. We don't look at each other, just at this shared thing, and we sit in a comforting silence, like the stillness after heavy rain.

CHAPTER FIVE

I spend some time clearing the kitchen after we've finished eating. I put away the rest of the cans and throw the rotten food into a plastic bag. I'm nearly sick with the smell. By the time I go back into the living room, Mum is asleep, her head resting against the side of the chair. She needs to see a doctor. Maybe Tess will know someone who can help her, or I'll get her to a hospital?

I go back down the stairs, throw the rubbish into an overfull dustbin, and see the glass of the front door glowing a warm orange. The sun is almost up. I've stayed too long. I put on my UV jacket, trousers, mask and gloves and head outside. Even just a few metres from Mum's flat, sweat is already dripping down from my head into my shirt, and from my legs into my shoes. When we were young, we were told not to go out in the midday sun without protection, but now, even a few minutes of exposure to the morning sun could kill you. We've retrofitted our world to be able to live, but the light always gets in, however hard we try.

In the early days of the Soundfield, I tried to convince Mum to follow the advice given by experts and scientists, but she refused to listen. She knew better. It was just good weather, she said, it wasn't going to hurt her. I was still a child in her eyes, so she didn't want to hear me. Mum spent too much time outside during those years, not covered, not protected, and it's going to kill her. I don't know when, but it will take her life. I know there have been times when Mum has been happy since her diagnosis, I sometimes see it in her eyes when she talks about Theo or when she looks at me, but these moments are becoming rarer, like she's spent all her hope.

My walk turns into a jog, then a run. The world is empty. I'm running through the shining streets, my body completely covered apart from a thin slit for my eyes. Across the river, I see someone in the distance. An officer. I slow down, then stop. He looks at me but doesn't move. He doesn't lift his gun. I can't control my breathing. I feel dizzy from the heat. I start walking again, slowly. By the time I get back to Mandalay House, almost everything is painted in bright light, and only a few shadows cling to the ground. My top is soaked in sweat, and I can taste salt on my tongue. I open the door and rip my outer layer off, leaving only a vest and my shorts. I wipe my brow, and liquid flings off my fingers. I look back through the front door. No one's there. I turn around. With one hand, Jarvis puts his forefinger to his lips, and with the other he gives me a small towel.

'He's been sleeping for about half an hour,' he says.

I dry my forehead and arms and catch my breath. Isaac is lying on the sofa, his knees and arms tucked into his chest, a tinny sound leaking from his headphones. I take them off, pause the music – he'll want to listen to the rest tomorrow – and put both straps of my bag round my shoulders. I slide my hands under his warm body, he stirs a little, and I lift him up. He's getting heavier, but his arms still feel thin, like every bit of food is going into growing his bones and there's nothing left for his muscles. Isaac wakes up a little and puts his legs round my waist and his arms round my neck.

'Thank you,' I say to Jarvis on my way out. He smiles and gives Isaac give a sleepy high-five. The day has reset.

By the time I get Isaac to the bedroom, he's nearly asleep. I lay him down on the bed, remove his top and socks, and close the shutters, then the blinds. The room disappears into darkness and all that's left is a thin column of light that will move from my bed to Isaac's during the day. I tuck him in, pushing the sheet underneath his legs and torso, and he makes a little contented noise. He pulls his hands from the under the sheet and signs to me, sleepily, with his eyes closed.

'Sing something,' he says.

'Okay,' I whisper.

I think of something Mum used to sing to me when I was young.

'Star light, star bright,
First star I see tonight;
I wish I may, I wish I might
Have the wish I wish tonight.'

The star light is our home now.

I leave Isaac asleep, with his CD player on the floor next to him in case he wants it, and close the bedroom door behind me. I put away the new food, throw some mouldy slices of bread in the bin, wash my face with cold water and close the shutters to block out the last of the sun. I do everything to avoid going to bed, because I know I won't be able to sleep. But Isaac will want me there, so I go back into the bedroom and lie on top of my sheets, waiting for dusk.

I'm at the edge of a beach, at the edge of the sea. Theo is in the water. He's calling out for me, so I swim to him. It's cold and the salt stings my mouth. I try to call for him, but I can't. My lungs are empty.

I'm awake. The thin streak of light coming from the blinds has dimmed and is now passing over Isaac's bed. I guess it's about an hour until the sun sets. My mouth is dry. I get up, aching, and go to the kitchen. As I drink, I pull open a shutter to let the sun in, and light passes by my left shoulder. I'm safe standing here, in the shadow. I look down to the street below. On the corner is a pub next to a row of shops, some of which are still in use, some boarded up. One has the word *Electronics* written in aggressive capitals on the front, with faded sparks coming off the letter *E*. Fifty years ago, this street would have been full at this time of day. Busy, and full. Now, it's like a de Chirico painting, the ones that show cities and towns bathed in light, with sharp blue sky and shadows, and the façades of ancient buildings, but completely empty. Not empty – abandoned.

I go to close the shutter – I should try to sleep if I can – but I see something. A person, running down the street. He's dressed in black. Black trousers, a loose black top, and a black scarf around his neck, face and head. From somewhere behind him, there's a distorted shout, a voice through a megaphone. The man stops quickly. We're close to each other – he's twenty feet away, two floors down. He looks back, waits a moment, then turns his head. He's looking straight at me. How? I'm in the dark. He can't see me, can he? But his eyes are on me. They're brown. I can see them from here. A deep brown. He is seeing me, and I'm seeing him. His hand goes up to his head and he removes the thick scarf. His face is in shadow, but I can see every detail. There's a scar on his cheek, just above his lip. His expression is calm, almost subdued. I move closer to the window and stretch my hand out, pressing it against the glass. He stretches his hand out too, spreading his fingers, holding my hand across the air. The air cracks, I blink, and he's on the ground. The Soundfield roars – a deafening bass note. I slam the shutter closed and throw myself into the wall, putting my hands over my mouth to muffle my cries, biting my finger so hard it bleeds. I look at the bedroom door. Nothing. Isaac is still asleep. I sit in my sweat, breathe deeply, and close my eyes until I can't see anymore.

The alarm on my watch wakes me. I'm slumped against the kitchen wall. My head hurts. I had dreamed that I had a hole in it, that it was opening outwards, and I've made my mind ache. I push myself up using the edge of the cabinet next to me and the wood creaks under my weight. I softly open the door to the bedroom and see Isaac still sleeping, curled into the sheet. His CD player is on the floor playing to itself. I pause the music and gently squeeze his shoulder to wake him.

He makes his way to the kitchen to find something to eat, headphones on, and I tell him I'll be with him soon. I sit on Isaac's bed, rest my hands on the side of my head and pass my fingers through my hair, expecting to feel a wound, or for them to be held back by dried blood. The man's blood is stuck in me.

I need to get going. Isaac needs to eat.

'We have some fresh bread today,' I sign when I've caught his gaze. I get the new loaf out, along with a small knife and a small plate, and I force myself to feel normal. Isaac has a piece of bread with a little butter, rocking his head to his music as he eats, removing the crusts to save for last. I envy how content he is. He was born into a world of nothing, so nothing is everything to him. Bread and some butter. I need to feel like that; I need to multiply the small sparks of hope until they become a galaxy.

CHAPTER SIX

'Come on,' I say as I take Isaac by the hand. He's still bobbing his head to the music as we make our way down the stairs, but he stops when he notices Jarvis isn't at his desk. He runs ahead. 'Wait for me there,' I say. The door to Jarvis's office is closed. 'I'm sure we'll see him later,' I say when I catch up.

'Hannah? Is that you?'

Jarvis's voice is muffled.

'Yes,' I call out. 'Are you okay?'

'I could use some help. Can you come in?'

I tell Isaac to stay in the corridor, and he jumps into Jarvis's big chair, sinking in and spinning himself round a couple of times. I open the door and see Jarvis standing with his back to me in the corner of the room, struggling to remove an oversized UV suit, like the outfits they give to officials or police officers.

'Can you help me take this thing off?'

I step into the room, leaving the door open behind me. I've never seen one of these suits up close, always from a distance from my window when I can't sleep. They look uncomfortable and heavy, and I feel hot thinking what it must be like to wear one in direct sunlight. The police walk in them as if through mud, pulling their bodies through thick air and sweat. Jarvis turns around and I see his front. It's covered in blood.

'Jarvis. What happened?'

'Clean-up on the street outside. Someone got shot. They took the body, but they made me clear it up. I can't get these fucking things off. Can you help?'

I grab his forearm with my right hand and use my other hand to pull a glove off. Blood goes onto my skin.

'Thanks. I've got it from here.' Jarvis pulls the second glove off, then his hood. His hair is matted and wet. I go to wash my hands in the small sink in the corner. They're shaking.

'Who was he?' I look in the mirror in front of me, hoping to see Jarvis's reaction.

'Babylon, I think. There's a new Representative in the building. He made me put on the suit and clear it up. I didn't even know we had one.'

'Is he the bald man?'

'Yeah, he lives a few doors down from you. I think they're placing them in flats now.'

'Why?' I ask, but I know the answer. I know why they want

to put them where people live. It's where we feel safest. Parents will lower their guard, and they'll let their children sing. But it's not safe. I'm not safe. I leave the room before Jarvis can reply.

'Hannah?' he calls out, but I don't turn back. Isaac is still on the chair.

'Stay there for a bit,' I say to him. I open the front door, and head out to the street with the old pub on the corner. The sun has nearly set, but the last few beams of light are still scattering through the air. I can see the place where the man was killed. Jarvis has cleaned up all he could, but the dark blood has stained the tarmac, leaving marks where it thickened around his head and then ran into the gutter a few feet away. I drop down, put out my hand, stretch my fingers and lay them flat on the ground. I don't know what I expect to feel, but I'm left cold. I get up, breathing deeply, and notice a piece of fabric blowing in the wind in the alleyway a few feet away, dancing in the warm air. I step over the blood-marked spot on the road and walk towards it. It's the man's scarf. I look around, open my bag and force the scarf to the bottom, under Isaac's CDs, the packets of food, my crumpled papers.

Isaac looks a little annoyed when I return, scrunching his face into a childish scowl. I lift him off the big chair and call goodbye to Jarvis, and we make our way out past the old pub to the river, Isaac's small legs tripping over themselves as we walk. We're late. I want to move faster but

Isaac holds me back, and I settle into his pace. I don't know if what I did was wrong, taking something that's not mine, but no one's coming for him, or to finish cleaning the place where he died, so no one's coming for his scarf. I'll keep it safe.

We turn left down a long set of steps, and into a small tunnel that takes us to the station. Even at the top of the steps, I can hear her. The preacher woman has set herself up in an empty doorway in the tunnel, pushing her back against a service door to keep out of the stream of commuters. Her voice is loud out in the open, but in here, it sounds like she's shouting, like every note of her voice is being amplified by the tiles and asphalt. Isaac hears her through his music and tries to spot her through the legs of the people in front of him. I tighten the straps of my bag, and lift him up, taking his weight under my right arm, grabbing onto the loop of my bag with my hand to keep him stable. As we get closer to the woman, Isaac lowers his headphones. Everyone else is covering their ears, trying to block her out, but Isaac wants to hear everything. He doesn't care, or even know what she's talking about, he just wants to feel her voice. As we pass by her, I slow down a little and Isaac reaches out his hand, stretching out his fingers like I did a few hours ago to the man on the street. I'm being pushed from behind, so I speed up. When we're out of the tunnel, I put Isaac down, he replaces his headphones, and I look into his eyes.

'Why did you put your hand out like that?' I sign.

'To say hello,' he signs back.

'Did you see me at the window?' I ask, but he stares at me blankly.

In the station, we head straight to our platform. It feels hotter than normal. The air smells like liquid metal. The train is heaving, so Isaac stands under my arm, leaning on me, listening to his music. A few people get off, then more at the next stop, and Isaac takes a seat. After a moment, he looks down at his belly, takes the CD player out of his front pocket and starts fiddling with the on-off switch. I drop down and see a flashing symbol of an empty battery on the small display. I didn't check. I open my bag and look for the batteries, but everything has moved around. I start pulling things out – my notes, packets of food, a bottle of water – and see the small paper bag with the batteries in, nestled in the black scarf. I wonder what he was doing, or what he had done, the man on the street. He knew what was going to happen to him, and he had accepted it. I could see it in his eyes. But he didn't look like someone who deserved to be killed. I've watched the news reports about Babylon – violent protests, arson, explosives, always against the government – but he didn't look like the type of person who could do anything like that, who could hurt people for no reason. I'm not even sure you can tell that by looking in a person's eyes. But they weren't angry. They were sad. And I can't get them out of my head.

I come back to the train. Isaac is singing. People are

staring, turning their backs to him. I grab the player out of his hand, causing the headphones to fling off his neck onto the lap of the person next to him, who pushes them carelessly onto the floor, gets up, and moves away from us. I open the small housing on the back of the player and lever the old batteries out. They fall to the ground and roll away. Isaac is still singing as I clumsily slot in the new ones. I'm being watched. I pick up the headphones and put them back round his ears. I toggle the power switch, waiting for a sign of life, and press play once the display re-animates. The CD starts spinning again, and I return the player into Isaac's front pocket.

'To yourself,' I sign. He's looking up past my left shoulder. I turn his head towards me with both of my hands and repeat the sign.

'To myself,' he signs back, and he stops singing.

There's a man in dark clothes in my peripheral version whose gaze seems to be fixed in our direction. I turn my head, and he's looking at Isaac. I get up, pushing my hands against my knees, trying to move slowly, trying not to react. He looks at me, back to Isaac, then away. He's wearing some sort of UV suit, but its more tight-fitting and lighter than the one Jarvis was wearing earlier, like he wears it more often, like it's been altered for him. He's young, maybe in his mid-twenties, and he doesn't look like the other government officials, but sometimes you can't tell. They're sometimes undercover. Children have been taken from trains in the past. The man reminds me of Theo.

I look back at Isaac. He's signing *hello* with his right hand in the way that makes it look like he's saluting. But it's not for me, it's for someone behind me. I turn my head. It's a girl. I recognise her. She's in my class – the one with the tattoo on her leg. She's shaved the hair down to the skin on one side of her head since yesterday. She's standing close to me.

'Hello. How are you?' she signs to Isaac. He thinks for a little while, rocks backwards and forwards a few times, pulls his hands out from under his legs and signs *hot*. The girl laughs.

'Sorry,' she says, 'my dad, he was deaf.'

'It's alright.' How does she know he can't speak? He's always been in my office during lectures.

'You're in one of my new first-year classes?' I say.

'Yeah.'

I nod. I catch myself looking at the man in the UV suit.

'I've always loved genetics and human studies,' she says, 'so I was one of the first to sign up. I love your class. Where did you study?'

I let the question sit and give an opaque answer.

'Here in the city, at UCS.'

She probably doesn't know what UCS stands for, but she doesn't ask. She's either eighteen or nineteen, born after the Soundfield, and to her, the world before must seem chaotic, built out of complicated acronyms, private institutions, and choice. Too much choice.

'What else have you signed up for?' I ask.

'Molecular biology with Dr Rayner, epidemiology with Jackson, biochemistry with, I can't remember who gives those . . .'

'Dr Manners.'

' . . . and then the Atavism lectures, of course.'

It shouldn't be called that. It's genetic anthropology. She looks at Isaac, sensing my discomfort.

'How old is your son?' she says.

'Six.'

'Has he always had difficulty with hearing?'

'No, he's not deaf. He just can't speak. How did you know he could sign?'

She looks confused, waits for a moment, then replies. 'I saw you with him, I think.' She drops down to Isaac and sees the cable running from the player in his front pocket to his hood.

'What are you listening to?' she signs.

Isaac stares at me, eyes wide.

'It's alright, you can answer,' I sign.

He looks back towards the girl, smiles and spells out B-A-C-H with his hands.

She doesn't seem to recognise the name and gets up.

'He's a composer from hundreds of years ago,' I sign to her.

She smiles brightly at Isaac and gives the sign for *cool*. I don't think he's ever seen this sign in this context.

'It means she likes the music,' I sign, and he puts his hands back under his legs.

She gets out a thin book from the cloth bag hanging over

her shoulder and starts to read. I look back down the carriage for the man with the tailored UV suit, but he's gone. At the next stop, the girl takes an empty seat a few feet away from us and continues reading. I glance at her occasionally, but she doesn't look up. When did she see us?

CHAPTER SEVEN

We've lost the girl by the time we get to ground level. Isaac and I are always slow-moving, as a pair. We make our way along our set path, lit by the streetlights, and as we turn the corner to the TEU I can smell diesel. It must have been a military or police truck. I think of the time Theo tried to teach me to drive, when I was fifteen, a year before the Soundfield appeared.

'What do I do?' I said, sitting in the driving seat of Mum's old SUV.

'Just go,' he said. 'It's easy.'

I stalled twice, he laughed, I shouted at him, and he told me something about 'feeling for the biting point', whatever that meant. I tried again, stalled again, got out of the car, and told him to take me home. I never learnt to drive after that, but I never needed to.

Isaac and I join the back of a line leading up to the entrance to the TEU, and wait to be scanned in. Isaac tugs on one of the loose straps hanging off my backpack with his free hand, but we haven't got time to stop.

'Passes, please.'

I don't recognise the voice. I hand our ID cards to the guard and he scans them.

'You are cleared, but the boy isn't.'

'My son has permission to enter with me. He won't appear on your scan because he isn't over eighteen.'

'I'm sorry, I can't let him in if he hasn't been cleared.'

'Your scan' – I point at the machine in his hand – 'only checks the passes of eligible students and teachers. As he is neither of those, he doesn't appear. I have a letter from Dr Manners.'

This hasn't happened in months. I'll need to talk to Peter again. I open my bag and search for the letter. It's buried somewhere in between my notes.

'Can you remove his hood for me?'

I glance back. The guard is looking at Isaac, whose face is hidden in shadow.

'Son, please remove your hood,' he says coldly.

'It's fine, I'll do it,' I say.

I bring Isaac over to me, shielding his body from the guards. I remove his headphones, pushing them back behind his neck, into the gap between his top and T-shirt, and I lower his hood. I continue looking through my bag. I try to calm my breath.

'Here.' I get up and hand the letter over, still in its envelope. The guard looks at Isaac, then down to the paper in his hand.

He reads carefully and, turning his back to us, mumbles something into his radio. He waits, holding the speaker to his ear. After a beat, a static voice comes back to him but I can't hear the words. The guard looks at me and nods.

'You can enter,' he says. He hands the letter back to me. 'Have this ready next time.'

We pass through the barrier. I can feel my pulse in my throat.

I sign in quickly and walk down the corridor as fast as Isaac will let me. Dr Manners leans out of his office, causing us to stop abruptly.

'Your class is waiting.'

'I know. I was held up by the guards. Can you take him to my room?'

I look at Isaac, who's staring up at some old gum stuck to a tile on the ceiling.

'Please?' I say.

Peter comes out of his office, hands in his pockets, tie loose.

'Fine,' he says, sighing.

I get a half-eaten packet of crackers out of my bag and give them to Isaac, then sign for him to go to my room. He runs on ahead, and Peter follows behind.

'Lecture Hall Three,' Peter says, without turning to look at me. 'Oh, and I need to speak to you afterwards.'

'What about?'

He ignores me and continues walking towards Isaac, who's now arrived at my door and is staring expectantly at me.

'You'll be okay,' I sign. 'I won't be long.'

I put my bag back over my shoulder and head to the lecture hall. When I enter, the chatter dies down a little – like a thick blanket has been placed over the room – but it doesn't go silent.

'Sorry I'm late,' I say, too quietly for most people to hear. I catch the eye of the girl from the train, the girl with the tattoo, sitting on the right-hand side of the front frow. She smiles at me and I can't help but smile back. It's like a reflex. When someone hits your knee, you kick. There are no guards in here today; I wonder why. I take out my now crumpled notes and try to arrange them in a way that makes sense.

'Okay. Let's continue where we left things.'

Some students keep on talking.

'At the end of yesterday's lecture, if you remember . . .' I find where we had reached, ' . . . yes, we had just started talking about the *Forkhead Box P2* gene, or *FOXP2* for short, and its relationship to the genetic language disorder exhibited by sixteen members of the KE family in the 1980s and 1990s.' I pause and slow down. 'It really was a remarkable find, a gold mine for geneticists. Sixteen members of the same family, all exhibiting symptoms of developmental verbal dyspraxia, impaired processing, and low verbal and performance IQ. Soon after the family were discovered, a genome analysis of these sixteen members found a linkage on the long arm of chromosome 7, in the part that we now call the *FOXP2* gene. *FOX* genes make transcription factors, proteins that alter the behaviour of other genes by binding to specific places on DNA – some activate the expression of genes, some repress them. The FOXP2 protein does both, and acts all over the body, from the lungs to the heart to the digestive system and, of course, the brain.'

Everyone's quiet now and taking notes.

'Every member of the KE family that had developmental issues all shared the same mutation in exon 14 of the *FOXP2* gene. A G-to-A substitution that caused a histidine to be swapped for an arginine in the primary sequence of the FOXP2 protein.'

I write these conversions on the board.

'A simple mutation that caused one amino acid to be replaced for another, but that had disastrous consequences for sixteen members of this family. It might seem like a cruel thing, that we can often only find out about the function of a gene by studying people with sometimes life-altering disorders, but it really is the fastest way to understand the complex genetic machinery that controls our lives. Before a find like this, it's like you're wandering in the dark, looking for a match, and then, all of a sudden, someone turns on the light and you can see *everything*.'

I'm playing things up today. Maybe it's for the girl?

'And once we knew where to look, it was then just a matter of time before we found out the true nature of this new gene and its associated protein. The FOXP2 protein is highly conserved amongst humans. In a study of forty-four partici-pants from every major continent, no amino acid polymorphism was found in the protein, and in another study with ninety-one participants, only one case of an amino acid replacement was discovered – an inconsequential insertion of two glutamine codons in the second polyglutamic stretch.' I can see I'm losing them, and I trip over my words a little. ' . . . in short, the FOXP2 protein does not vary amongst humans, and neither does its gene.'

I look down at my notes and find my place. I know what's coming next, I didn't need to check.

'And they've also barely changed throughout the course of evolution.' I look up. 'In the time between the common ancestor of humans and mice and the common ancestor of humans and chimps – a period of around one hundred and thirty million years – only one amino acid change occurred in the FOXP2 protein, within the orangutan lineage. Over one hundred million years of changing landscapes and climates, natural disasters, habitat destruction, new worlds being formed and destroyed, and only a *single* change in the protein structure. And then in about seven million years, an evolutionary blink of an eye,' – this gets a laugh – '*two* amino changes occurred in the FOXP2 protein within the human lineage, caused by mutations in exon 7 of the *FOXP2* gene.'

This still electrifies me as much as it did when I was twenty-one; I can't hide it, even in this run-down hall, even in front of these people who I'll never know, or who will never know me. The girl with the tattoo is smiling widely. They're all listening to me. They all want to know.

'And what happened during this time?'

I pause and hold the room.

'We developed language. The *FOXP2* gene is a language gene.'

CHAPTER EIGHT

At the end of the lecture, I leave quickly and return to Isaac. I can still feel the adrenaline in my veins. I used to think that the science was enough by itself, but I know now that it has to be shared to stay alive, like music. When I get back to my office, Isaac has rooted himself at the desk and has found the score he was looking at yesterday. I go in, put my bag down, and kiss him on the forehead. I can't pretend this is just for him; it's for me too, to keep me alive.

'I'm just going to see Peter,' I say. 'I'll be back in a few minutes.'

I head down the corridor to Dr Manners' office and notice someone in there with him. I lean back against the wall and wait. The sounds of the building come alive in the stillness: the Hum of the Soundfield through the cracks in the windows, the dull noise of students moving in the rooms and halls above and around me, a lecture being given in the room next to

Peter's office. I can hear every word through the door. It's
Alice, delivering one of the Atavism lectures. She's a few
lessons ahead of me.

'There are many theories about how music and language evolved
in humans. Some researchers approach each communication
system separately, believing they evolved independently, but many
believe that they both arose from a single system of communication, one that preceded both music and language, a musical
protolanguage. Our hominin ancestors experienced seismic
changes in the way they lived, hunted, and reproduced. Their
landscape turned from dense forest to open plains and savannahs,
their communities grew in number and complexity, their diet
changed from a plant-based one to one based around meat . . .'

I realise I'm mouthing the words with her.

' . . . a need for more complex communication,' Alice
continues. 'Facial expressions, gestures, body language and vocalisations would have been used to signal the presence of predators,
prey, and food for foraging, but also to pass information from
one individual to another across open stretches of land, and,
most importantly for our discussion, to express emotions: happiness, anger, love . . .'

We inferred these things from beautifully preserved fossils,
near-complete human skeletons from millions of years ago.
Lucy, the Turkana Boy, the Taung child.

' . . . found in our ape relatives, and even in dogs, but the
variety and intricacy of emotions expressed by humans is unlike
any other species on Earth and is a consequence of the sprawling
and multi-layered societal structures of our ancestors . . .'

Peter's door opens and a man comes out. I smile at him and he nods back.

'Hannah, come in,' Peter calls out.

He's sitting behind a wide desk. It has green felt on top and is scratched on every surface. A relic from another century.

He looks up and forms a weak smile.

'Please, sit.'

He points to the armchair facing his desk and goes back to his writing. The faux leather on the chair is peeling off. It feels warm. I can still hear Alice through the thin wall. She's near the end of the lecture.

' . . . *this protolanguage, this system that was a potential precursor to both music and language, could have been how early humans communicated, a language of holistic utterances that relied upon variations in pitch, amplitude and rhythm to express sometimes highly complex thoughts.* Hunt deer with me, share food with me, meet me at the river . . . '

I start before Peter can.

'I'm sorry I was late,' I say. 'Your guards held me up again. They wouldn't let Isaac in . . . '

'No, that's not what I wanted to talk to you about.'

He stops writing, carefully putting the lid on his pen, and rests his arms on the desk. He locks his hands together and looks down for a moment, holding the silence. When he speaks, it's in a dry monotone.

'There's no easy way to say this. We're being inspected from Monday. I'm going tell everyone about it at the meeting, but it's different from last year. They're bringing Atavism Representatives. They'll be in lectures and interviews . . .'

'Isaac,' I say calmly, cutting him off.

He pauses and breathes in.

'Yes. He can't be in the building, not even in your room. I'm sorry. I didn't want you to find out with everyone else. Is there anyone who can look after him?'

'Why didn't you give me more notice?' I ask.

'I couldn't,' he says. 'I only just found out. Really, I've been breaking the law by allowing it . . .'

'So, what? This is just a good excuse to get rid of him?'

'No,' he says abruptly, gesturing with the word. 'I know you might not think it, but I care about you and Isaac. I don't want what happened to David's son to happen to him.'

I hear Alice's voice again but all I want to do now is block it out. All I want is silence. Peter clears his throat and stares down at his notes.

'They're also going to be looking at the camera feeds,' he says. 'You need to be able to explain his behaviour.'

'There aren't cameras in the offices,' I say. Peter looks up.

'No, but there are in the halls and corridors.'

How many times has he sung in the corridors when no one was there? How many times has he sung out loud in an empty lecture hall?

'Can I have some water?' I ask.

He lifts an upturned glass and pours water out of a bruised metal jug. He passes it to me and I drink slowly.

'They may ask me about him,' he says. 'If they notice him on the cameras. I'm going to have to lie to them.'

'Why are you telling me this?'

'Because I want you to know what I'm prepared to do to keep you here.'

'You can do what you like,' I say.

He looks down and shakes his head slightly.

'I'm sorry it's come to this, Hannah. Is there anything I can do to help?'

I put the glass down and look away, my head lowered slightly. I hate that question. Do people ever want the answer to be yes?

'No,' I say.

Isaac is asleep by the time I get back to my office, his head nestled into his arms. I lock the door – I won't be long – and walk to Lecture Hall One. I'm one of the last to arrive. Peter is standing at the lectern at the front, talking quietly with one of the members of the physics department, drinking from a paper cup. Most people are sitting in silence; some are whispering to each other. The air feels heavy. I smell burnt coffee. Alice is in the middle of a group that's taking up a whole row, so I head to the back and sit by myself. Everything looks small from this angle, as if the walls are tapering towards the boards at the front, like one of those forced-perspective tricks in drawings.

Peter takes a step out from his lectern and the room goes quiet. In the fraction of time before he starts speaking, he glances up at the camera in the right-hand corner, then back to the group.

'Thank you all for giving up your break to meet. As I think some of you know . . .' I tune Peter's voice out to think. Why didn't I say anything to him? Should I talk to him again? I could convince him to allow Isaac to stay. He could be looked after by someone else for a week, maybe two, then he could come back. But I don't have anyone else. Mum can't even look after herself. Maybe Jarvis? No. It's too much of a risk, and he's done enough for me. I could stop working and give my rations to Isaac and Mum. But I wouldn't be able to buy batteries, or any fresh food, just cans. After two weeks I'd run out of money. I have nothing saved, and nothing of value to sell. But I can't leave him by himself in the flat, not with so many people around. He'll sing, like he always does.

Peter looks up at the camera again. I look too.

I wonder if anyone's watching. I wonder if they're listening. Do they watch my lectures? Do they watch me with Isaac? Do they know what he's really like? If they did, would he still be with me?

People have started talking over Peter. He has to half-shout to be heard. 'I'll put all the information outside my office today,' he says. 'This is going to be much more hands-on that it used to be. I'm sorry.'

'How can we prepare for this in one day?' A voice I don't recognise comes from somewhere near Alice.

'We don't have much choice. I was only told about it this morning, so it's been sprung on me as much as you. You'll have to do some work over the weekend, and I can talk with you individually after this if you have any questions.'

He pauses and looks down at his notes.

'There is one more thing.' Silence. 'The inspection team are going to be joined by two people from the Programme.'

'Why?' someone calls out.

'They've started sending Representatives to TEUs. They're looking to recruit more participants. So, in each of your interviews, someone from Atavism will be there alongside the inspectors. I don't know what questions they'll ask, or what they'll do with your answers, but they will be there, and they might come into your lectures as well.'

'Do we need to worry about our children?' Alice says. I stare at her, then at Peter. He looks small and alone. He glances at the door, sensing the noise of students gathering outside the room, and steps back behind the lectern without checking. He knocks his cup over. Black coffee spills across his papers and onto the floor. It pools outwards, seeping into the cracks between the floorboards. Peter mutters something to himself, then looks back to the room, annoyed.

'If you have any questions, Alice, or anyone else, I'll be in my office for the next half an hour.'

He leaves quickly, letting the idle chatter of the students filter into the room, leaving the coffee for someone else to clean up. People make their way down the risers, but I don't move. Instead, I look back at the camera. The red light on the side blinks twice then turns off. Maybe the recording's been stopped. Maybe the tape has been changed. It feels like a change, like something's been lost.

CHAPTER NINE

Isaac and I travel back to the South Station and make our way through the tunnel where we'd seen the preacher woman last evening. In the doorway where she'd been standing are some rags, two mismatched shoes and a plastic bag, but she's not with her things. Isaac drops his head and makes an almost cartoonishly sad face. 'She'll be back,' I say, although I don't know that for sure. People have disappeared without explanation in the past, and her things normally go with her when she moves from place to place. But I'd rather lie than make him sad. What I didn't expect was that I would miss her too.

I think I'll keep Isaac with me today. We walk along the river and turn off into Holland Market. I repeat my route, picking up two cans of beef, three cans of mixed vegetables, some soup, a packet of batteries and two bars of soap. But before I leave, I decide to turn back into the hall, heading down the slope to a brightly lit stall in the centre. Isaac squeezes my left hand tightly, and I squeeze back. In front of us are two large box fridges and a freezer. Fresh food costs three times as much as the dried things, but I feel like it today. I choose a single chicken breast, one large enough for the three of us – Mum, me and Isaac.

'Have you got any cod?' I ask the woman behind the counter.

'Only chicken, my love. Haven't had any cod for months.'

She wraps the breast in old newspaper and passes it over. I let go of Isaac's hand to put it in my bag, but when I lift my head, he's gone.

'Isaac?' I say. I look around. I can't see him. 'Did you see where my son went?' I ask the woman.

'No,' she says.

'He was just here. He's wearing a blue hoodie.'

'I didn't see. You still need to pay.'

I pass over the ration cards, throw my bag over my shoulder, and start searching between the stalls.

'Isaac?'

People swear at me as I push past them. I reach a dense crowd circling a newspaper stall. I call out Isaac's name again, but my voice is drowned. I see a child with a blue top and force myself towards them. 'Isaac?' I'm shouting now. People look at me, stare. I reach the boy and turn him round by the shoulders.

'I'm sorry,' I say. 'I'm sorry.' A woman pulls the boy away from me and they shrink into the crowd. I run back to the first stall. He's still not here. Is this how it happens? Do they not tell the parents? Do they just take them, and you find out later? How did they do it without my noticing? No, he can't be gone. Not like this. There are bright lights on heavy stands behind every stall, flooding the market with white light. I push my way past one of the lights and I can feel the heat radiating downwards. A vendor shouts at me, and I look back. I trip over something sticking out of the ground and hit my face on the concrete. My head cracks. I quickly push myself up, find my balance and move into the dark, empty half of the room.

'Isaac?' I yell.

The noise from the market has become a rich echo. I can hear the Soundfield now. 'Isaac?' I call, even louder this time, and my voice comes back to me twice. No, three times. I run. I'm alone in a sea of sound and moonlight. 'Where are you?' I whisper. My eyes are adjusting to the dark and a few metres away, towards the back of the hall, I see a huge object reaching tens of feet into the air, lying in shadow. On the wall behind the object are three words painted in tall white letters. *We will rise.* From the direction of the object, I think I hear something.

'Isaac?'

As I get closer, I start to make out some details in the object. It's a human, or human-like statue on a wide base. Two wings stick out from the sides, wrapping themselves around the torso. The body is split vertically. Half of it is normal, covered in skin, naked, but half has had its skin removed, showing the plastic organs and muscles and bones underneath. It's pregnant. I go round the back to look at the half with no skin and see a child curled up in a womb, with its thumb in its mouth, and, underneath, I see Isaac sitting up against the right leg of the figure, listening to his music, humming to himself. I climb on top of the base and walk over to him, stretching my hand up to touch the underside of the sculpture's belly when I'm close, standing on my toes to reach it. I sit down next to Isaac, put my arm round his shoulder, and he leans into me. He keeps humming, sleepily, and I shadow his melody in a breathy voice. Our song flows into the room, one voice chasing after the other, and is lost in the air around us.

We're hidden back here, in blue-black silence.

I squeeze him tight.

'Why did you run off?' I say.

He stops humming and gazes up at me.

'Too loud,' he signs.

'Okay,' I say. 'I'm sorry.'

I can't even keep him safe when he's with me.

'Are you okay?' he signs, pointing to the top of my head as he finishes his action. I put two fingers to my temple and feel something cold. My blood is jet-black in the light. I wipe the rest off with my sleeve.

'I'm alright,' I say, and he nods and starts crying. I wrap my arms around him. 'It's okay, it's just a cut.' We rock back and forth a few times and he finds a way to hold back his tears.

'Isaac . . .' Is this the right time to tell him? Maybe there is no right time. ' . . . you know how you always come to work with me? Well, from next week that can't happen. Something's changed which means you can't come with me anymore. It's just for a bit. But I'm going to find someone to look after you, or I'll look after you and not work.'

He lets go of me and looks into my eyes. They glisten in the half-light.

'Can I read the books?' he signs.

I laugh.

'Of course,' I say. 'I'll bring them to wherever you are, and you can read them. How does that sound?'

'Can't you read them to me?'

'Maybe,' I whisper, and I kiss his head. 'Maybe.'

Then, silence. Through the broken panels in the ceiling, the Soundfield sings out a soft melody, one I haven't heard for years. It starts on a high, held note, and descends slowly, gradually getter quieter, like it's moving away from us. Isaac bends his neck back, trying to chase the dying sound. He brings his hands to his chest with his fingers flat against each other and moves one hand vertically down against the other.

Pass, he signs. *Pass.*

'What does it mean, *pass*?' I hear Mahesh asking. He was looking through a one-way mirror at EK who was sitting by themselves in a small room. They were surrounded by toys, musical instruments, speakers attached to the walls and ceiling. 'What's passed?' he said.

The song dissolves into the hall and the Hum reappears. For a while we sit and hold each other, listening to the Field, looking up at the white words written on the wall in front of us. *We will rise. We will rise.* I close my eyes to try to store this moment, like when you're in the sun and you blink, and all that's left are the outlines of the brightest things.

CHAPTER TEN

I sometimes think about what Theo would have been like with Isaac. Just before the Soundfield appeared, some friends of his had a daughter – Emma, I think her name was – and they made Theo her godfather. During the years when we all pretended life was going to go back to normal, they stayed in touch, and he was close to Emma.

About a year after the Soundfield appeared, Theo offered to host Emma's eighth birthday at Mum's house. Emma's parents were looking after refugees from Sudan at the time, and they didn't have space for a party. During lunch, Theo argued with them about taking in refugees, saying it was unsustainable to house people and that it wasn't our job to help them. 'They'll get used to the comfort and won't want to leave,' he said. 'They'll have to go back to where they came from eventually.' He spoke in clichés, but we all thought the Soundfield was temporary. We thought people would be able to go back to their homes once the water had become drink-able and the air had become breathable.

After lunch, Emma's parents were tired, so Theo looked after her. He played with her for hours, working through a huge puzzle book with stickers. I kept myself busy, helping Mum with the washing up, getting people drinks and cake, but I couldn't help noticing how happy Emma was. There were times when we were young when he made me feel that happy, and I cried thinking about them when everyone had gone. I like to imagine he would have been the same with Isaac, but I don't know. Isaac isn't like Emma.

There are still some people outside as Isaac and I make our way across the bridge: the last of the commuters, a group of teenagers throwing stones into the water, two officers sending people back to their homes. On the embankment, blinds shut as we pass as though it's been choreographed, protecting the people inside from something that no one can see. The sun is rising and the metal and glass of Mum's building catches the first of the light, shining a warm white. For a moment I imagine it's beautiful, not a place that's been made with no care. Isaac realises where we're going, lets go of my hand and skips on ahead. I catch up, stroke his head, and open the door with the key. Before I go in, I glance to my right at the ground-floor flat where the men had been yesterday morning. The broken glass is gone, but so is the old man. His cat is licking an empty bowl.

As the front door closes behind us, it squeaks – metal on

metal – producing a few sliding notes which Isaac sings back with perfect accuracy.

He looks at me at the end of his song.

'Flat twenty-four,' I say.

He starts jumping up each step with two feet, timing it to a set, slow beat. I walk past him up the stairs and wait for him on Mum's floor, sitting on the top step. When he reaches me, he jumps up and throws himself into my arms, forcing me off balance for a moment. I centre myself, and laugh, and he laughs too, producing a small, musical sound. He's never spoken a word in his life, but he has more control over his voice than anyone I've met. If you've only ever spoken German, or Japanese, or Afrikaans, your mouth and muscles are formed around that language like tree roots wrapped around rock. That's what it's like for Isaac. His voice is musical because music is his language.

I let us into the flat.

'Hi, Mum,' I call out. 'I've got Isaac with me today.'

Isaac takes his CD player out of his pocket, presses pause, and runs into the living room. I go into the kitchen, put the cans in the cupboards – attaching one cupboard door back on its hinge – and put the chicken in the fridge. It smells better than yesterday.

Isaac comes back into the kitchen and pulls me by the hand, leading me to the living room. Mum is sitting in her chair facing the window, her head leaning to one side.

'Mum?'

Isaac jumps onto the sofa, bouncing up and down a little

on the hard springs. I squeeze Mum's shoulder gently. 'Mum? Are you okay?' She moves a little, and half opens her eyes, drowsily.

'Are you alright?'

'Hmm.'

She tries to sit upright, but it's too much for her, and her eyes close.

'Isaac is here?' she says, softly.

'Yes, Mum. He's here. How long have you been sitting here? Have you been in this chair all day?'

The curtains are drawn and the blinds are up, like she's waiting for the light to appear.

'Did you open the blinds, Mum?' but she doesn't reply.

She adjusts her position, grabbing her left arm, and turns her head away from me. I roll the sleeve up her arm and see the bandage I applied yesterday thick with blood. She winces, and I cover it up again.

'It's okay. Isaac and I are here. I'll make you some food. I've got fresh chicken. No cans, I promise.'

She eases back down into the chair and opens her eyes a fraction. Her face is red, and her eyes are shining. I tell Isaac that I'm going to the kitchen, and he nods. He stretches out on the sofa, puts his headphones on and clicks play, lying with his head on the armrest. He stares out of the window with Mum.

There's only one frying pan in the kitchen which has years of grease and fat burnt onto the surface. I try to clean it with a dirty scrubber and cold water but only manage to saturate the brush with thick black oil. I manage to cook the chicken breast after fifteen minutes and boil a tin of vegetables to go with it. When I'm done, I take the two plates through to the living room, one for Mum, one for Isaac, and place them on the small table next to Mum's chair. I'll eat whatever either of them leaves.

Isaac is still listening to his music, in another world.

'Come on,' I say. He glances over, rolls off the sofa, landing on the carpet with a little thud, and shuffles forward on his knees to the table, sitting back on his feet as he reaches his plate. I cut up his chicken into small pieces and pass him a fork. He drops his headphones down, the music still playing, and starts to eat, one mouthful at a time, keeping the chicken and vegetables separate. Mum looks at me.

'A tray . . .'

She points to the end of the sofa where a few trays are stacked amongst some old newspapers. I pick one up, blow off some of the dust and put it on her lap. She tries to pick up her plate with her good arm but gives up. I put the food on the tray and place a fork in her right hand. She's shaking slightly. She starts to eat, clumsily piercing a piece of chicken, bringing the fork up to her mouth and pushing her head forward to reach it. After she's finished chewing, she puts the fork down, and waits for the energy to have another piece. She looks at her left arm, which lies like a dead weight on the armrest.

Isaac manages to get through six or seven small pieces of chicken and a few mouthfuls of sweetcorn and peas before he's had enough. He looks at me to see if he can stop, and I smile gently. He puts his headphones back on, lies down on his front next to Mum's armchair, and ejects the CD from his player. I go back into the kitchen, find the three discs I have in my bag, and lie down on the floor next to Isaac, propping my head up with my left hand. I lay the discs out in front of him, and he points at the Bach Cello Suites. I click the CD into the player, close it inside, and place my ear against his ear and listen with him for a moment, the singing cello escaping through the plastic and foam. I get up. Mum has stopped eating, and is sitting back in her chair, looking away from me, softly crying.

I take the tray from her lap, place it on the floor, and move the small table with Isaac's food out of the way. I sit down next to her, leaning on the armrest, and hold her left hand with both of mine. She's like a child, broken.

'It's okay, Mum. I'm here. Is there anything I can do?' I ask, but I know there's no good answer to this question. 'I love you,' I say. 'I'm here.'

Isaac looks at Mum and pauses his music. He takes his headphones off, pushes himself up and stands in front of her chair. He holds the player and the headphones in his outstretched hands. Mum wipes her cheek with her good arm and looks at me.

'Can you translate?' she says in a thin voice.

'Of course,' I say.

She stares into Isaac's eyes, maybe for the first time.

'Is this for me?' she says to him.

Isaac places the player onto her lap and drops down onto

his knees. He makes a fist with his right hand and bobs it back and forth.

'Yes,' I say to Mum.

'What do you like to listen to?' she says.

Isaac glances at me and I smile back.

'Go on,' I sign.

'I don't know,' he signs. 'I like the piano.'

'He likes piano music,' I say. Mum looks at me, then back to Isaac.

'Your Mum used to play, you know. She was very good. She'd play for hours sometimes, making little tunes up . . . when . . .'

'When I was young,' I say.

'Yes,' Mum continues. 'When Theo was alive.'

Isaac closes his fists and, with one hand, touches his extended thumb to his forehead then brings it back down to meet his other thumb.

'He remembers,' I say. 'He remembers me playing.'

Mum looks at me, confused. But then her face slowly changes, to one of sadness or understanding; it's hard to tell the difference sometimes. 'Of course,' she says. 'Yes.' Her eyes shine like dew.

Isaac gets up, walks round to the other side of the chair from me, and picks up the headphones from Mum's lap. He pulls the cups carefully around her ears, leaning over the armrest to reach her left side. I have to help him. He can't quite reach. He sits down in front of her and presses play on the CD player.

Mum shuts her eyes and listens, gripping my hand with everything left in her.

I'm on the sand, curled into a ball, a cord coming from my belly reaching up beyond my head. All the grass and trees have gone. Endless beach and endless sea and sky. I'm wet and shivering. Next to me is the brown-eyed man, lying on his back, his head blown through, his scarf blowing in the wind.

I'm awake. The Soundfield. A Call.

I'd fallen asleep on the sofa. Mum's in her chair, snoring lightly. I hear Isaac singing to himself in the next room. He knows the song as well as I do. I get up, go to the bedroom, and quietly open the door. He stops.

'It's okay,' I say softly. I close the door behind me, lie on the bed next to him and hold him tight, singing with him until the song finishes and we're both asleep.

I wake up before Isaac and go into the living room.

'Morning, Mum,' I say as I pull up the blinds, filling the room with evening light. I squeeze her shoulder and she opens her eyes a little. She smells of body odour and dried blood, but also of peppermint.

'Did you sleep?' I ask. She shakes her head and re-adjusts her position in the chair. 'Do you want anything?' I say, but she doesn't reply. I move as if to leave, but she takes my hand. Without opening her eyes, she speaks to me in a broken half-voice.

'I can't do this, anymore . . .' she says. 'I can't . . .'

'I know, Mum. I know . . . We're going to go home to get washed, and then we'll come back. How does that sound?'

She lets go of my hand.

'I'm sorry,' she says in a barely audible whisper.

By the time we're ready to go home, Isaac is cut off from the world around him, listening to his music. I tell him to go ahead, and I look in on Mum one final time before leaving. She looks calm, like in that fraction of a second before sleep, when you feel your limbs becoming too heavy to lift. Isaac makes his way down the stairs as I shut the door to the flat, doing his thing of jumping down each step with two feet.

There's a family with three young children outside Mum's building – a girl and two boys. One of the boys is leaning over the edge of the railing, trying to look at something in the river below, his father gripping his waist. As we pass, he lifts the boy up onto his shoulders and they walk with us for a while. Isaac is looking at them and pulls on my hand. 'Can I?' he signs. I look at the father with his son then stoop down to Isaac's level. He jumps up onto my back, and I carry him for as long as I have the strength.

As we get closer to New Bridge, more people appear from side streets and buildings. Elderly couples getting some air, teenagers ambling in groups of four or five, a few people by themselves looking out over the river.

People go through life in units, and sometimes their units grow, and sometimes they don't. We can count the people that matter to us on one hand because we can't share ourselves with everyone, otherwise there'd be nothing left for us. All these people around me, the families, the officers, even the people alone and desperate for company, can't know that my mum is dying not because they wouldn't care – they would – but because they're full, like me. Every part of me has been given to my son and my mother, and every part of them has been given to me. And now there's nothing left for anyone else.

CHAPTER ELEVEN

I see Jarvis through the glass in the front door of Mandalay House, and Isaac sees him too. He takes his hand away from mine.

'He's here,' he signs.

'I know,' I sign back.

'He's not normally here in the night.'

'No, he's not,' I say. 'You can go ahead.'

Isaac smiles, pushes the door open excitedly and runs to Jarvis's side, putting his hand up as he gets there. Jarvis looks surprised.

'Hello, Isaac,' he says, completing the high-five. Isaac runs into Jarvis's room and starts looking for something on the shelf, another part of our routine.

'Isaac?' I call out, but he doesn't come back to me. I look at Jarvis. 'What are you still doing on shift?'

'Alexey hasn't turned up,' he replies.

I've hardly seen Alexey since he arrived. He doesn't really speak English and is a little intimidating. He's twice my size.

'Did you stay at your mum's last night?' Jarvis says.

'Yes,' I say, and Jarvis smiles at me in a way people only do when they know something's wrong. I can't hide how I'm feeling; it seeps out of me like sweat.

'Thanks for your help yesterday,' he says.

'It's okay.'

I glance into his room and see Isaac sitting on the sofa with his legs crossed, clumsily shuffling the cards. Hanging on the wall next to him is the UV suit Jarvis was wearing last night.

'Did you get the blood out?' I ask.

'Most of it.'

When we get back to the flat, Isaac skips to the kitchen table, puts his player down and starts clicking the previous button several times to return to the beginning of the CD. In front of him are piles of drawings, done on fragments of newspapers and blank pages ripped out from old books. He starts doodling on a fresh piece of paper with a blue crayon – the only pencil left – and hums along to his Bach. I go to the table, put my bag down, and guide his face towards mine. His skin is so soft. He knows what I'm going to say, and stops singing, re-directing his energy into kicking his feet and scribbling.

The drawings he does are of nothing at all, really. Other children might draw people, or houses, or animals, but Isaac doesn't often draw objects; he prefers lines and shapes. A set of orange pictures as he worked through the orange crayon, a set of green ones as he worked through the green crayon. The most recent set of drawings, all of them blue, have large semi-circular bands at the top, reaching beyond the edge of the page, some of them linked together to create larger sketches. It could be the sky, but I don't think it is. I think it just looks that way because of the colour. Isaac always listens to music when he draws, so I sometimes think that when I'm looking at his pictures, I'm looking into his mind, and that maybe if I look hard enough I might be able to see his thoughts.

I leave Isaac to his drawing, and go to the bathroom, closing the door behind me. I turn the shower on, take my clothes off and brace myself to step into the cold water. It's hot. My body sighs and I let out a small noise. Most days, the cold is a relief from the sun, but even in the heat, I still crave warm water.

I haven't looked at or felt my body in a while. I can see my rib cage under my skin. My muscles are thin and weak, and I feel small, small like someone years older than me. I look at the bruises on my leg – still yellow – and find a new mark on my arm next to my scar, but I don't know how I got it. I feel the scar tissue a little, pushing at the skin on either side, and I wonder if it will ever fade. When Theo tried to pull me out of the frozen lake the first time, I fell back in and caught my right forearm on the sharp edge of some ice. I remember seeing blood pouring out of my arm and into the water around me, but I don't remember feeling it. After he got me out, he ran to get Mum and I sat on the ice, shivering so much it hurt, blood staining the white ground around me. He arrived back before her and stood a few feet in front of me, repeating the same lines over and over: 'She's coming,' he said. 'She'll be here soon.'

I heard Mum screaming my name before I saw her. She shouted at Theo, then took off my wet clothes, wrapping my young, naked body in her huge coat to keep me alive. She held me as we waited for the ambulance, and I gripped my arm as tight as I could.

I'm gripping my arm now, sitting on the floor of the shower. I let go, and the skin expands to fill the deep grooves left by my thumb and fingers, leaving red marks behind.

I hear something from the kitchen.

'Isaac?'

I get up quickly, turn the shower off and rub my eyes. Isaac is singing.

'I'm coming. You need to stop,' I shout.

I dry myself with an abrasive towel and put my clothes back on, my body still damp. I hear a knock on the front door. I can't move fast enough; the clothes are sticking to my skin.

'Isaac, I'm coming. Please, stop.'

I open the bathroom door and see Isaac still sitting at the kitchen table, drawing, still listening to his music. Another knock on the door, this time harder.

'Can you open the door?' A man's voice, muffled.

I go over to Isaac, remove his headphones, and turn his head towards mine.

'You have to stop singing. Please. To yourself,' I sign.

'To myself,' he signs back.

The knock becomes a thump.

'Open the door,' the man shouts.

'I'm coming,' I call out. 'Go to the bedroom,' I sign to Isaac, 'and shut the door.'

Isaac runs into the bedroom, leaving his things behind, and closes the door with a quiet thud. I wait a moment, then another, throw my bag over Isaac's drawings and look to the bedroom to check he's out of sight. I walk slowly to the front door and pull it open a fraction, placing my foot at the base to stop it opening any further. The bald man is looking through the gap.

'What do you want?' I say, failing to hide my anxiety. A large capital 'A' is stitched into the front of his UV jacket. He sees me looking at it.

'You know who I am. It's your choice how you want this to go.' His voice is deep and clear.

'I don't know what you mean,' I say.

'I heard a child singing. It is your legal responsibility to declare any child who exhibits musical abilities to your local Atavism Representative. Open the door, ma'am.'

'I'm sorry, you must have mis-heard. It's just me in here.' I try to push the door closed, but he throws his shoulder into the gap. I haven't got the strength to hold him back.

'I heard a child singing. You have a legal responsibility to have your child taken for tests. Failure to comply could result in a prison sentence or execution. Do you understand?'

He pushes harder. The door swings open and I trip back a few steps, hitting into the kitchen table.

'Where is the child?' he says coldly.

He takes a step into the flat.

'Are they in the bedroom?

'No, there's no one here,' I say, in a half-voice, paralysed. 'There's no one . . .'

The man strides forward, opens the bedroom door, and looks in.

'Come on, son.'

Son. He's not your son.

He goes inside and pulls Isaac out by his arm. Isaac screams.

'No, please,' I say desperately. I try to take Isaac's hand, but the man pushes me to the floor. Isaac is crying softly, reaching out with his free arm, his eyes red and small. The man stares at me.

'Under the Atavism Act of 2043, your son is being adopted.' His tone is officious, short. He's reciting a script. 'Accordingly, he will undergo genetic testing at your local centre, and if he passes, he will be taken into the care of the State. If not, he will be returned to you. Do you understand?'

'No, I don't. I don't.' My heart is cracking. 'Please don't take him. I'm . . . I'm Dr Hannah Newnham. Do you know that name?'

He waits and stares at me, but there's no sign of recognition. He turns sharply towards the door, taking Isaac away from me.

He's taking my son.

'Please,' I say, quietly.

He's nearly out of the door. I push myself up and grab

something without looking from the kitchen table. I run towards the man and hit him as hard as I can on the back of the head. He falls forward, out of the doorway, taking Isaac with him, and he collides with the metal railing outside the front door. A dull thud – metal on flesh, on bone.

I drop what's left of the object I'm holding.

The man is on the ground. So is Isaac.

'Isaac?'

I rush down to Isaac and pick him up. He throws his arms round my neck, and I hold him tighter than I've ever held him. There are specks of red on his neck and shirt.

I look at the man. Blood is seeping from his ear. On the floor next to him is Isaac's CD player, broken into three pieces.

CHAPTER TWELVE

The man's body is lying half in my flat, half in the corridor. I bend his legs at the knees and push them away from me, tucking them into his chest. The pool of blood around his head spreads outwards.

I shut the door. Isaac is sitting on the floor, crying, trying to put together the pieces of his broken player. I take the fragments out of his hands and put them on the kitchen table. The CD inside is cracked, split between the *B* and the *a* of *Bach*.

'We'll get another one. I promise.'

I take Isaac to the kitchen sink and splash his face and neck with cold water, washing most of the blood off with my hands. He scowls, like when I try to make him eat when he doesn't want to. My hands are shaking. I remove his top, turning it inside out, and throw it into the bin in the corner. I pick up my bag, take Isaac by the hand, and lead him back into the bedroom, retracing the steps he just took.

'We have to get your things together,' I sign. 'Only essentials. We can't take music.'

I pull open the drawers under his bed and remove all of his clothes. I choose a new T-shirt at random and put it on him. He's still crying. I draw him close to me.

'It's okay. I'm so sorry about the player,' I say softly, and he wipes a tear from his face. I remove the lecture notes and spare CDs from my bag and replace them with some shirts, one pair of shorts, underwear, and another pair of shoes for Isaac and a couple of tops, spare trousers and underwear for me. The bag is almost full. Isaac picks up a CD and hands it to me.

'No. We can't. We can't take them. It won't work,' I say.

He looks like he might start crying again.

'I'm sorry. I'll get you another player, I promise,' I say.

'You promise?' he signs.

I cross my heart.

In the kitchen, I fill an old plastic bottle with some water from the tap, grab whatever dry food we have left – crackers, a couple of boxes of raisins, a can of meat, some bread – and force them into the top of my bag, pulling it shut. Isaac's blue crayon is sitting next to his broken player, on top of a half-finished drawing. He climbs onto the chair next to his things, sitting on his knees, and picks up the crayon.

'We have to go,' I say impatiently.

He holds the drawing up to me.

'No, we can't take it.'

'It's us,' he signs.

I look at the picture. I see the characteristic semi-circular band of blue at the top but, underneath, something new. A tall rectangle with a smaller one nested inside. In the smaller shape are loose lines that look like figures.

'Us?' I say.

'All of us,' he signs after putting the drawing down. He then brings his hands into a circle around his chest, outlining the shape of a ball. *The world.*

He looks at me with wide eyes.

'Okay, you can bring it . . .' I say.

I pick up the drawing, fold it into some extra paper, and push it into a side pocket in my bag along with the last remaining crayon. I have to keep him living, not just alive.

We're ready to leave. I'm standing here, looking at the door, Isaac's hand in my hand, not knowing where we're going or what will happen, and I can't move. I'm fixed. It's like when you're dreaming and you're looking at yourself from above. You try to speak or move your arms, but you're stuck in sand and your voice is silent. You try so hard to say something that you wake your living body. You kick in your sleep, or you make a noise, and suddenly, you can move again, you can think again.

Isaac pulls at my hand, and I come back to the room. A kick to wake me up. I drop down to him. My heart is racing.

'Isaac, I want you to close your eyes when we leave. I'm going to carry you, but you need to keep your eyes shut as tight as you can, okay? Don't look,' I sign and speak at the same time, doubling up the message. He squeezes his eyes shut. I pick him up and he wraps his legs around my waist. The combined weight of the bag and his body makes me stumble, but I won't need to carry him for long. I find my strength and turn the door handle. The man's legs slide into the room.

'Keep your eyes closed,' I repeat.

I place one foot on the left side of the body, trying to avoid the blood, and use my right hand to hold on to the doorframe to keep me stable, and to pivot round to the left. I push myself past the man and look back, just for a moment. His head moves, then his right arm. I rush to the end of the corridor, drop down into the stairwell, and put Isaac down once we're out of sight of the man. There's wet spray-paint on the wall next to me and the smell and the exertion makes me feel nauseous.

'You can open them now,' I say.

His eyes are red, and he's still crying a little.

'I just need to do something,' I sign.

'No. Stay,' he signs back.

'It's okay. I'll just be a minute.'

I leave Isaac on the step with my bag and run back to the flat. I pull the man's legs into his body and go to shut the door, but stop. I look inside, and feel empty, not because I liked living here but because Isaac's pictures are sitting on the kitchen table next to his broken player and I'm leaving them behind. They're the only things left in the place that I love.

When we get to the bottom of the stairs, Alexey is sitting in Jarvis's chair, hunched over the desk. He's playing with Isaac's cards. As we approach, he looks up, makes a small grunt of recognition, and I nod back. The door to Jarvis's room is closed, and for a moment I imagine he's in there, still trying to remove his UV suit. He calls out my name and I go in and help. I remove his gloves and wash my hands, but I don't go outside to the street this time. I don't arrive late to the TEU, and when I wake up in Mum's flat the next day, I stay with her. I don't go back home. I don't attack the man at my door; Isaac still has his music; we still have our little life.

We leave Mandalay House and find a dark space under the awning of a disused restaurant, hidden from the glow of the streetlamps. The dirt on the window is thick, and our reflections in the glass are dulled.

'We are going away, now, and we might not come back here for a while,' I sign. 'Do you understand?'

He nods.

'I'm hungry,' he signs.

I open my bag and take a piece of bread out of some crumpled brown paper. I split it in two, and we both start chewing.

'Where are we going?' he signs.

'I don't know,' I sign back.

'Why are we going? I don't want to go,' he signs, his hands hitting hard against his chest.

'I know,' I say, and I hold him, and the blurred reflection in the window turns from two people into one.

Without thinking, I start walking to the South Station. Isaac looks up at me, confused. He knows we shouldn't be going there now. It's not a work night. But I don't say anything. I have to think. We pass through the tunnel and head into the station. We need to get away from home, that's all I know. Isaac sees the alcove where I'd usually check his player. He lets go of my hand and runs ahead. He's stuck in his routine like me. I call out to him, and he glances back. He collides with a woman walking in the opposite direction and falls to the floor. She looks back, irritated, but hurries on. I'm twenty feet away from him. Closer are two police officers, and a man in a tight blue jacket. The man in the jacket looks at Isaac and strides towards him. He lifts Isaac up by his arm and when I reach the scene, I see the white *A* stitched into his breast pocket. Formal wear for public-facing officials.

'Is this your son?' he asks, gesturing towards Isaac. His voice is mannered like someone pretending to be years older than they are. He can't be over twenty-five.

'Yes,' I say in a thin voice. 'Thank you. We should go. Come on, Isaac.'

'No,' he says. 'Talk with me. I'm always keen to converse with members of the public.'

'We have to . . .'

'Where have you got to go?'

His stiff smile makes me feel nauseous. How do they get them so young? I look behind his shoulder at the two officers. One of them is gripping his assault rifle, looking at me, the other is speaking into a radio. I can feel my heart.

'Okay,' I say and I return his fake smile with one of my own.

He turns around and walks slowly back to his post. He waves impatiently at one of the officers and they move out of the way. I take Isaac's hand and we follow. The man stops at a circular table. Next to him is a life-sized poster showing a girl running through a field. She's smiling, her arms outstretched. It's daylight in the picture, taken before the Field. Below the girl is some white text. *Atavism: working towards a better future, together.* The table is littered with pamphlets.

'Have you ever considered getting your son tested?'

'Tested?' I say, feigning ignorance, or stupidity.

'Yes, genetically tested. How old is he?'

'Six,' I say.

'As I thought, he's too old to have been tested at birth. It really is a very simple process. A small sample of your son's blood is taken, and we run what's called a *single variant test.*' He gives each of these words a staccato accent, like he's speaking to a child. 'This is where we look for a simple mutation in your son's DNA. If we find this mutation, your son could make a vital contribution to the Programme.'

'No, we've never done that.'

'You're not interested?'

'No, I am. I've been busy.'

'Hmm. Has your son ever exhibited musical abilities?' He doesn't look at Isaac when he talks, only at me, like Isaac isn't important to him, or like he doesn't exist.

'No. He likes maths,' I lie.

'Oh, good,' he says with mild enthusiasm. 'Well, we always need people like that.'

I look at Isaac. There's a small red mark on his right earlobe. Small enough for me to miss when I was washing him, but large enough to be seen.

'We should go,' I repeat. My heart is beating faster.

'Why are you in such a rush?'

'We have to go and see his father.'

'Where does he live, if you don't mind me asking?'

'Just north of the city.'

'What do you do for work . . . sorry, what is your name?'

'Hannah.'

'Your full name,' he says, pointedly.

'Hannah Williams.'

He turns around and scribbles on a bit of paper attached to a clipboard. Without looking back, he continues talking.

'What do you do for work, Hannah Williams?'

'I work in a TEU.' I can't lie to him. He'll check.

'So, you work in a TEU, but you don't know about genetics tests.'

'Well . . .'

'No, that wasn't a question. What do you teach?'

'I don't,' I say. 'I'm an administrator.'

He writes some more, then aggressively underlines a word. He puts his pen down carefully and turns back to me.

'Ah, well that makes more sense, doesn't it.'

Isaac lets go of my hand and signs.

'Can we get another player?'

'What did he say?' the man asks.

'He's hungry,' I lie.

The man finally looks at Isaac. He stoops down and ruffles his hair, like someone who has only seen parenting in films. A copy of a copy of the real thing. He reaches into his pocket and brings out a yellow sweet, wrapped in clear plastic film. It crinkles as he holds it out towards Isaac.

'No, thank you,' I say. 'Not for him.'

He looks at me and smiles.

'Oh, well that's a shame,' he says, getting up. 'Well.' He pauses for an uncomfortably long time. 'If ever you want to get your son tested, come to me.' He passes me a pamphlet and I take it.

'I will, thank you.'

I turn quickly and pull Isaac away. We head towards the platform, as if I'm going to work. When we reach the top of the escalator, I glance back. I see the poster with the smiling girl and the two officers. I see the man with his ill-fitting jacket looking straight at me.

I get on the first train that arrives. There are only three other people in our carriage: a woman with a scarf covering her face, and a man with his son sitting on the bench opposite Isaac and me. The boy is about the same age as Isaac, and he's waving at him, trying to get his attention. Their eyes meet, and they stare at each other for a while until Isaac gives in. He clambers onto my knee and puts his arms around my neck.

'It's alright,' I whisper. 'It's alright.'

Within two stops, he's asleep in my arms. I smell his hair. Sweet, slightly musty. The smell would normally make me tired – it's the last thing I experience in the mornings – but nothing could make me sleep now, not even the heat. My mind is racing. I feel naked and spotlighted. More people get on at the next few stops. I try to look for signs of official uniforms – white letters, blue jackets, badges, guns – but there are too many people. The woman with the scarf is still in the carriage. She's leaning forward in her chair, her elbows resting on her legs, fiddling with a ring on her left hand.

Isaac is awake. He shuffles in my lap and hums a few notes to himself.

'Isaac, quiet,' I say into his ear, but his song continues and gets louder. I drop him into the seat next to me and lower myself to him. He won't look at me. He's gazing all around the carriage. His hum opens up into a bright *ah* sound. I take his cheeks into my hands and direct his eyes towards mine.

'Stop singing, please,' I sign.

The woman in the seat next to Isaac gets up and shuffles down the carriage, away from the noise and attention. Everyone's looking at us.

'Please, stop,' I sign. 'Please.' He won't stop. He's waiting to listen to music. That's what normally happens, that's what he's learnt.

I pick Isaac up. It takes all my strength. He wraps his arms round my neck.

'Where are we?' I half-shout, to no one in particular. My voice is unstable.

A young girl points at a station on the map on the wall next to her. We're way past our stop for the TEU. We've gone north, further north than I've been in years, nearly out of the city. The train approaches the next station, and two men in suits stand up and look in our direction.

'It's okay,' I whisper in Isaac's ear. 'I'll protect you. I'll protect you.'

Someone pushes past me, as if they're making their way to the door. They're standing right next to me. 'Come with me at the next stop.' A woman's voice.

'What?' I can't see her face; we're looking in opposite directions.

'Those two men, they're Atavism Representatives. They were

looking at your son. Come with me if you want to keep him safe.'

The men in suits start walking towards us, forcing themselves through the crowd. Isaac has stopped singing, but it's too late.

'Who are you?' I say.

'Not now, just follow me.'

I put Isaac down and take his hand. The train comes to a stop. The doors open.

'Come. Quickly,' she says.

She moves out of the carriage, turning right towards the exit. It's the woman with the black scarf. Her face is still covered. I follow her blurry outline amongst the mass of people. She moves lightly, like she has no weight on her. Isaac is dragging his feet. I pull him along the platform.

'Come on,' I call. He stops suddenly and snatches his hand away from mine. I look back. His arms are crossed.

'I want my music,' he signs.

People push past him.

'Not now,' I say. 'We have to go.'

I glance behind me but I can't see the woman. Did the men get off the train?

'Please,' I say desperately, putting out my hand. 'Please.'

He considers it for a moment, then unfolds his arms and takes my hand. I pull him close to me. I search for the woman's scarf, but I can't focus. Everything's lost its colour. What was she wearing? There are too many people. But then I find her, standing still in the middle of the writhing crowd. She's looking straight at me. I see her eyes. A deep brown. I see them so clearly, like lightning in a storm.

We run to catch up to her. She moves past the exit, and heads to the end of the platform. Warm air flows from the black tunnel and the light dims.

'In here,' she says, glancing back at us. She pushes open a door and I look into a dark room. A train rushes past.

'Inside,' she barks over the noise.

I head in and the woman locks the door behind us. It's black. We're alone.

CHAPTER THIRTEEN

I'm standing in the dark, holding onto Isaac. I'm trying to catch my breath. The room smells of rust and cleaning fluid.

'How did you know they were Atavism?' I say.

'Keep quiet,' she half-whispers. She has an accent that I can't place. My eyes find what light there is in the room. The woman has her ear pressed against the door. My breathing is slowing but my heart is beating fast. The woman flicks on a small lamp next to her, casting orange light onto a metal desk covered with paint pots and brushes. The light makes the room look sick.

'Your son makes a lot of noise,' the woman says, still whispering.

'How did you know who they were?'

She waits before answering.

'I've seen those two before. They're known to us.' She looks at Isaac. 'They would have taken your son.'

I let go of Isaac's hand and wipe the sweat from my fore-head. My hands are shaking.

'Where are we?' he signs.

'I don't know,' I sign. 'It'll be okay.'

The woman steps back from the door and sits down on an upturned bucket in the corner. Her face is still partly covered by the scarf. She looks at me and plays with the ring on her left hand again.

'I'm Layla.'

I think for a second whether or not to tell her my name.

'We need to leave,' I say.

'Not yet,' she says. 'What's your name?'

I hesitate.

'Hannah,' I say, putting my hand to my chest, 'and this is Isaac.' She nods. I haven't met anyone new in years, and I've forgotten the way I used to introduce myself. When you're young, saying your name is like a game where you get to make up the rules, but when you're an adult, it becomes fixed.

Isaac looks up at me. His eyes are tired and anxious. 'It's alright,' I sign. 'Which station is this?' I say to Layla. 'We have to leave now.'

'They'll be looking for you. You should wait.'

'No, I need to go.'

But I can't go. I can't go to Mum's, or back home, or to the TEU. The man will be conscious by now, or they will have found the body. Mum is all by herself. I've left her.

'We have a place not far from here,' Layla says. 'You can

stay there for a while, if you'd like, till you work out what you want to do.'

She removes the scarf from her head. She's beautiful, but her face is thin like mine, like she's also giving her food to someone else. The lamplight shines in her eyes. They're almost black in the dim glow of the room. She has the same look of hope as the man I saw die on the street. She has the same eyes.

'Okay,' I say. She smiles and gazes at Isaac, who's sitting on the floor next to me with his legs crossed. 'Why are you helping me?' I say.

'We have to stick together,' she says, still looking at my son.

'How old is yours?' I say.

'She's turning four soon.'

We wait in silence in the small room, Layla sitting in the corner, Isaac drawing with his blue crayon. The air feels compressed. I try to order things in my mind, but every move I make dislodges something else. A knot in my head that I can only make tighter. What time is it? I feel my naked wrist. Layla has an old mechanical watch with a broken face that she checks every now and then. She sees me looking at it.

'It's nearly five,' she says. 'We'll need to leave soon.'

After a while, Layla gets up and nods. I take Isaac's hand as she opens the door. Light flows in – harsh, yellow light.

'Follow me,' she says. 'It's not far.'

I could leave now, not go with her. Do I have a choice? Maybe, I don't know. She looks into my eyes.

'Are you coming?'

'Yes,' I reply.

The platform is almost empty. The men have gone. We make our way up three flights of stairs, with Layla running ahead of us, taking two steps at a time. The air outside is cool and still in the early morning. I breathe it in. There are people around, but all heading indoors: shutting blinds and curtains, tightening locks, calling to each other across the gaps between buildings, saying *sleep well* instead of *goodnight*. Within twenty minutes, there's no one left. It's exhilarating and terrifying to be left alone with the rising sun, like the first time you deliberately broke the rules as a child.

'We're close,' she says.

Layla takes us into an alleyway which opens up into a paved road, an old high street. It's lit up by the low-lying sun like it's channelling the waves of light and heat. Across from us is a wide building with boarded-up windows that reaches five or six storeys into the air – there's a huge sign on the front, in big green letters, but I don't recognise the name. *Bidnalls*.

'We need to put our suits on,' I say.

'There's no time,' she says. 'We can run.'

She covers her face with her hand and darts across the street into the shadow of the building opposite. I lift Isaac up and he wraps his legs around my waist.

'We'll be okay,' I say into his ear. 'We'll be okay.'

It'll only be a few seconds of exposure, I tell myself, and it's morning, so the atmosphere will protect us from the worst of the radiation. I run as fast as I can, holding Isaac's head to my chest to shield him, but when the light hits my face I nearly stop. In the summer when I was young, when the days and months stretched out like water over hot stone, I would chase the evening light until it died. The warmth of sunlight can't be recreated by lamps, or electric heaters, or even fire, it's never the same as the sun's warmth, and, for a moment, I think about staying in the light forever.

We reach the other side, but before I can catch my breath Layla moves into a street on the right of the building.

'Come on,' she says.

I put Isaac down and we follow her round the corner, my breathing still heavy. The street is dark. The stench of stale urine makes me gag. We pass a ramp that leads down into an underground car park full of rows of hibernating cars and trucks. Layla looks back down the street, gets out a key and opens a small door a few feet beyond the ramp. She goes in and we follow closely behind.

The door slams shut. We're in sudden darkness and it takes some time for my eyes and ears to adjust to the lack of light and noise. I hear a click from Layla's direction and a tube-light flickers on with a high-pitched ring. I'm in a narrow corridor. Beside me is a desk with a sliding glass panel and the word *Reception* written above it. On the other wall, there are noticeboards covered with leaflets and posters reminding people to sign in and out, or to join the new healthcare scheme, or advertising someone's old ride-on lawnmower.

'What is this place?' I ask.

'It's an old department store.'

Layla walks past Isaac and me, stops at the end of the corridor and looks back. I wonder if she's going to say something, but she doesn't. I drop down to Isaac.

'Are you okay?' I ask.

'Sleepy,' he signs.

'Not long now,' I say, and I hug him.

Layla opens the door and light floods into the corridor – natural light. She takes us into a cavernous, open space lit by the morning sun. I walk slowly forwards, stop next to one of the heavy concrete columns and look up. Above are clean glass panels forming a complex geometric pattern. They cut up the light into pieces, casting black lines onto the concrete floor. I walk slowly across the shining tiles, staying in the shadow of the floor above me, and look inside the remains of old shops. Some are closed and boarded up, but some are still open: a clothes shop with wintry coats still hanging on racks, a jewellery store with plastic necklaces and fake diamond earrings littering the floor, a restaurant with empty fridges. I used to come to places like this. Mum and I would spend a few hours together, looking at things that were too expensive to buy and buying things that were too cheap to survive.

'This way,' Layla says.

She heads up a broken escalator to the first floor. As Isaac and I get on, we both lose our balance and trip forwards, pre-empting the movement of the stairs. Isaac laughs, and I can't help but laugh too. Once he's stable, he runs up a few steps, then back down to me, and then up again, and I walk slowly behind him.

I hear voices ahead.

'Let me do the talking,' Layla says when we get to the top. On the wall on my left are three words written in white paint.

We will rise.

Layla walks ahead, leading us to a store in the far corner. The noise gets louder as we approach and I imagine we're in a scene from the old world, one in which Mum and I are wasting time shopping and there's no danger, only hope. I'm holding Isaac's hand tightly. The front of the store is completely open and above the entrance is a symbol that I vaguely recognise, the logo of a technology company that died soon after the Soundfield appeared. Inside, there are several small groups. No children, just adults, some lying on the ground, some sitting, most crowded around things: maps, folders, guns leant against walls, a cluster of screens on one wall displaying black-and-white images.

'Wait here,' Layla tells me. She approaches one group surrounding a large wooden table in the centre of the room and talks to a man with a short beard wearing a bullet-proof vest. Their eyes move between us and the other members of the group as they talk, and I feel looked at – not seen, but observed.

I drop down to Isaac, turning my back to the store, shielding him.

'What are we doing?' he signs.

'We're going to stay here for a bit. Okay?' I sign back.

'I don't want to.'

'It'll be alright.'

People are watching us speak our secret language. Layla walks back to us.

'You can stay,' she says. 'Pedro's always a bit hostile to new people, but he says it's alright. We've got a spare room for you.'

'Thank you.'

'No problem,' and she smiles at Isaac.

As we leave, I glance back in the store and see the man Layla was talking to – he must be Pedro. There's no warmth in his eyes. He's staring at me, or is he staring at Isaac? Layla takes us round the corner, past more shops, but unlike the ones on the ground floor, these have life in them. There's a classroom with wooden school desks in neat rows and a blackboard at the front, bedrooms with small cots in their corners and bedside tables with lamps on them, stores for food and supplies, a library, and in one room, a group of children being read a story surrounded by a fort made of cardboard boxes and old sheets.

'It's the same on every floor,' Layla says. 'Right up to the top.'

'Who are all these people?'

'They're just like us. People trying to survive.'

'Are you Babylon?'

She waits before replying.

'No, some of us are . . . but it's not what you think. This isn't a cult, we just all want the same thing.'

We reach the end of the hallway and Layla shows us into a room that's one half of an old fast-food restaurant. The kitchen at the back is still intact, but the tables and chairs have all been removed and the room divided into two by a thin strip of wood. In our half, there's a camp bed against one wall, a writing desk on the other, and piles of bedding pushed up to the food counter. Several glass figurines, some pens and pieces of writing paper have been arranged into neat piles on the desk. The sheets on the bed are scrunched into a ball.

'This looks like someone else's room,' I say.

'It was.' She pauses. 'But it's yours now.'

CHAPTER FOURTEEN

The sun is filling the department store with light. I get up and walk over to the metal shutters at the front of our room. We're set back here, but the light still finds us, radiating out from the well in the centre, past the wide columns, and into the buried edges of the building. It filters through the small, repeating gaps in the metal in front of me, creating a pattern of elongated rectangles on the walls and floor of the restaurant we're sleeping in. It's not dangerous to us now. I put my hands through the light, and the shapes distort in my palm. I stretch out my fingers then close them into a fist to try to grab the packets of energy.

How did this happen? How did I end up here? I should be used to things changing this quickly, but it still hurts. My mind aches from the jolt.

It's mostly quiet in the building apart from a few conversations which echo in the space, dissolving like the daylight.

When we were young, Mum used to throw dinner parties for her colleagues, usually after they'd landed a big deal, or signed a new artist. Theo and I would be allowed to join for the first part of the evening but were sent to bed when the main course was served and people started to drink too much. I remember being surrounded by my thick duvet upstairs and hearing the laughter and voices fill the house. I loved that sound.

I look back at Isaac's bed. His sheets are crumpled, but he's not there.

'Isaac?' I say.

I hear something. Movement, metal bending. I walk to the shining counters at the back of the store and lean over to the other side. Isaac is slumped on the floor, his back pushed up against the counter. He's gazing at something in his cupped hands.

'Can't you sleep?' I say. He shakes his head.

I go around the end of the counter and into the kitchen. The room smells of burnt cooking oil. Nothing seems to have changed since it was last used. Ovens, friers, an ice-cream machine with stickers for different flavours. I sit down next to Isaac and look at the object in his hands. It's a pin – red and pink concentric circles radiate out from a green plant at its centre.

'Where did you get this?' I say.

He shrugs.

'Was it in here?' I say.

He shrugs again.

I try to take the pin from his hands. He pulls it away and scowls.

'Isaac, please give it to me.'

He shakes his head.

'Isaac?'

He puts it in his pocket and signs.

'You won't let me keep it.'

'I'll give it back in a bit, I promise,' I say, clearly.

He takes it out of his pocket and puts it in my hand. I turn it over. There's something scratched into the back. *Sasha, No. 12.*

'Can you take me to where you found it?'

He pushes himself up, holds his hand out flat and looks at me with cross eyes. I put the pin onto his warm palm and close his fingers.

'Just for now,' I say and he nods.

Isaac takes my hand and leads me through a small gap in the dividing wall between the two halves of the restaurant, then through an open door into a storage room with its metal shutters still up. There are piles of boxes and newspapers, large paintings still wrapped in plastic, teddy bears piled in one corner. Isaac pulls on my hand and leads me out into the corridor. The sun bounces off the white concrete and makes my eyes hurt.

I blink.

*

I'm being led by the hand, by Theo. My brother is taking me somewhere. I was nine, maybe. I remember him waking me in the middle of the night.

'Come on,' he said, 'I've got to show you something,'

He took me out of the house and into the woods.

'Where are we going?' I said.

'You'll see,' he said.

It was summer, but it had been raining all day. I was sleepy, stepping in puddles and mud. My pyjamas were getting wet. They had ducks on them and I worried about them getting covered in dirt. Theo took me to the lake, and we stood at the water's edge. He pointed to the island.

'You see that?' he said.

'See what?'

I rubbed my eyes and looked harder. The island was covered in light. Small specks of darting white light. They surrounded the trees, skimmed off the water, made the air dance.

'What are they?' I said, but he didn't answer.

Isaac takes me down the corridor, past the makeshift school and the room with the cardboard fort towards a narrow store with a pair of golden glasses painted above the door-frame. The windows are boarded up, but the door has been removed.

Isaac lets go of my hand and runs inside.

'Wait!' I say, but he ignores me.

He skips to the back of the store and up a staircase. His

footsteps make small thuds which fade to nothing as he climbs higher. On both sides of the store are rows of dark bookcases separated into sections. *New Fiction, Science-Fiction, Thriller, Travel, Romance.* In the biography section, one book takes up a whole shelf: several copies stacked in neat piles, a few standing open. *My Premiership.* I remember his face. The last US president before the Field.

I hear voices from above.

'Isaac?' I call out.

I move to the back of the store, past narrow tables with more piles of dusty books and head upstairs. There's light, artificial and dim. I reach the top and see Isaac standing still, the pin resting on his outstretched palm.

'I thought I'd lost it,' a man says. His speech is slurred, heavy. His accent is Spanish, South American maybe.

I go up the final few steps and put my hands around Isaac's shoulder, pulling him close to me. The windows are blocked up here too. The only light comes from a small lamp pointing towards us. The man is sitting at the back of the room in an armchair. I can't see his face.

'*My flesh and my heart may fail,*' he says, holding his right hand in the air, '*but God is the strength of my heart and my portion forever.*'

He brings his hand down quickly as if he couldn't hold it up any longer.

'Do you know where that's from?'

'I'm sorry,' I say. 'We shouldn't be here.'

'I said, do you know where that's from?'

He reaches forward, picks up the lamp and puts it on the table next to him. It's the man Layla was talking to earlier. Pedro. He takes a drink from a half-empty bottle. Some liquid spills out of his mouth and onto his shirt.

'It's from a psalm,' he says. His speech is laboured. *'Those who are far from you will perish; you destroy all who are unfaithful to you.'*

'We should go,' I say.

'No, stay,' he snaps, and Isaac closes his hand over the pin. 'Stay, please,' he repeats more softly. He slumps back into his chair and closes his eyes.

'Do you believe in God, Hannah?'

'I don't know,' I say impatiently.

I uncurl Isaac's fingers and take the pin from him. It leaves a dark indent in his skin.

'It's here, the pin,' I say, putting it down onto the table next to me.

'If you don't believe in God,' he says in a quiet voice, 'then what is the point of living? *The body is a vessel for the soul.* Where is your soul going when you die?'

'I believe in science,' I say.

'Science won't work,' he says, half-shouting. 'It's not enough. There's something from Hebrews . . . What is it? What is it?' He's muttering to himself. 'Yes! Yes. This is it.' He breathes in deeply. *'By faith we understand that the worlds were framed by the word of God, so that the things which are seen were not made of things which are visible.* Science won't save you . . .'

Pedro reaches for the bottle and knocks the lamp to the floor.

'Fuck,' he says, but he makes no attempt to pick it up.

It lights up the wall behind him. There are hundreds of pins on a cork board, arranged by colour. A green section, a yellow section, a multicoloured section, a hole where one is missing.

He opens his eyes, looks at the shining board, then at us.

'You know what happened to my country? My people?'

His eyes are bloodshot and damp. What am I doing here?

'It's gone. All gone. Nothing left.'

He falls back into his chair and closes his eyes. '*My flesh and my heart may fail*,' he whispers. '*My flesh and my heart may fail*. You know what that means? It means we will die; you will die, your mother will die, son. *Es el destino*. It's what it is. It's fucked. All of it.'

I turn Isaac round and take him down the stairs and out of the store. I don't look back or say anything. I take him to his bed and tuck him in. With his eyes closed, he rotates his fist in small circles on his chest, over and over.

'Sorry,' he signs.

I'm woken up by the mechanical noise of the metal shutters rising. It's still light.

'Sorry to wake you.'

Pedro is standing in the now open space at the front of the restaurant.

'It's okay,' I say quietly. I bring the sheet up over my body, shielding myself.

'I'll take you to breakfast,' he says. His voice is monotone, harsh. 'I'll wait out here.'

I put on the clothes I was wearing yesterday and get Isaac dressed. The man nods curtly when he sees me and starts walking a few feet ahead. He's tall, with broad shoulders. I can see the muscles under his shirt. He reminds me how men used to look in films. We head past the bookstore with the boarded windows. On the doorframe there's something scribbled in red pen. I slow down to read it. *Sasha's hideaway*.

Pedro glances at the writing.

'My daughter,' he says.

'You scared my son.'

He looks at Isaac.

'I'm sorry,' he says in a way that makes me believe him. 'Layla told me someone was going to take him?'

'Yes,' I say.

'I'm glad she could help,' he says. 'We've known each other a long time.' He walks on. 'At the beginning, there were only fifteen of us, in this huge store. Prophets in a new land,' he says, looking around, holding his hands out. 'It was my mother who told me about the building. We came to this country when I was a boy. Escaping war, not the heat, but it's all the same. We're people with no homes. Unable to live where we were born, hated by the country we end up in. My mother worked in the supermarket on the ground floor, stacking shelves and cleaning up shit in the toilets. It was boarded up after the Field, but she still had her keys. She took me inside, and I found our home. Layla came not long afterwards. She helped set up the first school in the old stationary store, taught science and maths. She was only a teenager, but she was clever. There were only two kids back then. Now, we have over thirty. We have a school timetable, and classrooms. We have bedrooms for everyone. There are a hundred people living in this place. And how do we keep it safe? *Confianza. Trust.* We've managed to keep it safe because we trust our own. We trust that people will do what's best for the community.'

He stops and looks at me.

'Can I trust you, Hannah? Layla says I should. She found you on the train, yes?'

I nod.

'But how do I know you're not working for the government?'

'I'm . . .'

'A few years after we moved in here,' he says, interrupting me, 'Layla's brother, Samir, went to a protest in the city centre. Things got ugly, he was attacked, and a stranger looked after him. Samir was bleeding heavily. The man bandaged his arm, and Samir brought him back here. The stranger said he believed in what we do, that he wanted to help refugees. I didn't want him here, but Samir convinced me. Three days later, someone overheard the man talking on the radio to a government official. He saw them, there was a fight, and my friend got stabbed in the neck. I shot the stranger in the head as he was trying to escape, and my friend died. Since then, no one has come here without checks. But Layla . . .' He pauses. 'Why did you go with her?'

'I don't know, it happened so fast . . .' I reply.

'You had no knowledge of this place before you came here?'

'No,' I say firmly.

'What do you do for work?'

'I'm a lecturer, a scientist. I work in a TEU.'

'And what do you parents do?'

'They're dead,' I say. Was this a lie?

'Hm . . .'

He looks away.

'You can trust me,' I say.

He stares back at me, then at Isaac.

'Not yet,' he says.

We climb broken escalators up two flights, and I hear a sound that I haven't heard in years. The restaurant is just like one from before the Soundfield: tables with cutlery and napkins; an open kitchen stretching across the back wall with a section that juts into the restaurant; large trays of cooked food under heat lamps. There are chefs, servers, people eating and talking, and a faded map of Italy on one wall with the most famous cities highlighted – Rome, Florence, Siena. All places that are empty now.

Pedro turns to me.

'Thank you for bringing the pin back,' he says. 'It means a lot to Sasha.'

'It's okay,' I say.

He nods. 'Well, anyway. Eat. If you need anything, ask Layla.'

He points towards a table, and we sit down. It has a rough paper cloth, like the ones that used to be clipped to plastic tables at seaside resorts. I see it blowing in the wind as Theo and I eat ice cream and we talk about our secret trip to the lake when Mum is out of earshot.

CHAPTER FIFTEEN

Layla brings us our food. Runny eggs, toast. People are looking at us.

'We don't get many newcomers,' Layla says as she sits down. 'They'll stop staring eventually. Why did Pedro want to see you this evening? He said he wanted to wake you.'

'I'm not sure,' I say, and I cut up Isaac's toast into rectangles. 'You can dip them,' I say, and I show him what to do. '*Soldiers*, that's what my mum called them.'

Pedro is sitting on the far side of the restaurant with a young girl. He's helping her too – cutting up her food, pouring her water. She looks older than the other children, in her teens, I think. Or maybe it's just that she seems older because she doesn't smile.

'Is that Pedro's daughter?' I say.

Layla glances over her shoulder.

'Yeah,' she replies. 'Sasha.'

'Does Pedro run this place?'

'Sort of,' she says. 'No one person is in charge.'

Sasha says something to her father and stands up. Pedro gently grabs her arm, but she pulls it away, tripping slightly. She looks over at our table and walks in our direction. She moves slowly, holding her stomach with one hand.

'Hello,' she says to Isaac, speaking in a soft voice. 'I've got a little gift for you.'

She brings something out of her pocket and holds it out in front of her.

'I hear you liked the look of this one,' she says, 'and I want you to have it. It's one of the first ones I found, so it's quite special. That means you need to look after it.'

Isaac looks at the pin with the green plant and radiating circles, then back at me.

'Isaac can't speak,' I say, smiling, 'but he says thank you.'

'Oh,' she says. 'Well, let me help you put it on.'

She sits down on the chair next to Isaac and clasps the pin to his dirty white T-shirt. Her skin is thin, almost translucent. The whites of her eyes are yellow.

Pedro appears behind Sasha, carrying his bullet-proof vest in one hand.

'Anything about Samir?' he says coldly, directing his question to Layla.

It feels like he's trying not to look at his daughter and Isaac, like he doesn't want to see the exchange.

'Nothing,' Layla says.

'I'll pray for his return,' he says. 'Unit 12 is heading that way this evening. They may find him.'

'Okay,' Layla replies quietly and Pedro walks off. I try to catch Layla's eye, but she doesn't look back. Isaac peers down at his new pin and smiles.

'There's one more thing I want to show you,' Sasha says to Isaac. 'If that's okay with your mum?'

I nod.

'Okay,' she says brightly. 'Well, I think you're going to like this.'

Sasha takes us up to the top floor and Layla comes with us. On every level, we pass more bedrooms, storerooms and play areas. Every part of the building is being used. Life has found a way into every part. It's the opposite of where I live – lived. Sasha is walking ahead with Isaac, pointing things out to him: a store full of comfy sofas and armchairs; children sitting in a circle reading a book out loud to a patient teacher. The kids stare at us with fascination as we pass. A little boy waves enthusiastically to Isaac and he waves back.

'Do you still teach here?' I ask Layla.

'Teach? Oh, Pedro told you. No, not really. They have enough people to help now.'

I can hear bright voices from above.

We head up one more flight to the top floor and I see children playing. There's a huge toy store with painted walls and a patterned carpet; shelves full of stuffed bears and plastic toys. Next to the store is a play area with a ball pit and slide and a racetrack painted onto the floor. The Soundfield's Hum is drowned out by the laughter.

'Do you want to go and play?' I sign to Isaac. He looks into the toy shop, then back at me. 'It's okay. You can go. I'll be right here.'

'I'll help you,' Sasha says.

She holds out her hand and Isaac takes it. They walk slowly into the store and Sasha points at something. Isaac glances up at her, then runs to one of the shelves. He picks up a train with a blue engine and two blue carriages and shows it to Sasha. She smiles and picks up another train – a red one – and leads him to the beanbags a few feet away. She sits down, and Isaac falls onto the bag next to her, kicking a cloud of dust into the air. Sasha starts pushing her train across the floor, opening and closing the doors periodically to let imaginary passengers in. Isaac imitates her in the way he would have done if he'd had a brother or a sister.

'What's wrong with her?' I say quietly to Layla.

'Sasha? We don't know,' she says, looking at me. 'There's a doctor here but they don't have any equipment. They can't do any scans or any tests, really. And Pedro won't take her to a hospital. He thinks he'll lead them to us. Anyway, he believes God will help her. I've tried to convince him to go. I've taken Yara, my daughter, in the past. For small things.'

'Which one is she?'

She looks away – to the back of the floor, or to nothing at all.

'She's not here. She's with her father in the countryside. It's not far.'

A girl of about three or four joins Isaac and Sasha and asks if she can play too. Isaac gazes over at me.

'Go on,' I sign, and he slides one of the carriages over to the girl who starts pushing it along the ground too, imitating the sound of an old steam train with her mouth. How does she know what they sounded like?

I look at Layla, but she doesn't look back at me.

'Why are you doing this for us?'

'I wanted to help you,' she says calmly.

'People aren't that altruistic,' I say.

She stares at her feet. Her mouth is slightly open, as if she's waiting for the words to appear.

'I know who you are. You're Dr Hannah Newnham.'

I don't know how to react. I look at Isaac.

'How do you know that name?' I say.

'You did a series of lectures on the Field in 2038. I went to every one of them. I wanted to know more about the Soundfield, and I saw your talks advertised. I hadn't really been interested in it much before that, but the way you spoke . . . I didn't realise that science could be like that.' She looks away from me. 'When the Soundfield came, I thought it was the end, but you made me think differently about it. You made me see it as a problem to be solved, not something to be scared of . . . I actually still have a flyer from the lecture series with your bio and picture on. It's a little sad, I know . . .' She laughs. 'Those lectures meant a lot to me, Hannah.'

I didn't think anyone would have remembered them. Elias had asked me to do them at the last minute, and I'd never spoken in public before. The moment before I delivered my first lecture, I was shaking, with excitement or fear, I don't know, and it felt like there wasn't enough air in my lungs. But Elias helped me through it, and I stood on stage and shared what we'd been working on.

'So, is that why you helped me?' I say. 'You wanted to meet me?'

'No, I helped you because I would have wanted someone to do the same if it was Yara instead of Isaac. Look, this isn't calculated, and I'm still trying to work things out, but there is a way you can help us. It's not why I did it . . .'

'I could just leave.'

'Yes, you could, and I wouldn't stop you . . .' Layla looks at me, and I see her eyes again, deep brown, warm, ' . . . but I need to show you something before you go.'

I ask Sasha to look after Isaac and sign to him that I'll be back soon. The little girl on the beanbag next to him has found three more carriages and has attached them to Isaac's engine. As I leave, they start pushing their train together, making chugging noises in unison.

I follow Layla down one flight of stairs and to a room at the end of a long corridor. Her bedroom has the feeling of being lived in, of being loved. She has a proper single bed, with a thick mattress, a dining table, and an area at the back with two sofas and a round coffee table in the centre. The walls have been decorated with posters – abstract art, a cityscape that looks European, a rock band from a century ago – and any signs of what the room was once used for have been covered up or lost. The only thing left of its past life is a faded sign on the back wall with a white arrow and the words *Dressing Room* written in slanted letters.

'Did you have first pick?' I say.

'Oh, the room. Nearly. I chose this one because of how it smelt. I liked the smell of new clothes.'

I didn't do much to my flat in Mandalay House but was probably there as long as Layla has been here. Maybe I hoped it would be temporary, so I told myself that I didn't have space for clutter, but clutter is made of the things you care about too much to get rid of.

'It's in here somewhere.'

Layla is rooting through a filing cabinet at the back of the store.

I put my bag down, sit at the dining table, and look at the posters on the wall above Layla's bed. There's one with dozens of people posing in front of a kick drum and a flower bed. I don't recognise the album, but I recognise the band. Next to it is a poster of two people holding a sign saying *WAR IS OVER! If you want it.*

'Who are they?'

Layla glances at the poster and carries on searching.

'John Lennon and Yoko Ono. The selection wasn't great in the store, but I liked that one. My grandparents used to listen to The Beatles, and they told me about Lennon. He was killed in New York. Shot in the back.'

She pulls out a document and looks at it, but she doesn't turn to me.

'You're going to ask why I have this, and that's fair. I will explain, but I need you to see it first.'

She turns around and sits on the chair opposite me and slides the document over. The title reads *Evidence for the genomic basis of communication with the Soundfield*.

CHAPTER SIXTEEN

'How did you get this?' I say.

'Is this you?'

Layla points to the first name in a list at the top of the page. *Dr H. Newnham, Prof. E. Larsson, Dr M. Singh, Dr F. S. Harker.*

Elias let me put my name first.

'We had a contact in the Programme,' Layla says. 'He passed us documents when he could. This one came to us a few months ago. I recognised your name straight away. It is you, isn't it?'

Do I lie? It's too late for that.

'Yes,' I say quietly.

'I was the only one who could see how useful this could be,' she says. 'Pedro wasn't convinced, no one was, but I thought that if we could understand the science, we could actually make some progress. I spent weeks reading and re-reading it and trying to find all the papers and books you referenced.' She turns to the back page and shows me the catalogue of seventy-two references.

'I'd be surprised if you could find any of them now,' I say.

'It was hard. I got twenty or so. The Mithen helped a lot, so did the Darwin. The Pinker, not so much. There's an old bookstore at the north end of the high street which I broke into. The papers and journals I got from our contact. I thought I understood most of it, but . . .'

Layla turns back a page. Every line of the last few paragraphs of the paper is covered in thick black marks.

'Everything's redacted. I can't make sense of it without the end, without you, Hannah.'

I could recite the blackened lines by heart. In the days after we'd finished the paper, after I'd presented my ideas to a room full of faceless men, I would lie in bed next to Elias, whispering the words to myself, trying to work out where I went wrong.

'I can't help you,' I say, 'I'm sorry. I need to get back to Isaac.'

I get up to leave.

'Why are you scared of the work you did?' Layla stands up and holds the paper towards me.

'Whatever you're doing here,' I say, 'is *your* purpose. What you're holding in your hand was mine, but it's done now.'

'You can't save your son if you leave.'

'Don't . . .'

'There won't be someone to help you whenever he sings in public. You can't protect him from them, but *we* can.'

'You have no idea what I've had to do to keep him safe. I've lost everything.'

'You don't think I've lost people too? You don't think I hate myself for what's happened to the people I love?'

I look into her eyes and then I see it, the resemblance.

'Your eyes,' I say.

'What?'

'You have the same eyes.'

I stop, and for a moment I think about taking it back.

'What do you mean?' she says.

'Two days ago. I was looking out of the window in my flat, near the South Station, and a man appeared in the street down below. He looked straight up at me.'

'You saw my brother?' Her voice is hopeful.

'I don't know,' I say. 'What did he look like?'

'Black hair. A bit taller than me. Brown eyes.'

'It might have been him,' I say. 'I have something of his.'

I pick up my bag and reach to the bottom. I find it, tangled, but soft. I pull the man's scarf out and hold it towards Layla. She looks at it, and her expression changes.

'What happened?' she says with only breath in her voice, still looking at the scarf.

'There was a sound, a shout from somewhere behind him, police, I think, and then he . . . then he fell to the ground.'

Layla stares at the floor and I hear something that sounds like a muffled cry. She turns away from me, puts my paper down on the table and holds her hands to her chest. She breathes in slowly and the air stutters as it comes out.

'He knew the risks,' she says. 'We all do.'

'My brother was killed a few years ago,' I say. I see Theo's face in my mind, but his eyes are blurred. No, not blurred. Black. I feel hollowed out. 'I know it doesn't seem like it now, but it will get better,' I lie.

'Please go,' she says.

I look at my paper, open on the redacted pages, then back at Layla. I think about staying, but the thought goes as quickly as it comes.

'I'm so sorry,' I say.

Isaac is alone by the time I reach the top floor. He's lying on his back on the beanbag, flicking through the pages of a colourful book on dinosaurs, his knees pointing to the ceiling. I drag a blue beanbag next to him and he shuffles towards me.

'Have you had a nice time?' I say. 'Where's Sasha?'

He shrugs and turns another page revealing a slightly faded picture of a pterodactyl with feathers and a large beak. He drops the book to his side, keeping the page open.

'Are these still alive?' he signs.

'No. They died out a long time ago,' I sign back.

'With the heat?'

He means the people in the southern hemispheres, the refugees who didn't make it north.

'Not with them,' I sign. 'These animals became extinct millions of years ago, when a meteor hit the Earth.' I use my hands to mimic an explosion, making a little noise with the gesture. 'We have to leave,' I say. He goes back to looking at the pterodactyl. 'We have to leave, Isaac.' He starts to cry a little and shakes his small head, and I hug him through the picture book.

'We'll take this, but don't tell anyone, okay?'

'Okay,' he signs through his tears.

I lift him onto his feet, put the dinosaur book in my bag, and take his hand. The children have dispersed a little, but there are still a few left: two racing each other in red and yellow cars on the track; one in the ball pit; a few in the far corner sitting under a plastic palm tree. Sasha is under the tree too, reading a book out loud to the group.

'Do you want to read first?' I remember Theo saying to me in an excited voice, hoping I'd say no. He was young, so was I. We were keeping each other busy on a rainy day.

'You go first!' I said. 'And do the voices!'

I can hear all the accents he did – a snarly voice for the fox, a high-pitched squeaking for the mouse, a sibilant whisper for the snake. But in my memory, I can't see his face. When I try to bring it into focus, all I see is Samir, Layla's brother. Their images are tied together in my head, and I can't seem to undo them. Or is it Theo's face with Samir's eyes?

I stop one floor down and look towards Layla's room. Isaac pulls at my hand and gazes up at me.

'I just need to do something,' I say.

I see the picture of John Lennon and Yoko Ono on the wall before I see Layla, and I repeat the words in my head. *WAR IS OVER! If you want it.*

'Layla?' She turns around and looks at me. 'I'll help you if I can.'

She walks over quickly and puts her arms round my neck. After a moment, I hold her back.

'Thank you,' she says. 'I have a place we can talk. It's private.'

We go through a door at the end of Layla's corridor and climb a set of rusting metal stairs to an old fire exit. When Layla opens the door, it brings in cool blue light and the deep sound of the Field – we're on the roof. It must have been raining. It smells earthy and sweet. I walk to the metal railing a few feet away – the roof looks out for miles across the city, exposing a patchwork of spaces lit by streetlamps and floodlights, places where humans have clustered. The air buffets across the vents and satellite dishes still clinging onto the surface of the roof, and I turn my face to the wind for a moment. It takes my sweat and heat away.

Layla joins me. 'Samir and I used to come up here to escape the others when things got heated,' she says, leaning on the railing. 'We had these little dens when we were young. Places where we'd meet where Mama and Baba – my father – wouldn't be able to find us. This roof was like one of those hiding places. No one else really knows about it, so we would come and sit up here, and just look out over the rooftops.'

I tell Isaac to stay away from the edge and give him his dinosaur book. He sits on a large pipe – one leg on either side – and opens the book to the first page. I go back to Layla.

'Thank you for telling me about him, Hannah. Pedro thought

he was dead, but I didn't want to believe him. He didn't really like Sam.'

She breathes out heavily.

'We always thought things might end,' she says. 'Every morning, we would say goodbye like it was the last time we'd see each other.'

'Why did you stay?'

'We had nowhere else to go, and the people here, they became our family.' She looks at me. 'You do know what you're getting into?'

'No, not really.' I glance back at Isaac. He's now lying on the pipe, book in the air, feet dangling.

'My brother, Theo, was in the army,' I say. Layla looks away from me. She knows what *in the army* means. I stare out at the city with her.

'I never asked what he did, but I know he was working at the coast. Mum told me that. I'd see pictures of hundreds of bodies on the shore, some with bullet holes, and I would think of Theo. It made me sick thinking about what he was doing, what he *might* have been doing . . . When he died, I was finishing off the research for my paper. Someone from the army came and told me he'd been killed, but I didn't feel sad, or not as sad as I should have. I think I felt relieved. I never understood why he wanted to join; it was like he was wired differently from me.'

I gaze at Layla.

'The Soundfield . . . the research we did . . . I thought it was the opposite of what Theo was doing. I was making something; he was destroying things. You have to understand that at the beginning, we never guessed what might happen. It was just exciting: a chance to work on something that no one else had worked on in history. I want to help you because I can't let it all be for nothing.'

Warm air blows past us and I hear the pages of Isaac's book rustling.

'What have you been doing since?' Layla asks.

'I teach, in a TEU. I give lectures on my research, actually, but under a different name, under my mum's maiden name. None of the original researchers are still talked about – Elias, Mahesh, Freya and me. We've all been erased. But I didn't want to take the risk. It was easy to fake a few documents.'

'Why?'

'Why don't I use my real name?'

'No, why do you give lectures on your research? Isn't it a risk?'

This question used to keep me awake in the heat of the day. I thought about doing something different – manual labour, administrative work for the few government departments left, selling food, ration distribution, care – but I chose to teach.

I answer Layla as honestly as I can.

'Because I don't how to do anything else.'

The night is deep now, and the city is alive. The high street below is less busy than it would have been on any day before the Field, but there are still enough people to fill the space:

a few groups gathered around pop-up stalls selling bread and canned food; a couple chatting on a bench; some kids kicking a ball against an old toothpaste advert stuck to the wall, trying to hit the same spot in the person's mouth every time. I wonder whether people would want to go back to a world where we lived in the day, and slept at night? There's a generation growing up who see this as *their* world, and who are we to take it away? Maybe they don't want to go back. Maybe I don't want to go back.

I look at Layla, and she smiles at me. She isn't pressuring me to share, nor am I pressuring her to tell me about her life or what they do here, about Babylon. But I think I can help her.

For the next few hours, I tell Layla my story, and she listens, and we watch the air begin to glow with the rising sun as Isaac reads to himself in the uneven light.

PART TWO

CHAPTER SEVENTEEN

Theo left six months after the Soundfield appeared.

He dropped out of school, signed up to the army and had moved out of the house by the spring. I overheard him talking to his friend a week before he left. Daniel, I think his name was. Theo said something about the tear gas that was being used against migrants in Europe. He paused, then laughed raucously. The news reports were always about the migrant crisis in those days, but they only told one side of the story. On some websites, there were suggestions that the gas was causing women to have miscarriages. I tried to speak to Theo about it, but I couldn't get the words out. Instead, I just told him that Mum didn't want him to leave. It wasn't a lie, but he didn't believe me. On the day Theo left, Mum and I stood outside on the gravel and watched him get into Daniel's car, and we waved him off. Mum hugged him tight, and said how proud she was, but when the car was out of sight she burst into tears and her knees gave way. I held her like she was a child, and she cried into my jumper in the cold air.

Mum's work had all but disappeared by this point. Before the Field, she was in music copyright, working with a record label in the city. She would deal with contracts, I think – I never really knew exactly what she did every day – but, as a child it meant we were always surrounded by music, and musicians. She often invited people round – producers, singers, her colleagues – and they'd spend an evening, or a whole weekend, with us, escaping the noise and smell of the city. Mum worked for a small company, and they had to work hard to get clients and harder to keep them, but I got the sense that she liked what she did. The big record labels survived longest after the Soundfield, but all of them were gone within two years. There was no money left, and no incentive to keep making music because no one was buying it.

Theo only came back home a handful of times in the years that followed, mainly at holidays, so he never saw how Mum really was. She spent a lot of time in bed during the day – this was before either of us switched – and at night, I would hear her crying to herself. I thought it was for Theo at first, but I think it might have been for her. She had lost her life, as well as her son. I tried to come up with ways to help her – walks by the lake, board games, listening to her favourite music together – but nothing really worked. She was in a room that was locked from the inside.

Unlike a lot of my friends, I stayed in school. I had nearly two years left, so I split my time between lessons and looking after Mum. After school, I'd come home, check on her, make dinner, do some cleaning, and after she was asleep I'd study in my bedroom using as little electricity as I could by only switching on a small desk lamp. One winter, a local power station was vandalised, and the electricity was off for three weeks. I sat in the cold – that's when it was still cold at winter – and read about chromosomal aberrations and genetic poly-morphism by candlelight. Mum and I spent our time wrapped in thick blankets.

At school, a new girl called Mia arrived from Italy. Her father was a climate scientist, and they were worried about her education being disrupted. She had an aunt who lived here, and so Mia moved in with her and came to our school for the last two years. She had blue eyes, and long black hair, and we dated for just over a year. I hadn't really done anything like that before, and it probably looked out of character to the people around me, but she had an energy about her that I couldn't resist. She wasn't like most other people in my year. She thought the Soundfield was exciting, and that it was the beginning of something new, and the end of a world that was dying anyway. She used to quote a line from an old movie that she liked that I hadn't seen: *Let the past die, kill it if you have to*, she'd say in a soft Italian accent. She thought that it was our chance to reinvent ourselves, to change everything, and I believed her.

For a while, she was my little secret, and I would go to her house to study – and do other things – but one weekend, I decided to introduce her to Mum. I told Mum we were a couple, sort of, and she was polite enough. Mum served lasagne to make Mia feel at home and talked about a holiday she'd taken to Siena as a child. But after Mia had left, without flinching or looking up from the plate she was scrubbing, she said to me that Mia was a fling and that I should get over her. I was angry, but she was right, of course. By the middle of my last year at school, Mia and I were spending much less time together and, in the final term, I saw her kissing a boy from my year in the chemistry corridor.

During those two years without Theo, Mum and I got into a routine and even became close. But she never asked me what I wanted to do after I left school. It became this unsaid thing that hung in the air between us. Maybe she assumed I would stay with her, I don't know, but whenever I brought it up, she would pretend not to hear, or would change the topic. I loved my mum, and there was a comfort in the life we had built together, but during those years, I lay in bed at night listening to the Soundfield, fantasising about a life outside of those walls, imagining what I could learn or achieve.

Theo's leaving should have been the hardest, but mine was. Mum wasn't really there; she hugged me, but it was sterile.

'Good luck,' she said, without feeling.

I couldn't convince her that it was worthwhile me going to university.

'There are so many things you could do here, Hannah,' she said at dinner a few days before I left. 'Teaching at the school, volunteering in a hospital, delivering food – Sarah next door has only had two deliveries in the past week because her man has gone – you could be doing *anything*. People need you here. You're being selfish.' I yelled at her when she said this, saying childish things like *you don't understand*, and *how could you keep me here*, but maybe I shouted because she was right. In the end, we just gave up talking about it, and she went back to crying herself to sleep, rounding the circle that began with Theo leaving.

My university was one of the early adopters of night-working. The labs and halls were getting too hot during the day, so we became one of twenty or so institutions – mainly governmental departments and schools – to switch first. Mum was worried I wouldn't be able to see her, but I told her that everyone would have to change eventually, and that I could always come and visit after re-timing for a couple of days.

To prepare for the switch, I stayed up for a day and a night, then slept through the next day. I woke up at seven in the evening, stayed up for another night, and slept again at dawn. I did this for five more days, and then on the Tuesday of the week after, I did my first night of work. We had lectures from ten till midnight, then labs in the early morning. On that first night shift, I finished my work as the sun rose and I watched the light find its way into the room, catching the edges of the metal and glass around me, making the place shimmer. It was beautiful. I called Mum, but she didn't answer. I called Theo, but he didn't answer. I even called Mia, but she didn't answer.

I sat in my lab and looked out of the window and caught the first glimpse of the day, and was alone.

There wasn't much socialising outside of the anthropology department, not that I was aware of. But we did all eat together – professors as well as students – before restaurants and shops made the switch. At half-past twelve every night, we'd be given food in the canteen, and we'd talk a little about our work, but mainly about our lives before the switch, and we'd pretend that this was only temporary. I was struggling with sleeping through the day, most people were, so it was nice to tell yourself it wouldn't last long. Most things about working at night were the same as working in the day, except the stillness. I walked down windowless corridors by myself, and could feel the night: the heavy, quiet air stacked in thick layers upwards, unmoved by the dark. But there was something beautiful about the quiet; it let me work harder than I've ever worked in my life, and I could escape in it.

I missed Mum, though.

When I was back from university one holiday, before she had switched, I found her outside in the sun. It was in my second year, I think, and July and August had become so hot by that point that it was impossible to stay outside in the day for any length of time. It hurt even to half-open your eyes in the light. That morning, I was in the kitchen clearing up my breakfast – I had woken up late – and I saw Mum out on the lawn, lying on the grass reading a book. She was wearing a vest, exposing a small V-shaped area of her chest, and her arms and legs were uncovered. I opened the door and called for her to come inside. She ignored me, so I called again, and she waved her hand dismissively in my direction. I went to the hall, grabbed a black raincoat, put the hood up, put my hands in the pockets and bowed my head to the sun as I went out.

'Mum, you have to come back in,' I shouted.

'It's nice. Leave me be.'

She muttered something about me looking stupid in the raincoat under her breath but came in eventually. Her arms were bright red. I pressed my thumb into her left shoulder, and it left a white mark that stayed for nearly a minute. I told her she should never go outside without being covered, that she had to stay indoors in the middle of the day. But this obviously wasn't the first time she'd done it. Experts told us to avoid going outside during the day unless absolutely necessary, but even this was too lenient. Research later showed that UV levels four years after the Soundfield appeared – the year I caught Mum reading outside in the dry heat – were high enough to cause mutations in skin cell DNA with only thirty minutes of exposure. Melanomas worldwide peaked every year for a decade, with every record set by the previous year being decimated by the next. Eventually, people listened. UV suits were properly designed and the makeshift ones that we all wore, most people wore, were pulled apart and put away. In the years after she got sick, we never talked about why it happened, but I didn't love her any less for not listening to me.

CHAPTER EIGHTEEN

I met Elias for the first time in the canteen when I was a few months into my doctoral studies. He sat opposite me and introduced himself as a member of the atmospheric physics department, but he didn't ask me what I was doing. He ate quickly, corrected someone who had mis-quoted Niels Bohr and left within five minutes.

Our next meeting was also in the canteen. I was having a cup of coffee, looking through some papers, and he was sat at the table next to me bending over his laptop. Something about my work caught his attention.

'You know I wrote that one?'

He nodded towards a paper buried under a few others. *The Physical Properties of the Soundfield, Prof. E. Larsson et al.*

'I'm Elias. Sorry I was rude the other day.' He smiled with his eyes. They were opal.

'You weren't, don't worry.'

I honestly hadn't thought anything of it. The more scientists I met, the more I realised we were all the same, trapped inside our heads.

'What's your thesis?' he asked.

'It's on the evolution of music.'

'That's clever.'

'How do you mean?'

'Well, you have to do something on the Soundfield, right? So, evolutionary musicology *seems* like it's related to the Field to lay people, but isn't really. It's tangential at best. *Tell all the truth but tell it slant.* Isn't that what Dickinson wrote?'

I laughed. 'Well, maybe my research will finally give us some answers,' I said, with a smile. He laughed back.

His paper was brilliant, but I had a lot of questions. I had a good understanding of physics from my time at school and from my own reading, but some things were still unclear to me, so a few days after we talked in the canteen, I went to his office. I thought he might send me away – young doctoral students didn't really speak to people like him – but he invited me in and answered every one of my questions. If he was annoyed, or thought what I was asking was stupid, he didn't let it show. In fact, he seemed happy to be talking to me. Elias's research was fast-moving, and he produced a new paper every few months. As soon as one was published, I would read it quickly, then would go to his office to ask him about it. It became a routine of sorts, a small part of both of our lives.

'You don't think like my students,' he said one time. 'They're too rational, too stuck. I'm beginning to wonder if I should get rid of them all and replace them with you.'

Elias's team discovered nothing alien in the Field. From the weather balloons sent up to the stratosphere, they found it was composed of a mixture of atmospheric gases, as expected – mostly nitrogen, around one fifth oxygen, some water vapour, and a few trace gases like radon and carbon dioxide – but also things that shouldn't be there: small dust particles, inert minerals and silica, and some living organisms like bacteria and fungi. It was air mixed with earth mixed with life. When the Soundfield arrived, Elias concluded, it took a microscopic layer off the ground as it rose and held it in suspension about thirty kilometres above our heads, creating a thin, fragile dome that sealed the Earth.

The first few of Elias's papers were about the composition of the Field, but he quickly moved on to thinking about how it was producing sound. Collecting data for this part of his research was much more difficult. They tried sending small rockets up to capture footage in slow motion, but most over-shot the correct altitude and were destroyed by the Field, or the video was too blurry to glean anything useful. Flying up there was the only option. It was too high for a helicopter, so Elias pulled every string he could to charter a plane. They attached fourteen cameras to the outside of the aircraft set to record at different frame rates and in different parts of the electromagnetic spectrum, and the pilot flew five hundred metres below the Field at night. He was the only person on the plane and Elias didn't know if it would kill him being so close to the Soundfield. He told me later that someone above him had lied to the pilot about the chances of surviving the journey. Elias was in the control room during the experiment, but he had to leave to be sick.

'Do you know about the Chernobyl nuclear disaster of the 1980s?' he said to me a few weeks after the flight. I was in his office, drinking coffee.

'Of course,' I said, surprised. I remember this question coming from nowhere.

'Well, after the explosion, the cooling pipes that were meant to carry water to the reactor in case of an emergency ruptured, causing the basement underneath to be flooded. The fuel from the reactor was still somewhere over a thousand degrees Celsius and was mixing with the graphite from the fuel rods and the concrete of the reactor floor to create a lava-like substance that was eating its way through into the basement. If this substance were to reach the water underneath it would cause the water to vaporise so quickly that it would result in a second explosion. A massive one, big enough to throw tonnes of radioactive material into the air. So, there was only once choice. The water had to be drained. But it could only be done by hand . . .' He paused. 'Three men were sent in to open the sluice gates. They were given respirators, diving suits, dosimeters. But the water by this point, it was like toxic waste. As far as the people in charge were concerned, they were dead men.

'When I used to hear stories like this, I tried to imagine

what I would have done if faced with the same situation. I
told myself that I would have done things differently, that I
would have found another solution, or sacrificed myself instead
of others, but . . .' He looked at me. 'The three men who
opened the gates actually survived. Did you know that? People
often forget to say that part of the story, but they did. They
survived all that radiation . . .'

He stopped and looked away.

'The pilot. James. He died from UV exposure two days ago.'

I didn't see Elias for a few months after that. He took some
time off, and his research was put on hold whilst his team
waited for him to return, but this only heightened speculation
about the experiment and the footage. I didn't want to talk
to anyone about it, out of respect more than anything else,
but one morning, I came across a group of undergraduates
looking at something on a laptop in the canteen, whispering
to one another. It started with only three students, then a few
more joined, then more still, until twenty people were crowded
around the computer.

'What's going on?' I asked someone who had just returned
from the group.

'It's a video from the plane,' they said.

Someone in Elias' team had leaked a six-second shot from
one of the jet's upwards-facing cameras, one recording in the
visible spectrum. I shouldn't have gone over, but I did. I
couldn't help myself. I stood at the back of the group, trans-
fixed, trying to work out what I was watching. There was

nothing in the image to parse the scale – no reference objects or measurements – and it was recorded at hundreds of frames per second, so getting a sense of how fast it was moving in real terms was difficult, but it *was* moving. It was like *waves*, crisp waves passing across the screen, like how a snake pushes itself across the ground. It was pulsing, alive.

After I saw the footage, I said nothing and left.

I went outside into the warm darkness, looked up in silence, and, for a moment, I thought I could see the air and dust vibrating: layers of a shifting world hanging above my head folding into each other like surf on a wave, and all I wanted to do was swim in its waters. Later, we would find out that the air in the Field is moving so fast that it's almost invisible to the human eye, like the beating of an insect's wings, but that didn't change what I experienced that night. I saw the Soundfield for the first time in that empty courtyard, and I knew I had to find out why it was here.

Elias was back by the end of November, and he produced the first paper on the pilot's footage three months later. It confirmed what we had all seen in the canteen that day.

'The Soundfield is best compared to a diaphragm in a loud-speaker,' he wrote. 'It's a thin, taut membrane that vibrates thousands of times a second, manipulating the air to produce soundwaves. This explains the phenomenon that we now colloquially refer to as the *Hum*. Further research will be required to explain how the *Calls* are produced.' At the end of the paper, he added a dedication to the pilot who lost his life. But after the Atavism Programme began a few years later, this was removed.

It took me a while to work up the courage to talk to Elias about what had happened during the flight, but in the meantime we could always talk about work – science was objective and rational, unlike people. A week after he published the paper on the Soundfield's Hum, he asked me into his office.

'What do you make of this?'

He pressed play on a small device sitting on his desk and sat back in his chair. It was one of the Soundfield's *Calls*, but it sounded different to how I'd heard them before. It was clearer, like if you've only heard someone's voice through a wall, and suddenly you're standing right next to them, and they're speaking into your ear, and you can hear the way their jaw clicks as they talk.

'Was this recorded by the pilot?'

'Yes.'

'How many seconds do we have?'

'This is it.'

'Does it sound like it's trying to speak to us?'

Elias looked at me as though I'd said something to offend him, but his expression slowly changed to one of confusion. He looked away.

'Sorry,' he said, 'it's just no one's ever said that before.'

Elias let me take the recording with me, and I would sometimes play it to myself when I wanted a break from writing. One day, I fell asleep listening to it, and it worked its way into my dreams. I saw a long, matte black surface with sand floating just above it, stuck in the air, vibrating thousands of times a second as if the ground was making music.

Nine years after the Soundfield arrived I completed my doctoral thesis. I decided to go back home for a week or two after my Viva to check on Mum. She hadn't switched yet, so I re-timed for her. I stayed awake for a night and a day and slept through the following night. I should have done more rounds – I was exhausted – but I had nothing to do at home other than read and sleep. Mum was happy to see me, but when she hugged me on the doorstep, she winced. I asked her if she was alright, and she said she was fine. After dinner, I asked her again.

'Skin cancer.'

That was all she said. No context or preparation, just those lonely words.

'How long have you known?'

'Just over a month.'

'Why didn't you tell me?'

'How could I? You've switched. I barely know what times you're awake.'

'What did the doctor say?'

'They can't operate or won't. They want to give me drugs, and to do radiotherapy, but it's a night clinic, so I can't do it. There have been thousands of people like me. I'll be fine.'

Over the next two days, I convinced her to accept the treatment and said I'd switch with her so she could attend the clinic. We stayed up one day and one night, slept the next day, and repeated the pattern for two weeks until we were both tired enough to sleep fully during the day. To keep ourselves awake at night, we played board games and read books, and we ate every meal at the kitchen table. Rationing had just started, so I didn't eat much. I gave most of my food to Mum.

The week after Mum switched, I took her to the clinic for her first bout of chemotherapy and sat with her in a brightly lit room as the drugs dripped into her left arm. She was staring at a poster of a cat dangling on a rope with the caption *Hang in there*. I wanted to rip the poster down.

'Does Theo know?' I asked.

'No.' She looked at me. 'Don't tell him, Hannah. Please.'

Theo had only been back to see Mum once in the two years leading up to her diagnosis. He had been posted to the south coast, she said, part of a group used to keep order on the beaches, and to round up refugees that had survived the crossing. Thousands died in boats before getting here. They had to decide between travelling at night – when it was easier to hide but harder to navigate – or travelling in the day – when the sun was so hot that they could die of heat stroke or UV exposure. And if they made it across the water alive, they were then met by people like Theo. Men with guns. Maybe I should have told him about Mum? Maybe it would have changed him? It's too late for that now, and it was probably too late then.

'Please don't,' she repeated as I put her to bed later that morning.

'I won't,' I said.

I stayed with Mum for a few months after that first appointment and said I'd be with her when she started radiotherapy, but at the end of October that year, Elias came to visit.

CHAPTER NINETEEN

I was in the garden when he arrived. Elias still had a car when everyone else I knew had sold theirs in the scrappage scheme or abandoned them. His research came with perks, even access to fuel.

When he got out of his car, I hugged him, and I hadn't realised how much I missed him. 'How was your journey?' I said, as if I'd been expecting him, and he said it was fine. He came into the house, and we ate together. Mum was in bed but she woke up to be sick a few times. Elias asked what was wrong and I told him everything. It was the first time I'd spoken about it. Mum didn't talk much about her pain or about her treatment. It was like she was living two lives: one where she was well and with me and another where she was ill and alone. So, everything came out. Elias held me afterwards and I was finally able to ask him how he was. He talked about the pilot and his time off. He said that in the weeks after James's death, he had considered following him: walking into the sun, and letting it burn him. It had taken all his strength to keep going. He cried. Before that night, I saw Elias as someone so confident in their own intelligence and abilities that I thought nothing could break them, but I was wrong.

That day we fell asleep in each other's arms in my childhood bed, and I began to fall in love with him.

In the evening, I woke up before Elias, and heard Mum downstairs. I washed and got dressed and went to explain why there was a car in the drive. Mum didn't seem to mind – I think she was in pain – and when Elias got up, the three of us ate breakfast together and made polite conversation. Afterwards, Mum was tired so went back to bed, and I asked Elias why he had come.

'To see you,' he said. 'But also for something else. We're struggling, Hannah. We've got as far as we can with the data, but there's something holding us back . . .' He shifted a little in his chair. 'I have dozens of people working on this, brilliant minds, but we're making no progress. Maybe everything happened too fast at the beginning, I don't know. We know so much about the properties of the Field, about what it is, about how it makes sound, but we have no idea why it's here, or what any of it means.' He got up and turned away from me. 'Things are changing, Hannah. I keep getting called into meetings with new people asking me the same questions over and over. They want answers, and I don't have them.' He looked back at me. 'I need you to come and work for us.'

'I've never worked on the Field before.'

'But you know everything about it. You've read all my papers; you know more than most of my people. We need a new perspective. You can see things that other people can't.'

'But my mum. I can't go.'

'I know. I know this is difficult, but you could help us; you could help me. You don't have to give me an answer right now.'

Elias left straight after we'd talked. He told me to say thank you to my mum and to think about his offer, and so I did. I went back into the house and up to my room and found Elias's audio recorder. For the next ten minutes, I sat on my bed in the dark and listened to the recording of the Soundfield's music on repeat, clicking the back button every sixteen seconds. Pinned to my wall was a piece of manuscript paper dated the sixth of August 2028, the day after the Soundfield arrived. I took the paper off the wall, put it into my bag along with the recorder and waited for Mum to wake up.

I didn't think I'd have to leave her again, but it was easier this time – she understood that I had to go, even if I couldn't tell her why. But it was still hard. I worried Mum might spiral after I left, and that she wouldn't complete her treatment. I had my work to sustain me, but what did she have? Theo wasn't coming back, and her friends had all switched months before her and had moved on with their lives. But at least I could call her in the night now. I could check to see if she'd been to the doctors or had bought some food, or we could just talk about nothing.

Elias had moved into a new building by the time I returned. He had twice the number of labs and offices, and his team had ballooned. At first, I felt lost in the sea of new names and faces, but I had no time to learn them. I'd read a lot about the Field, but I wasn't prepared for how much data had already been accumulated: over one hundred hours of recordings, attempted categorisation of the sounds, chemical and physical data, video footage, musical transcriptions of the Calls. I sat in my office alone and read, watched, and listened to it all. I had to form my own opinions about what had been collected before I spoke to anyone. Every person working on the Field would have their own interpretations of the data, and I couldn't be clouded by them.

Once I was ready, Elias put me in charge of a group of doctoral and postdoctoral students, and the first thing we did was to create a definitive categorisation of the sounds produced by the Field. The *Hum* itself was not a fixed thing. The pitch changed – sometimes it was made up of hundreds of different frequencies like white noise, sometimes it was only a few frequencies – but the amplitude and timbre of the sound also changed, depending upon the local weather but also where you were in the world. We had recordings from every country, even those that had been deserted, and the character and quality of the Hum was different in different places. The Soundfield could localise its music, like every part of it was the mouth of the instrument, or like the mouth could move.

We classified the Soundfield's Hum by its fundamental frequency but the melodies, or *Calls* as we named them, were harder to categorise. By the time I started working on the Field, I had access to hundreds of recordings of different Calls, some taken at ground level, some at higher elevations. There were only three that repeated with identical pitches every time. One was the Call that was heard when the Soundfield arrived, which I named Common Phrase 1, or CP1 for short. The morning after its first iteration, when I was sixteen and living with Mum at home, I made a transcription of this Call. I woke up in Mum's bed, left her sleeping, went to my room, and on a small piece of manuscript paper wrote down what I remembered of the melody that I'd heard the night before. I knew there would be recordings of it everywhere on the internet – from people's phones or from CCTV footage – but this was how I heard it; it was my version. When I left Mum to join Elias and his team nearly ten years later, I stuck my scribbled transcription onto the board in my office, and whenever the Call appeared, I would read through my score as I listened. I only heard CP1 twice, maybe three times during those years, but it would become the most common melody in the years after the executions began.

The two other two repeated Calls – CP2 and CP3 – were short, and easily recognisable. One started with an upwards slide moving to a held note, a slightly flat C natural, and the other began with a short, attacked note which turned into a three-note sequence, characterised by wide intervals. These three Calls were the only ones that retained their pitch identities between iterations, but another approach was needed to categorise the remaining Calls. And on a rainy night in the sixth month of my research, I came up with an idea.

CHAPTER TWENTY

'*Phonemes*,' I said to Elias, who looked at me quizzically. 'In linguistics,' I continued, 'phonemes are the units of language, and the way we distinguish one word from another. So, something like *push* for example has three phonemes – /p/ for the consonant at the beginning, /ʊ/ for the vowel sound, which can be vocalised at any pitch, and /ʃ/ for the sound at the end. And I think the Soundfield has its own phonemes. There are phrases, sometimes only two or three notes long, which keep reappearing in different Calls, but often at different pitches, like acoustical building blocks of the Soundfield's language. Look . . .'

I brought up a database of musical phenomes that I had been putting together with my team. Elias leant over my desk to look at the screen.

'This one,' – I pointed at a cell showing a sequence of four notes: long, short, short, long – 'this has appeared in over forty

Calls. Its pitches change nearly every time, but the sequence of intervals is always the same.'

'So, this is combinatorial?' Elias asked.

'Possibly. Music is combinatorial, like spoken language, so maybe the Soundfield's language is too?'

I thought about how that might work.

'Phonemes in language combine to make words, which then combine to make phrases and sentences. And music does something similar. It's made up of notes, which stack vertically to make harmony and horizontally to make melodies. These then add together to produce musical phrases.'

I looked at Elias.

'The Soundfield could be building a language out of these musical phonemes. But without knowing what the individual phonemes mean, I can't work out what the "words" mean, let alone a whole Call. And of course, these phonemes could be acting like words in tonal languages, where the same word voiced at a different pitch can mean something different. So, in Mandarin, *ma* pitched high means *mother*, but if the vocalisation starts low and ends high, it means *hemp*. Or all of this could be wrong and, instead, the utterances could be holistic, with each Call having its own singular meaning and the phonemes by themselves meaning nothing.'

I stopped and breathed deeply.

'That's of course if there's any meaning at all,' I said.

Elias looked at me and saw my tiredness, and I saw his. We were desperate to understand the Soundfield, but it was like trying to read a text written in a language that died out thousands of years ago that had no dictionary, no translations of any words, and no relation to any other language living or dead. It was like trying to describe something that you'd once seen in a dream, that felt concrete in another world, but that ran from you like water in your hands when you were awake.

'*Hope is the thing with feathers, and sings the tune without words, that never stops at all,*' Elias said. 'We'll get there.'

For the next few months I continued my categorisation of the phonemes, and had a database of hundreds of sounds by the end. I hoped that if I continued working, losing myself in the repetitive nature of the task, new ideas would come to me. But I was too tired to think, and I was getting distracted by the world around me. Everyone had been forced to switch by then, so at least we didn't feel so alone at night, but the world was heating up fast, and so were the people. Elias wasn't meant to tell me, he said, but we were receiving threats.

'A group called Babylon,' he said. 'Religious extremists. They think we're being punished by God and only the worthy will survive, like Noah's flood.'

'Babylon? The tower of Babel?' I said.

'The tower that joins Earth to the Heavens, yes.'

I had heard about the story when I was young. In the Old Testament, the people of Babel built a great tower, and when God saw it, he punished them for what they'd done. He destroyed the tower, and scattered the people of Babel across the world, turning their one common language into several so they couldn't understand each other anymore. Elias showed me one of their threats:

> *You are not worthy to communicate with heaven. You do not deserve to speak the Lord's language. Only the chosen will rise, those for whom God has designed the language, those who are blessed to speak it. We will rise.*

'We will rise,' Elias said. 'Bit dramatic, isn't it?' I laughed but it scared me. I had heard things about attacks on police in the cities and in camps, and Babylon had claimed responsibility for some of them. One of my team, Mahesh, had a cousin who had been with Babylon for a few months, and he told a group of us about them one morning.

'He was taken in by the food,' he said.

'By the food?' someone else said.

'Yeah, they have these little societies, cults, and you join and listen to their rubbish, and they ply you with food and alcohol, and get you to do their shit for them.'

'What did your cousin do?' I asked.

'Nothing, really. He wasn't there for long. Left when they started talking about an attack on the Exchange Building.'

I largely ignored the news in the years I worked on the Field, but I had a vague sense of what was happening. Refugees were arriving in the country by boat in their thousands, I knew that, and the police and army couldn't stop them. I pictured them coming ashore, pushing their small boats up the sand, their feet and clothes wet, their skin blistered. I see them calling for help but being blinded by searchlights or shot at from a distance. I knew churches and halls were being converted into makeshift shelters. I knew some people were helping and some were fighting against the government, independently of Babylon. But I couldn't imagine what the people dislocated from their homes were doing or feeling when they got here. How would they know what to do in a world that they couldn't understand, surrounded by people who didn't speak their language? Scattered and confused. Mum told me that the village hall had been given over to the refugees, and she made some comment about people taking up space and rations. I told her not to talk like that, but I didn't know what it was like for her. I was protected, and everything in the news felt like someone else's reality, something happening thousands of miles away. But that feeling wouldn't last forever. It was broken on the day Elias showed the Colonel into my room.

'Dr Newnham?'

A uniformed man appeared at the door to my office, standing next to Elias.

'Could I have a moment of your time?' the man said. I gestured towards the chair opposite my desk. He sat down, took off his beret and straightened his flat, greasy hair with his right hand.

'Dr Newnham, my name is Colonel Fran Miller.'

'Is this about the threats?' I said.

'Uh, no, it's not,' he said, and he paused. 'Threats?' I had forgotten Elias wasn't meant to tell me, so I said nothing. 'I work with your brother, Lieutenant Newnham. I'm his commanding officer.'

He stopped, as if he expected me to say something.

'I'm sorry to tell you that yesterday evening, Lieutenant Newnham was shot by a refugee. An illegal immigrant stole your brother's sidearm and fired twice into his chest. He was taken to a hospital, and operated on, but he couldn't be saved. I'm very sorry, Dr Newnham.'

I didn't respond and he looked at me with confusion.

'Do you have any questions?' he said hesitantly.

'What happened to the man who shot him?'

'I'm sorry?'

'The refugee? What happened to him?'

'He was arrested, I think.'

'Is he alive?'

'I don't know. Why?'

I didn't answer, and turned back to my work, pretending to write something on the paper in front of me.

'Lieutenant . . .' He stopped. 'Theo was a good man. He was loyal. You should be proud of him.'

When the Colonel had left the room, I put my pen down, and let go of the air that I'd been holding inside me for the last minute. In the silence, I thought about the final conversation I had with Theo before he left for the army. He was in his room watching TV. I could hear it from the corridor. I knocked on the door and he pulled it open with his foot. He was watching a rolling news channel. I remember hearing gunfire in the background as we talked.

'Mum doesn't want you to go,' I said. He didn't look at me. 'Theo?'

'Yes, she does,' he replied, still staring at the screen.

'No, she's putting it on.'

'I'm watching,' he said.

'I don't want you to go,' I said quietly.

'What?'

'I don't want you to go,' I repeated. He looked at me with little emotion.

'I've already signed up, and Mum's happy.'

'She's not, she's pretending.'

'I'm already gone.'

'Why do you want to do this?'

He shrugged. 'I don't know. Looks cool.'

'That's not a reason,' I said.

'I don't need to give a reason. I want to and that's it.' He looked at me. 'What are you going to do to help?' He had such contempt in his voice.

'What do you mean? I'm still at school.'

'Yeah, but after, how are you going to help?'

'I don't know. You're not helping by being a solider, or whatever. That's just making it worse.'

'Someone needs to do it,' he said, nodding at the TV.

I looked at the screen. It was playing footage from the uprising in Germany on a loop. Armed civilians were storming a building. A car was on fire. There were charred bodies on the ground.

'But why does it have to be you?' I said, almost shouting.

He looked at me again and thought for a moment. I

wondered if he knew the answer to my question, or if he was just trying to work out whether or not he wanted to tell me. After a while, he went back to watching and muttered something under his breath.

'Because I have to,' I think he said, but I was too cross to ask him to repeat it. I used to believe that it was Theo who pressured his friends into joining – Daniel, and the others. But maybe it wasn't as simple as that.

There were only five of us at Theo's funeral: me, Mum, Elias, an officer who left straight after it finished, and a girl I didn't recognise who sat a few rows behind us. Elias held my hand as my brother's body was cremated, and as my mum collapsed under her grief. I cried for her, and Elias squeezed my hand tight. At the end, he took Mum home, and I stayed behind to collect the ashes.

'Hannah?'

The girl was walking towards me.

'Hello,' I said. 'I'm sorry, do I know you?'

'You do. Well, you did. I'm Emma, Theo's goddaughter.'

I recognised her then. Her blue eyes, and curly hair. She was now a young woman, sixteen maybe.

'Oh, of course,' I said. 'Are you still living around here?'

'No, I had to take the train. I thought I wouldn't get here, actually, but I wanted to come. Do you have a minute to talk?'

I said yes, and we sat down.

'Do you remember when we had my birthday party in your house? I think I was eight, maybe nine?'

'I do, yes.' I see our living room full of presents, a cake at the side, adults standing in twos and threes making polite conversation. 'Were your parents looking after refugees at the time?'

'Yeah. They were staying with us. I remember they used to spend all weekend downstairs. They were nice, but two of them couldn't speak English. I liked the teenage one, Levi. Anyway, Mum and Dad were cross that day and, well, Theo was really lovely to me. Everything had been pretty difficult since the Soundfield, actually, and I'd felt sort of forgotten with everything going on. But he was really kind. I talked to him about Mum and Dad and I said I was worried about things. They were arguing a lot, and I used to hear them from my room in the attic, and he said something which I've never forgotten . . . He said I should be more like *you*.'

'Like me?'

'Yeah. He told me all about what you were doing, about your science and things, and how clever you were, and how I should look up to you. I don't know exactly what you're doing now, but I'm sure it's amazing whatever it is. I just wanted to say thank you, I think, for being someone I could look up to . . .'

'That's . . . Is that why you came?'

'No, not really. I wanted to say goodbye to Theo. Mum and Dad say hello, by the way. They wanted to come but they couldn't. They let me go by myself . . .' She stopped and looked to the front of the chapel. Two men drew a heavy curtain, revealing the platform that had just held Theo's body.

'I saw him recently, about six months ago. He came to visit us, and he couldn't stop talking about you even all these years later. But he said you'd fallen out, or something? That you don't speak?'

'Well things have been a bit . . .' I realised I couldn't lie to her, not after what she had just said. 'We didn't see eye to eye about some things, but he was a good brother. What was he saying about me?'

She told me that Theo didn't know what I'd been working on, but that he knew it was important, and that it was something to do with the Soundfield. She said he'd heard it all through Mum, but I'd only told her what I was allowed to, which wasn't much.

Emma tailed off, and our conversation came to a natural end. She said it was nice to see me again, got up and walked to the end of the row.

'Emma?' She turned and looked at me. 'I know you might not be able to answer this, but . . . was Theo happy when you saw him?'

She paused for a moment.

'I don't know. He was happy to see me, and Mum and Dad. He looked tired, but he seemed okay. There . . . there was one moment when he said he regretted things. But I didn't really know what he was talking about.'

When we got home, Mum went to bed and I picked at some cold food with Elias. We ate in silence. The night was warm, so I headed out by myself to the lake, following the path Theo and I had taken when we were young. I pushed the same branches back, climbed over the same gates, picked at the leaves of the same hedgerows. The lake lay flat and still above the sky, catching the white moonlight and scattering it into the trees that lined the water's edge. I thought about what Emma had said and I felt a hollow guilt. I sat down on the beach, looked up at the Soundfield through the thin clouds, and rubbed the scar on my right arm.

After my accident in this lake, I spent two weeks in bed. The cold was inside me, and it would take a long time for me to feel warm again. Mum brought me hot soup, she changed my dressing, and I watched re-runs of old sitcoms on the square TV in my room. Three days after I fell in the ice, Theo came to see me. It was the first time we'd spoken since it had happened. He was holding something behind his back: a boardgame – Scrabble, I think – and for the next few hours we played together. I used my left arm to pick up pieces, and the effort to think of new words distracted me from the pain and the cold. Every day for the next week, he'd bring a new boardgame, and he'd sit on the bed and play with me. It was the most time we'd ever spent together and I think of those days when I feel my scar. I don't blame him for the accident. I blame him and myself for all the times we could have got on but decided to argue instead. I thought a lot about Theo in the weeks after his funeral – I wanted to change the picture of him in my mind.

I heard Elias behind me. I turned, smiled, and he sat down on the beach by my side. I held his hand. His skin was soft.

'Are you okay?' he said.

'I will be.'

CHAPTER TWENTY-ONE

Elias lay back down on the pebbles, and I did too, and we looked at the stars together, watching the air dance. There used to be artificial specks of light in the sky, the flashing wings of planes, satellites, space stations, junk: markers of our need to colonise the air as well as the land. Now, no planes fly, no satellites are replaced, and no one can go beyond the reaches of the Soundfield. I sometimes think about the two astronauts who were on the ISS when the Field arrived. They would have seen the world vibrate, dust clouds fill the air, and lights going off in cities on every continent. They would have tried to radio down to Earth, but no one would have answered, and they would have spent their last days looking down on a quiet world, not knowing if they were inside the prison or outside of it.

As Elias and I lay on our little beach, the Hum from the Soundfield dropped away.

'A Call,' he whispered into the silence. Five slowly descending notes appeared, the last of which lingered for a few seconds then died with a small slide upwards. We didn't speak for a moment, waiting for the Hum to return.

'Which one was that?' Elias asked after the Field had reset.

'P26A, I think. I'd have to check.'

'You know I have a theory? About how the Soundfield makes its Calls.'

I turned my head towards him, but he continued to stare at the sky. His face was lit by soft moonlight, and I could see what he would have looked like as a younger man.

'Something has to be changing within the Soundfield when it produces its Calls – it has to be manipulating the sound somehow.'

He wasn't saying anything new, just working through his thoughts, so I waited for him to continue.

'What if I've been thinking about the Soundfield all wrong,' he said. 'I've been trying to find out how it works by comparing it to instruments, or artificial ways of producing sound because, to us, it's unnatural, it's artificial. We didn't make it, but *someone* or *something* did. Maybe it's more natural than we think? Maybe it is more like the human voice than any instrument or device that we've made? You've been thinking about it like that for months, with your phonemes idea, and I've been wasting my time trying to find physical explanations and analogies for how it produces its Calls, but maybe you've got it right.'

Elias pushed himself up and started pacing slowly.

'*We* produce different pitches by altering the speed of vibration of our vocal cords, or by altering the rate at which air is passed through the cords, yes?' I nodded. 'And so, maybe it's as simple as that? The Soundfield is changing its speed of vibration of its "cords", whatever they are, and so producing different notes, different hums, and Calls. The quality of the sound doesn't change because the cavity in which the sound resonates – the space between the Field and the Earth – is always the same, but maybe it can produce music in the same way that *we* produce music, more human, less robotic, less manufactured . . .'

Elias stopped at the edge of the lake and looked outwards.

'There's also something else that's bothering me, that we haven't really talked about.' He looked back at me. 'The Calls have slides in them.'

'Glissandos?' I say. 'String instruments, lots of instruments can produce slides.'

'Yes, but isn't it the most *human* sound?' He looked to the sky. 'When you want to represent grief musically, what do you do? You write descending notes, or a descending glissando. Why do you always say that the cello is the most "human" instrument? Yes, it's partly because its register is similar to the human voice, but it's also because it can slide between notes, like us.'

Like us, I thought.

He sat down on the ground next to me, and stayed quiet for a few minutes, listening to the Hum, but he broke the silence eventually.

*'That music always round me, unceasing, unbeginning – yet
long untaught
    I did not hear.'*

That day, as we lay in bed together, I dreamt of our night on
the beach. I imagined I could understand the Soundfield's Calls
and answer back. I spoke to it as if it was an old friend and I
asked it to descend back down into the earth, and it listened.

Elias went back to work the next evening, but I stayed with
Mum for a few days to make sure she was okay. We didn't
speak much – she mostly wanted to be alone – and it reminded
me of when Theo left for the army. I thought about that
moment on the gravel when he stepped into his friend's car,
stepped away from us. When people leave you, that's when
you lose control. Even before Theo's death, I'd been thinking
that Mum should move closer to me, to the city, and I
suggested it to her the day after the funeral. She didn't like
the idea, of course, but she would come round to it eventually.
It would just take a while.

I returned to the city and to my work a week after Theo
had been killed. People asked me why I was coming back so
soon, and I told them it was because I wanted to distract
myself. The truth was that I couldn't stop thinking about what
Elias had said at the lake. *Like us*, he had said. *Like us*. On
the train back, I scribbled some thoughts into my notebook,
and made a list of books to find. I hadn't touched three of
them since my undergraduate days, and there was one book

on the list that I'd never read. I had an idea which was too radical to present without proper research. I had to construct my argument carefully.

For the next few weeks, I locked myself in my office and read. When you think of people making discoveries, you imagine the point of inspiration, the moment when every idea comes together into a single thought, but in reality, science is just work. It's weeks and months of reading, writing, and checking and double checking. But it's also a process of finding questions that you can't answer, or not even finding the questions at all.

There's was only one book I read during that time that wasn't about science. I had it with me one evening when I was in the cafeteria.

'The *Gita*?' Mahesh sat down opposite me. 'My mother used to read that to me at night. A children's version. She had these different voices for Krishna and Arjuna.'

He put on a scared, high-pitched voice and continued:

'*O Krishna, seeing these, my own people, standing before me, eager to fight, my limbs fail, my mouth is parched, my body is trembling. My bow slips from my hand and my skin is afire!*' He laughed and so did I. 'Sorry, I'll let you eat, it's just seeing it again . . .'

'It's fine,' I said, smiling. 'Actually, you could help me. Do you read Sanskrit?'

'Enough,' he said. 'But it's been a while.'

'How would you translate this?' I pointed at a stanza and covered up the English translation below it.

He stared at it for a while.

'*The Lord said: I am time*, yes, *time,* I think. *I am time, the source of destruction that comes to* . . . *samāhartum,* annihilate . . . *comes to annihilate the worlds.*' He looked at me. 'Oppenheimer?'

'Yes,' I said.

'*Now I am become Death, the destroyer of worlds.* The Trinity Test?'

I nodded.

'What does it really mean?' I ask.

'Well, Arjuna is about to fight in a war, but he stops and puts down his bow because he sees his friends and family in the enemy ranks. So Krishna, who is the god Vishnu in human form, tries to persuade him to fight. Arjuna is eventually convinced and asks to see Krishna in his godly form. That was the best bit,' he said, excitedly, standing up. 'Mum would get up and hold her arms out like Vishnu and say: "*Like a thousand suns bursting in the sky all at once!*"' He sat down again. 'After that, Krishna says the famous line: *Now I am become Death, the destroyer of worlds.* That's the one Oppenheimer thought about during the first atomic bomb test. But the translation of *kālah* is not *death,* it's *time.* Time and Fate are the destroyer of worlds. Krishna is saying that people are going to die whether or not Arjuna fires his arrows. People think that that Oppenheimer quote is about his guilt, but it's not. Everyone gets that wrong. It's about fate. Why are you reading this anyway?'

'No reason,' I said. He gave me a curious look and smiled, then I carried on reading.

Oppenheimer had once said that the scientists working on the Manhattan Project had blood on their hands from the bombings in Hiroshima and Nagasaki, but he also said he didn't regret working on the project. He'd even advocated for dropping the bomb on a city instead of empty land to show its destructive power and had suggested the correct height and weather conditions for the explosion to inflict maximum damage. He believed it was fate that the atomic bomb would be made and that he was just doing his duty as a scientist. If he hadn't done it, someone else would have, he thought. I wanted to read what he read not because I wanted to think like him, but because I didn't. The consequences of science are not set, I told myself. They're not inevitable. We could control them.

After a month, I had brought all my research together into a five-page summary. I went to Elias's office with the paper in my hand. His door was open, and the desk lamp was on, so I waited for him to arrive, but he didn't show. I walked down the corridor to see if he was in his lab – there was no one there – so I kept on going, through two double doors, and then a final door on one side of the corridor into a huge lecture hall. Elias was sitting in the back row by himself, lit by a single row of strip lights.

'You found my hiding place,' he said. He put his lid on his pen, got up and started walking towards me. 'I come in here when I'm being bombarded by too many questions from junior researchers. They need to learn to think for themselves.' I met him halfway up the stairs, and we sat down on a long wooden bench and looked down at the stage together. There were loose papers on the desk at the front, but nothing written on the three enormous rolling boards. They were all empty.

'Are you alright?' he said, still looking ahead. 'Sorry if I've not been to see you much.'

'It's fine, I've been okay.' I was nervous. 'How's the drone development coming?'

'It's slow. I'm not even sure we're going to be able to finish it. They're still saying it's impossible, but it's the only option. Have you spoken to your mum?'

'Once, but . . .' I looked at my paper. 'You remember what you said to me when we were down on the lake?' Elias was surprised by the change in topic, but he nodded anyway. 'Well, it made me think. The first time you played me the recording of the Soundfield, the one made by the pilot, I said that it sounded human.'

'Yes,' he said tentatively.

'At the lake, you said that it sounds like *us*, the slides, the way it moves between notes, and to an extent that's true. But it doesn't sound like us *now*. If it did, wouldn't we be able to understand it?'

I got up.

'After I got back, I couldn't stop thinking about an idea . . . It's what I've been working on for the past few weeks. I probably should be taking time off, after Theo, but I had to get it out of my head.' I handed my paper to Elias.

'What's this?'

'It's my thoughts, my idea. I want you to read it.'

'Can't you tell me about it?'

'Why?'

'Because I want to hear it from you. We're in a lecture hall. Give me your lecture.'

CHAPTER TWENTY-TWO

I walked down to the front of the hall and turned to face Elias. He was sat waiting. I could feel my anxiety in my chest, pressure just underneath my sternum.

'Okay, first some context.'

I began by telling him about the KE family, about how sixteen members of this family exhibited symptoms of verbal dyspraxia and impaired processing and how this led to the discovery of the *FOXP2* gene on chromosome 7, known colloquially as the *language gene*.

'The *FOXP2* gene is highly conserved amongst humans,' I said, 'and its protein has only undergone two amino acid changes since humans diverged from chimpanzees and bonobos seven million years ago, caused by mutations in exon 7 of the gene. A threonine amino acid was exchanged for an asparagine at position 303, and an asparagine for a serine at position 325.'

I looked up.

'This will be related to the Soundfield, I promise.' Elias laughed. I thought he would ask me questions as I went, but he sat there in silence, not taking notes, just listening.

'Where spoken language came from is an open debate. Some believe language can't be compared to the communication exhibited by our closest ancestors – the calls and grunts of chimps and bonobos – but a lot of people, including me, believe language evolved directly from these rudimentary forms of communication. The mating calls of a gibbon, or the alarm calls of vervet monkeys, sound viscerally human, like there's something deeply rooted in us that connects our language to theirs. But spoken language isn't the only form of communication that separates us from our ape ancestors. There's also music.

'Music and language share a lot of features. As you know, they're both combinatorial, made up of individual units that stack together to give new structures. Words into phrases, notes into melodies and so on. But they're also both recursive and innate.'

I was beginning to imagine I wasn't just speaking to Elias. I could see rows of students.

'We are biologically programmed to speak, but also to listen to and produce music. Think about how we communicate with infants. Parents will sing to their children as much as they speak to them, and even when they talk, they will alter the prosody of their voices – the intonation, rhythm and stress – to make it sound more musical, helping them impart meaning and emotion to a pre-linguistic child. When a mother wants to employ an encouraging or exciting tone, she'll use higher frequencies, upwards-moving pitch contours, and longer vowels. And when she wants to do the opposite – a *stop* command, or a warning – the voice will go lower, and the vowels will become short and accented. Spoken language becomes musical.

'These two communication systems seem to be two strands of one thread. So, the idea that music and language co-evolved from a single form of communication, a *musical protolanguage*, is one that is not that difficult to comprehend. And it's an idea that has existed for as long as we have studied human evolution, going all the way back to Charles Darwin.'

Elias sat up as if coming to attention on hearing Darwin's name. I picked up my notes and read:

'In *The Descent of Man, and Selection in Relation to Sex*, published in 1871, Darwin wrote that, "*it appears probable that the progenitors of man, either the males or females or both sexes, before acquiring the power of expressing mutual love in articulate language, endeavoured to charm each other with musical notes and rhythm*".'

I put my notes down, looked back into the room, and the benches re-filled with students.

'There were a lot of things that Darwin got wrong in *The Descent of Man*, both culturally and scientifically, but maybe he was right here? He might have been off with his reasoning – that language evolved as a result of sexual selection – but maybe he was correct in his assertion that our ancestors communicated via a system that was comparable to what we now call *music*.

'About two million years ago, the human ancestor *Homo ergaster* appeared in the fossil record. *Ergaster* was the first fully bipedal hominin and was in the process of developing features that we'd now recognise as distinctly human, driven by the selective pressures created by the opening up of land-scapes in Africa, the creation of savannahs. Bipedalism came, in part, as a result of this change in habitat. Walking on two feet allowed them to cover greater distances in shorter times and kept them cool as they travelled, but it also allowed them to hunt a greater variety of prey. Their diet moved away from plants and towards meat, and so, in turn, their teeth and jaws got smaller and, largely as a by-product of walking on two feet, their larynxes dropped in the throat and became more flexible.'

I thought about the millions of things that had to have happened to allow me to stand here and deliver this lecture. The structural alterations in the vocal machinery, the neuro-logical changes, the genetic mutations, all subtly altering the way we interact with the world around us.

'The result of all of these small, sometimes accidental changes was that we gained the ability to produce more complex and controlled vocalisations. But in order to form language as we know it, there had to be an evolutionary *need* to produce these sounds, not just the means. It had to be *selected* for.

'And again, we can explain this by thinking about the change in habitat. Open landscapes required long-distance calls between members of a group. It meant more predators, each of which might demand a unique alarm call, as well as different prey, which all needed to be recognised and hunted. Hunting required careful coordination between members of the group, as well as non-verbal or subtle communication – via gestures or very soft sounds. And a more complex diet meant more people in each group – hunters, butchers, foragers, caregivers – leading to more complex social dynamics and emotions: love, anger, hatred, pain, loss, joy, all of which needed to be communicated in some form. And what about social cohesion? Could the emotional, musical part of this communication system have developed to bind these early human groups together, or to allow a mother to comfort her child as she's foraging a short distance away?'

I imagined a child I might have in the future. I had a name in mind, even back then, if it was a boy.

'This protolanguage, the predecessor to both our music and language, would have existed to serve all of these different functions, allowing increasingly complex human societies to flourish in their new world. But, maybe the more important consideration is not why this protolanguage evolved, but how it worked as a communication system. Or in other words, what did it sound like?'

I stopped and looked down.

'Are you alright?' Elias asked.

'Fine, it's just . . .'

At the time, I didn't know why I'd stopped. The situation wasn't the problem. It might have been for other people, but the formality of the lecture made me more relaxed, not less.

'Can we stop for a bit?' I said.

'Of course. Take your time. We can do this some other way if you'd like?'

'No, it's alright.'

I left the hall via a door to my right and entered a dimly lit corridor. On the walls, there were large posters summarising the papers of scientists who'd worked in these labs before the Soundfield. There was one to my left showing a novel synthesis for an epilepsy drug. It showed the synthetic pathway, laid out in minute detail, step by step – more than ten of them – with reagents carefully labelled, temperatures shown to the closest degree, and pressures and catalysts quoted. This was science that was unequivocal, certain. They had data to tell them that what they had done was not only remarkable but also correct. Someone might have been able to afford their medication as a result of this work. Someone's life might have been saved.

I went back inside the hall and took my place again, standing in front of the rows of empty benches. I looked up at Elias and suddenly felt small in the room, like I could only half-fill it with my ideas.

'How soon unaccountable I became tired and sick.
Till rising and gliding I wander'd off by myself,
In the mystical moist night-air, and from time to time,
Look'd up in perfect silence at the stars.'

'Who's that?' I asked.

'It's Whitman,' Elias said. 'One of my favourites.'

He paused.

'You can do this, Hannah,' he said. 'It's just me here. Just me, and the stars.'

I found my place in the story and began again.

'Working out what this musical protolanguage would have sounded like is . . . is a difficult task.' I shuffled the notes on the desk in front of me. 'But we can infer a lot about this language based on how contemporary primates communicate.'

'Take vervet monkeys. Vervets live in large social groups – up to seventy members – and are hunted by a variety of predators including cheetahs, eagles and snakes. When a monkey sees one of these animals, they will produce an alarm call that is specific to that predator. If a monkey spots a snake, for example, it will make a "chutter" vocalisation, a non-tonal, rhythmic and dry sound, standing on its hind legs to try to scare the animal away. When other monkeys hear this specific call, they will also stand on their hind legs and look to the ground.

'But if they hear the eagle call instead, they will look to the sky; if they hear the one for a cheetah, they will run up the nearest tree. These calls are non-semantic. The snake call doesn't mean *snake*, or the eagle call *eagle*; they are literally calls to *action* – sounds that act to manipulate the behaviour of other members of the group. And these vocalisations are also holistic. Some of them can go on for extended periods, but they only make sense when taken as a *whole*. These are complete messages – *run to the tree, look to the sky, look to the ground* – but no individual part of the vocalisations means *run*, or *look*, or *ground*.

'So, it's fair to assume that the shared ancestor of humans and chimps would have communicated in a similar way. And it's also fair to assume that by two million years ago, by the time *Homo ergaster* appeared, our ancestors would have been using and developing this holistic, manipulative language for over five million years. But unlike the predator-specific calls of vervet monkeys, early human calls would have needed to communicate far more complex actions and behaviours. A holistic call might mean *meet me at the large tree, bring arrows and bow, cut up carcass*, or *attack antelope with spear*. Again, these are manipulative, but they're also far more specific. As compared with monkeys, early human calls would have used a greater variety in pitch and rhythm, using slides and clicks, different phrase lengths, shorter and longer notes, all combined with gestures and actions, some of which might have mimicked the movements of animals. And they might have even used onomatopoeia, imitating the sound of an animal to help refer to them – a lion's roar, a bird's song, the chuttering of a monkey. This not only required greater flexibility of the voice, but also more cognitive power. The calls had to be remembered, repeated, taught to infants, and the message associated with each vocalisation retained across the group over time. What's the point of having a call for *collect water from river* if only a fraction of the group can understand what you mean?

'And, so, our brains got bigger, accelerating around six hundred thousand years ago. But during this time, something else also changed – our genetics. Two million years ago, in one part of chromosome 7, a point mutation occurred, randomly altering the sequence of nucleotide bases in the *FOXP2* gene. And maybe this small change allowed us to develop the parts of our brain that help us create, store and understand these more complex vocalisations?'

I took a slow breath in. My pulse was getting faster.

'I believe that the first change in the *FOXP2* gene in the human lineage corresponded with the development of this new protolanguage – a distinct form of communication from the one that we observe in contemporary primate groups. I believe this language is the one that dominated the lives of early humans for nearly two million years, and that it was used by hominin species in Africa and Europe until it died out with the Neanderthals around thirty thousand years ago. And I also believe that the second change in the *FOXP2* gene in the human lineage, which occurred around two hundred thousand years ago, corresponded with the division of the musical protolanguage into two new non-holistic and recursive communication systems. One of which was symbolic and referential – used primarily for imparting information – and another of which was non-symbolic and expressive – used for emotional communication and social cohesion. Language and music.'

I stopped and formed my next words carefully in my mind. I said them slowly, and clearly.

'I believe that the Soundfield's Calls are similar, if not

identical, to the way in which humans communicated before this schism.'

I could feel my heart beat in my throat as I said the final words of my lecture.

'I believe that what we are hearing from the Soundfield is the musical protolanguage used by our ancestors. *Our* protolanguage, a language that hasn't been heard on this planet for tens of thousands of years.'

Elias didn't move for a while. He stared down at the desk, and I wondered if I should say something.

'What evidence is there?' he said eventually. He was stern, almost like a parent talking to their child.

'None. Not yet, just a feeling.'

'Science isn't based on feelings.'

'Don't patronise me,' I said. 'Every idea has to start somewhere.'

'But how does it help us?'

'I don't know. Not yet. We need to find out if I'm correct before we can work out how we can exploit it.'

'Now you're patronising me,' he said.

'You've said it yourself, and other people would say it too if they weren't too scared. The Soundfield's Calls feel *human*, like a voice, and maybe there's some way we can understand it. So, shouldn't we try?'

Elias didn't reply to this straight away. I understood his reaction. He was afraid of the idea, and so was I.

'You're right,' he said, and he looked deflated. 'You need evidence, though. I can't tell anyone without it, but God knows how you'll get it.' He laughed nervously, and I felt my body relax. 'As you said, the last person who could speak the language died thirty thousand years ago.'

I walked back up the stairs and sat next to him. He noticed I was shaking slightly, and he held my hand.

'So, how did we get words from all this?' he said.

'We're not sure. Maybe we attached non-sensical vowels and consonants to the calls to begin with, and eventually these segmented into shorter phrases of one or two syllables which had definite meanings. Most of it would have been accidental – a sound shared between two holistic phrases that were referring to the same thing might have become a new word. So, say if *tulima* and *kalima* both referred to something a mother did, then *ma* became the word for mother.'

'And then they stuck?'

'Something like that.'

CHAPTER TWENTY-THREE

I told Freya and Mahesh the day after I had delivered my lecture to Elias.

I gave them my paper and after they'd read it, they sat in my office and asked me questions. We were there for three hours, but I could only answer a fraction of what they asked with any sort of certainty. They were excited to be working on a new idea, to be working on anything, and their reaction felt good after Elias's. At the end of the three hours, we had a developed a plan for how we were going to conduct our research, centred around the genetic components of the theory.

So, we began.

We put out a call for people who believed they could interpret the Soundfield's melodies, and hundreds came forward. We rejected most of them quickly and spent a week filtering through the remaining applications, finally selecting twenty participants for the first round of studies. We brought them in and played them extracts of Calls while analysing their neurological activity using functional MRI and PET scans, focusing on the parts of the brain associated with language – Broca's area in the frontal lobe and Wernicke's area in the temporal lobe. Every person had slight increases in blood flow in these areas when listening to the Soundfield's Calls, both when listening live and when played a recording via headphones, but the real test would be a genetic one. After the audio rounds were completed, we took samples of the participants' DNA but found none had mutations in exon 7 of the *FOXP2* gene. As a control, I put myself through the tests. Similar to the participants, the language parts of my frontal and temporal lobes lit up when listening to the Soundfield, but like every person we tested during those months, I also had a normal *FOXP2* gene.

My team was encouraged by our initial findings. They thought it partly confirmed the human connection to the Soundfield's Calls, but I said that it could just be a sign of our brains trying to make sense of information from a novel signal, not necessarily evidence that this is an ancient part of our brain responding to a dead language. So, we continued testing participants, hundreds of them, but the results never changed. We did this for over a year, until I stopped the tests. I gave everyone two weeks off and I saw their hope diminish.

During the break I went home to see Mum, and I cried in front of her but I couldn't tell her why. That first night back, she made me my favourite meal and I went on a walk to the lake by myself. A few days after I arrived, Mum was in the sitting room watching the news and I was reading in the kitchen. I had seen bulletins about the first execution on the journey down. They were advertising it like a sporting event. *Watch live. Exclusive coverage. In-depth analysis.* The news was all state-owned by then, so there was no one to argue the other side. I had decided not to watch, but Mum had the TV on so loud that I couldn't ignore it. I walked into the sitting room and stood at the door. On the screen was a smartly dressed man standing at the edge of a concrete building delivering his lines in a clipped accent.

'This is the Exchange Building. In the past, it's been used for trade and, latterly, for passing new legislation. Now, it's being used for the first execution since capital punishment was abolished nearly one hundred years ago.'

He lifted his clipboard and read.

'Last week a group of five men from the militia group known as *Babylon* attacked a police convoy escorting illegal immigrants to a detention centre south of the City. Three officers died in the attack and two were seriously wounded. The whereabouts of four of the five men is still unknown. One man, however, was captured and was sentenced to death for crimes against the state. And in a few minutes' time, at dawn, he will be executed via lethal injection.'

The reporter walked slowly out of the frame and the camera focused in on the building behind him. There were hundreds of members of the public in UV suits pushing up against a high fence – shouting, jostling for position – with lines of officers

wearing official black uniforms on the other side. The officers
were trying to keep the public at bay, holding their hands out,
gesturing with their weapons. The light was beginning to change.
The grey building turned yellow, then a warm orange, then
white. It lost all its colour as the sun rose. I heard a voice from
off-screen:

'The man is being led onto a platform at the centre of the
hall. His face is covered with a black cloth.' A pause. 'He is
in place now. The cloth is lifted.' Then distant boos, shouts,
cries, and the reporter spoke for a final time: 'May God have
mercy on his soul.'

Suddenly everyone stopped shouting and looked up. There
was no sound anymore, no Hum. I stood up from the sofa.
Mum didn't say anything. The silence was with us too, not
just on the report. A note appeared from above, first with us,
then on the TV. I knew what it was.

'CP1,' I whispered.

I pulled back the curtain and stood away from the light. I
watched the dust play in the morning sun as I listened to the
ten-minute Call. I started singing along in my head, and then
hummed out loud. Everything distorted like in a dream. When
it finished, I looked back at the TV. The camera zoomed in
slowly on the crowds. No one moved or spoke. The officers
stood still. The Soundfield's Hum returned, but still no one
moved. For what felt like a lifetime the camera remained
locked on the building, waiting for something to happen,
waiting for the world to end, or a new one to appear.

*

We didn't speak about the execution afterwards. It was easier to ignore it than to find some way to describe how it made us feel. Instead, we talked about village gossip and Theo, and the accident at the lake.

'Do you remember what you did after I got you out of your wet clothes?' Mum said one morning.

'No, what do you mean?' I said.

'You don't remember? You sang. In fact, I couldn't get you to stop singing.'

I laughed. 'No, I don't have any memory of that. What did I sing?'

'Oh, lots of things. You spent about ten minutes singing one nursery rhyme over and over. I think it was *Humpty Dumpty*. You were too old to be singing those songs but you wouldn't stop, even in the ambulance. I was worried you were losing your mind. Eventually, you gave up with the words and just hummed the tunes.'

'What did the paramedics say?'

'I think they were a little worried the cold had gone to your head. You hadn't sung any of those songs since you were a toddler. In fact, all you did when you were young was sing and dance. I thought you'd become a musician, not a scientist.'

'Maybe I should have been a musician.'

'You used to say that you wanted to sing forever. Well, you'd sing it. I had to work hard to get you to talk, do you remember? When you were learning to speak, you would sing everything instead, like there was a switch in your brain that hadn't been flicked yet.'

I did remember singing, or at least I remember watching videos of me singing as I span around the living room.

'I could have had perfect pitch,' I said. 'That would have been nice.'

'I thought you did,' she said.

'No, I have relative pitch. I can work out what note something is in my head, but it takes a little time. Not like people with perfect pitch. They know the note without thinking; it's instinctive. I read once that children are all born with perfect pitch, and that in the process of learning non-tonal languages like English, we lose the ability to recognise pitches, and we have to work hard to regain it. Maybe I would still have it if you hadn't made me talk,' I said, and Mum smiled.

I look back at this conversation now and wonder what the world would be like if it had never happened. There's a chance no one would have discovered the truth, and the Soundfield would have remained a mystery for my lifetime, and for Isaac's. But every other possible pathway was cut off that night, the night I reconvened my team and told them about a thought that had dug itself deep into my mind.

'I think we've been looking for the wrong characteristic,' I said to them anxiously. 'We have been looking for people who *understand* the Soundfield's language, but maybe we should have been looking for people who *speak* the language.'

They looked at each other, confused.

'I know that if I'm correct, this protolanguage died out thousands of years ago, but maybe the cases of it re-appearing in humans have been so rare that people have assumed it's a disorder?'

They weren't convinced.

'Imagine, as a thought experiment, you wake up in an Ethiopian forest one morning and you've lost all your memories, but not your ability to speak. Let's say, then, you come across a group of Gelada monkeys and you try to talk with them, thinking that you are one of them, and they try to communicate back using their primitive form of communication – calls, grunts, gestures, and so on. As far as they are concerned, you're not speaking a language they don't recognise, you're not speaking a language at all. To them, it's completely meaningless, and isn't this what the Soundfield is like to us? If someone was born speaking the Soundfield's language, wouldn't we assume they couldn't speak at all?

'There have been a number of cases of children, especially autistic children, who have exhibited language difficulties – aphasia – but also astonishing musical abilities. There was a boy born on a plantation in Illinois in the 1840s, I think it was, called Thomas Wiggins. Very early on, he demonstrated symptoms which we'd now see as signs of autism: rapid movement of his fingers, body rocking, and language problems. He had echolalic speech, which meant he often just repeated back what he heard instead of saying something new. But he was also exceptionally musical – he could imitate sounds, he had perfect pitch, he could recognise and repeat melodies from an early age, and he was giving concerts on the piano when he was eight. But maybe Thomas wasn't deficient in language at all? Maybe he could speak this *protolanguage*, the Soundfield's language, but the people around him simply couldn't understand?'

We put out a call for musically talented children who had also experienced language difficulties, and a few came forward. One, a two-year-old who we called EK as a nod to the family that began this story, was aphasic and had outstanding musical abilities. They were already making music, had perfect pitch, and could play the piano. We scanned their brain in various scenarios – when playing and listening to music, and when listening to the Soundfield – and every part of it lit up: the motor cortex, the auditory cortex, the emotional and memory centres, the frontal and temporal lobes, the cerebellum, the nucleus accumbens, as well the language areas of the brain. When listening to the Soundfield, the Wernicke and Broca areas of EK's brain were as active as someone speaking and processing language.

We also observed how EK 'communicated' with the Soundfield. We gave them access to a number of musical instruments and played them the Soundfield's Calls, adding in silence between the recordings to allow time for EK's response, replicating the natural pauses in conversation. At first EK imitated the Calls vocally, or instead transcribed them using one of the instruments. After a few days, however, they began to alter their vocalisations. Instead of exactly imitating the Call, they would change one or more pitches in the sequence, slide up instead of down at the end of a phrase, or alter the rhythm of a particular phoneme. Eventually, not only was EK producing entirely novel vocalisations in response to the Calls, they were also reproducing these vocalisations in response to a specific Call even if they hadn't heard it for days. This implied that they were storing their responses in their long-term memory.

Mahesh suggested giving EK some means to write or draw as they listened. We gave them paper and crayons and, alongside their vocalisations, they would sometimes draw swooping lines, or harsh, angular shapes – always abstract and visually similar to the sounds they made. If their singing was soft and warm, their drawings were soft and warm, and if their singing was angular and guttural, so was their art. Mahesh thought that they might write down words, but I pointed out that even if the Soundfield's Calls did have meaning – either the Calls as a whole, or the individual phonemes – EK wouldn't be able to translate them. The Calls had no referential or symbolic associations, so there was no way to interpret meaning.

'We only know a vervet monkey's alarm call for a snake "means" snake,' I explained, 'because the call only happens when a snake is around. EK has nothing concrete to attach to the Soundfield's Calls, so even if they could understand them, they couldn't tell us what they mean.'

EK's behaviour was remarkable, but the real evidence for my theory would come from their DNA. We took a sample of EK's blood and Freya sequenced their genome. She let me look at it before anyone else. I sat at her computer and focused in on exon 7 of the *FOXP2* gene. First, I looked at the area responsible for the asparagine to serine replacement first. It was normal. That was fine, we knew one of them would be. Next, I focussed in on the area that had led to the second amino acid substitution in the human lineage, and the sequence of three nucleotide bases which would normally read AAT read ACT. An adenine nucleotide base had mutated into a cytosine. This is what we were looking for. The second amino acid change in the FOXP2 protein had been reversed and, as a result, had resurrected a dead language. Freya ran to get Mahesh and I stared at the screen. I read and re-read those three small letters, over and over. *ACT. ACT. ACT.* I cried, out of exhaustion and happiness.

'Science is what makes the world come alive, Hannah,' my dad had said, and he was right.

I told Elias the news straight after I left Freya's office. He was unsure when looking at the neurological data, but when he saw EK's altered genetic sequence, he laughed.

'You did it,' he said. 'You did it.'

He continued looking at the computer for a while, then said something in a soft but clear voice.

'We have to get this right, Hannah.'

I've thought a lot about this moment over the years. The way he said those words – *we have to get this right* – it wasn't a throw-away line. It was rehearsed. But instead of asking him what he meant, I just said, 'We will.' He half-smiled, nodded gently and left the room. I found out later that he was being pressured by the government to make more progress. They threatened to shut down the research. They threatened to take his money. They threatened his life. Elias never told me about it at the time because he didn't want me to worry but, looking back, I wish he had said something. It might have changed everything.

After EK, things started to accelerate. We found nine more children with the same mutation in the *FOXP2* gene, all of whom demonstrated some form of communication with the field. We got them to listen to the Calls and we'd observe how they responded. A few of them played instruments, some of them sang like EK, one of the non-aphasic children even started saying words and phrases in response to certain Calls, but there was nothing to suggest that they were translating the Call. I had so many unanswered questions. What did their responses mean? Was there a way for humans without the mutation to produce this language? Why are children more sensitive to the Soundfield than adults? And what about group dynamics? One evening, when we were all on the roof looking at the stars and constellations – *clusters of light beyond the Field*, as Elias told the children – a Call appeared. During the song, everyone was silent, listening, waiting. Then one of the children started to imitate the Call. A few seconds later, the others joined in. They sang together as if they had rehearsed, as if they were speaking one language. After they had finished, I realised I was crying.

During those months, I worked and did nothing else. We collected mountains of data – video, audio, images, fMRI scans, PET scans – and at the end of it all, I started writing up our findings. It would take three months to finish the first draft of the paper, then another month to finalise it. When I was ready, I presented our research to a group of thirty government officials in a single lecture, in the same hall where I'd told Elias about my idea two years earlier.

On the board, I wrote the words *Evidence for the genomic basis of communication with the Soundfield* and I explained, as best I could, what we had discovered.

That would be the last night I would work on the Soundfield.

CHAPTER TWENTY-FOUR

'They told us they'd bring us back,' I say, 'but they never did.' Layla is sitting now, looking out over the quiet city. 'They stopped our research that night and sent us home, without any explanation, and I never saw Freya or Mahesh again. We couldn't speak about it; they threatened our families, made us sign NDAs. It felt like they were taking everything from us. I didn't even say goodbye to EK.'

'What happened to the kids?'

'I don't know,' I say softly.

Isaac stirs behind me. He's fast asleep with his head resting against my bag.

'So, where did you go?' Layla asks.

'I went to Mum's for a bit, and Elias came, and we waited for news. Elias tried to get back into the lab, but they wouldn't let him. There were armed guards at the entrances. He couldn't see anyone working inside. All my books, my notes. It was all

there, but they wouldn't let him in. I suppose that was the
point: they didn't want us hiding anything. I thought they
were on our side.'

'They never were, Hannah.'

'No, maybe not. But I never thought they'd react in that
way. Elias had been shielding me.'

The sun is almost up, and we'll have to go inside soon. The
streets are emptying, and the world is closing.

'What happened to Elias?'

'We stayed together for a couple of weeks, he even helped
me move Mum's stuff into her new flat, but something had
changed between us. I know it might sound strange, but it was
like we'd lost a child. Our research was the only thing keeping
us going. I fell in love with him because of his work and his
mind, so maybe it made sense that it fell apart afterwards. And
after the Atavism Programme began, there was no going back.'

'We should go inside,' Layla says.

She moves away from the railing, and heads back towards
the stairs.

'What is this for? Honestly?' I say, turning to look at her.
'Why do you want to know all of this?'

'Everyone here thinks we can only bring the Programme
down with force, but there has to be another way. Sam thought
so too. But we can't do it without the end of the paper,'
Hannah, without the redacted section.'

'Is that all you wanted to know?'

'No, I wanted to hear everything, but this isn't just about
us . . .'

'Those threats we received from Babylon weren't just threats.'

She doesn't say anything. She knows what I'm talking about, and I see the expression Elias had on his face when he told me. He was pale, ill-looking.

'That was . . . It wasn't good,' she says.

'You took one of Elias's team hostage and you threatened to kill her.' I'm trying to control my temper.

'Pedro did that by himself, and she was fine, in the end. We managed to convince him to hand her back. That's not what we do here.'

'What do you do?'

'I'll tell you, but we need to go inside.'

The light is crawling over the tops of the buildings. We'll be exposed soon.

'I need to know I can trust you, Layla, to tell you the last part of the paper.'

'I know,' she replies.

I go to Isaac and squeeze his shoulder. He wakes up, takes my hand, and walks sleepily to the stairs with me, still holding onto his dinosaur book.

'There's something I want to show you both,' Layla says to us when we're back at our room.

'How long will it take?' I say, looking at Isaac.

'Not long,' Layla replies. 'He'll be able to sleep soon.'

I lower the shutters at the front of our room and leave Isaac's book behind. Layla takes us up one flight, across to the other side of the building, and through a small door in the corner. We're in a long corridor. It's dark. It smells of wax. The only light comes from a small window at the far end. The window is covered with white cloth which blows gently in the morning air, so the darkness fluctuates like our star is breathing.

'Follow me,' Layla says.

In the moments when the corridor lightens, I can see the walls. They're black, so is the ceiling, covered with white marks. I run my fingers along the right-hand wall. It feels thick, bumpy, like tar mixed with rock. I look at some of the markings. They're drawings: small figures, houses, mountains, a deer on a hill, a candle with sharp lines radiating out from its flame, a woman kneeling in prayer, groups, children, parents, the sun exploding, planets, the moon covered by clouds, a cross. Every inch is covered, the ceiling too. There are stars, thousands of them. In parts, constellations are mapped out in detail. In others, the stars are scattered loosely and drawn in a way a child might draw them, with six sharp points like the Star of David.

'Who did all this?' I ask.

'We did,' Layla replies. 'When you join, you add a picture. Yara did that one.'

She points to a drawing of a large square house surrounded by a tight circle of crudely drawn trees. Two smiling faces peek out of the only window in the house. Isaac lets go of my hand and runs to the picture. He passes his hand along the outer edge of the chalk house. He looks up at me.

'Who is it?' he signs.

'Who's in the picture?' I ask Layla.

'That's me and her dad,' she says. 'That's what Yara told me.'

Halfway down the corridor is a set of double doors with a single word painted in large white letters above it. *Sanctuary*. Chalk lines grow out of the word like veins out of the heart.

I can hear music from inside; so can Isaac. His face has lit up.

'Come on,' Layla says, smiling warmly.

Layla opens one of the doors and the sound grows. It's like the Soundfield's Hum, but richer. Chords stacked on top of a deep drone. We follow Layla inside. The music is coming from a massed choir. Adults and children holding hands in a tight circle in the middle of wide, open room lit by candlelight. I realise that Isaac has never heard anything like this before. He's never heard *people* make music, only the Field. His mouth is open, like he's about to join in. His eyes shine like stars. At the outer edges of the circle there are others, in pairs and threes, watching the performance. Behind them are sofas and armchairs pushed together, TVs hanging on stud walls, computers abandoned on glossy white tables.

'We can watch from over here,' Layla says.

We walk round the edge of the room and join a group in front of a long glass wall. Layla greets each person in turn by pressing her forehead into theirs like I do with Isaac.

In the space behind the glass wall are room dividers displaying framed pictures. The candlelight bounces off the pictures and onto the glass, creating a complex pattern of flickering light and for a moment, I imagine I'm seeing one candle split between thousands of parallel worlds. There's one reality where this is still a store and people are in this room buying furniture at the weekend. There's another where the candlelight is a fire and the whole world is burning. There's one where I'm still with Isaac in our flat and he's sitting at the kitchen table drawing blue shapes.

The music dies away, like the Soundfield before a Call, and the circle expands slowly. A man dressed in a white robe walks into the centre. Pedro. He closes his eyes, holds one arm upwards and stretches his other arm out in front of him. Two people in the chain let go of each other's hands and someone fills the gap. Two more break the chain and a second person joins the first. A final pair open the circle, but the last participant does something different. She moves inside the circle and takes Pedro's outstretched hand. She walks slowly, holding her stomach. Pedro draws his daughter towards him and places both of his hands on her head. In a hushed voice, he speaks: 'What God has done, let him make whole. What God has done, let him make whole. What God has done, let him make whole.' He repeats the line until it turns into a chant. The circle contracts and, person by person, they place their hands on Sasha's head, then her shoulder, and, when they can't reach her, each other's shoulders, backs, and heads. People standing around the outside join in until almost every person in the room has added to the chain, Layla too. Pedro's chant gets louder and louder, turning into a shout, until he stops. He lifts his hands, flattening his palms, then brings them down again. Out of the mass of people, he lifts his daughter up and holds her in his arms. He pushes her higher and the people around him hold her up. Sasha is floating, held by the fingers and hands and hope of tens of people.

Out of the corner of my eye, I see Isaac running ahead of me. I call out under my voice, a thrown whisper, but he doesn't turn back. He pushes his way into the crowd then disappears. After a moment, Pedro looks down to his left. It's hard to see his face in the light, but I can see his smile. He drops down, then reappears not as one, but as two. Isaac is clinging to his back, like the way a new-born monkey holds onto their mother. Isaac leans his whole body forward and rests his right hand on Sasha's shoulder. Pedro supports her head like a baby.

'Lift her up, God,' he says in a broken voice, 'and take her sin.'

After it's over, people leave in silence, and I wait for Isaac in the middle of a thinning crowd. I find him. He's with Pedro, standing where Sasha had just been held. Pedro is crouched down in front of him, at his eye level, talking softly. He takes the pin on Isaac's chest between two fingers, says something, smiles, and, in return, Isaac puts his right hand out flat and moves it down from his head to his chest. I walk over to them.

'It means *he will*,' I say.

Pedro keeps looking at Isaac, nods, and rises.

'Your son has more faith than you,' he says. His voice has lost some of its edge since the last time we spoke.

'Come on, Isaac,' I say. Isaac looks up at me and takes my hand. 'Sorry if we weren't meant to be here.'

'You're sorry?' Pedro replies, staring at me. He waits for the silence to grow. It feels thick, heavy. 'Why are you sorry?'

'I'm not,' I say anxiously. 'It just felt . . . private.'

'Nothing is just for us, Hannah. God sees.'

I look back. Layla is waiting for us by the door.

'You go,' Pedro says, laughing and flicking his hand through the air. 'Run away.'

I turn and take Isaac towards Layla. The room is almost empty now. All that's left is the light.

'Hannah,' Pedro calls out as we're about to leave. I look at him. 'Maybe you should be more like your son. He knows more than you think.'

Out of the black corridor, Layla takes us back to our room. I put Isaac to bed, give him his book in case he wakes up, and close the shutters gently behind me. Layla and I sit down on the bench a few feet away from where Isaac is sleeping. She starts talking, quietly, as if we're still in the Sanctuary, as if our breath is still being held.

'Babylon have always been labelled as terrorists. Ever since the first execution. It's what the government wanted. They wanted you to hate them. They wanted someone to blame.'

I don't reply, not because I don't want to talk but because it's not my turn. It's hers. Light is flooding the store. It must be close to midday.

'I don't believe in God, not really . . . but I believe in Pedro, and everyone here. They're my family.' She leans forward. 'When we arrived here, in this country, we were put in this converted barge – Sam, my parents and me. I don't know if you remember it. It was huge, but they crammed hundreds of us in there. They put mats down on the deck and stripped the benches out to make space for cots. The four of us shared the second floor with dozens of other families. We were given a small area, much smaller than the room you're sleeping in now, and we had to do everything there. They gave us a bucket to go to the toilet, water twice a day and a slice of bread each once a day. We had travelled for over a week to get there. We had sat in the backs of trucks with crowds of other people. We had walked across borders, we stank, and what they gave us was worse than if we'd been in a prison. I was only thirteen. And my period had just begun, but they wouldn't give me any pads.'

She stops, and I look at her, but she can't look back at me.

'After a week we were moved to a camp on land, but it wasn't much better. We had a tent to ourselves which was just big enough for the four of us. On site, people started talking about Babylon, and about a month later some Babylon members broke into the camp. They brought us food, and told us about what they did, and who they were. They whispered about freedom and God and speaking the "true language". I saw through the religious stuff, even then, but they were the only people who were kind to us. Pedro was with them – that's where we met. They came back a few more times, with food, and even some magazines. And after we escaped, they looked after us, Sam and me. I'm not saying I agree with everything they've done. But they're the reason I'm alive.'

Layla tells me about her life in Cairo before the Field. Her
parents were doctors, and she had dreams of becoming one
too. She had a cat, and friends, and she loved her brother.
They lived near the sea and on days when it wasn't too hot,
they would go swimming together at the beach without their
parents. When the Soundfield appeared, older people were
the first to die, she says, of heat stroke, and then the houses
became too hot to live in, then reservoirs ran dry, and electricity failed. Those who stayed didn't last longer than a week.
The roads out of the city were jammed, and the tarmac at
the airport was melting, so planes couldn't take off. When
they left Egypt, Layla knew her parents were terrified, but
they were pretending not to be. They distracted her and Samir
by playing games, and by imagining what their new life would
be like in the north.

'Mama invented the *house game*,' she says, 'where each of
us would have to describe what sort of house we'd like to live
in. Mama would start with something silly like a mansion with
a swimming pool on the roof and a basement full of sweets,
and the next person would try to one-up her by imagining a
floating house in the clouds with inflatable walls and ceilings,
and the next person would describe a villain's lair surrounded
by lava and rocks, something like that. It all got a bit silly,
but I can remember laughing so much it hurt. When we got
to the barge, Mama and Baba didn't want to play the game
anymore, but Sam and I carried on anyway. We needed something to pass the time. But instead of imagining castles, or
villas in Florida, or anything like that, we came up with really

simple ideas: houses with a hall and a living room and a bedroom for each of us.'

'What happened to your parents?' I ask.

'They died. A few weeks after we arrived in the camp.'

I hold her hand, and I realise how alone she is, and how little I want to leave her. She looks at me. Her eyes are red.

'Where are you going to go?' she asks. 'I get the feeling you're not going to stay for long.'

I instinctively glance back at my room, towards Isaac.

'I don't know,' I say. 'There's one place I could go, but I'm not sure if I'll be welcome there.'

'Elias?'

'Yes. He has a house north of the city, in the woods. I went there just before Theo died.'

'I'll go with you,' Layla says.

'You don't have to do that.'

'I want to,' she says. 'You can't go alone, and I need to see Yara.' She pauses. 'Home is that way.'

CHAPTER TWENTY-FIVE

Sometimes, when EK's parents couldn't come and collect them, EK would sleep in the lab. It happened once or twice early on, but they did it more often as the weeks of research turned into months. We cleared out a disused office and put a small bed inside, and I spent some time making it nice for them. I found a rug and some colourful posters from one of the old common rooms and put a piano and a violin in one corner of the room. Whenever they slept over, two of us had to look after them. EK would eat with us in the morning, they would brush their teeth in the staff bathroom, having to stand on an upturned bin to reach the taps, and then we'd put them to bed. They were only two years old at the beginning. They couldn't express themselves other than through making music, so we learnt a shorthand for what they wanted, a gestural language.

Every evening, after EK woke up, they would go to the

keyboard in their room and sleepily play a tune – usually something of their own invention – and I would sit on the small chair in the corner and listen, or sometimes I'd play along with them, adding in countermelodies or harmony. They weren't trying to say anything, I don't think, it was just a ritual, and by the end of their song they were usually awake enough to start work. But I had my own ritual. Every night, just before we left the room, I would ask them if they were happy to continue, half-expecting them one day to sign *no*, and for the tests to stop, but they would always nod back at me, and I had to assume that they understood what I was asking.

Isaac stirs. I go over to him and sit on his bed.

'Evening,' I say.

'Hello,' he says, giving me a sleepy salute.

'Did you sleep well?' I say and he nods and turns over on his side.

After breakfast, we meet Layla in her room and she takes us to the old technology store on the second floor. *The hub*, she calls it. The logo at the front almost looks like it's glowing and I imagine a queue of people lining up outside, waiting to purchase the latest phone, or whatever they sold here. Now there aren't rows of laptops, but weapons and papers, and a stack of screens showing grainy footage of vacant stairwells.

'Here,' Layla says.

She goes to a pile of maps next to the screens and filters

through them. I follow her inside. The room is empty – everyone's eating or asleep – but it still feels like I'm not allowed in here, that Pedro wouldn't like it. I watch one of the CCTV feeds. It shows a dark image of an exterior wall with white text in the bottom-right corner that reads *East Street 4*. In the wall is a small door – the one we entered through. On the left-hand edge of the image, I can see part of the ramp that leads into the underground car park. There's a car at the bottom of the ramp with its front pointing up towards the street. In its windscreen I see the reflection of a light. I imagine it's green, like a security light. The light flickers.

'This is it,' Layla says.

She pulls out a map from the pile and unfurls it onto the large table in the centre of the room, covering the papers and maps that have already been stuck to the surface.

'Do you know where Elias's house is?'

Isaac stands on his tiptoes to see what Layla is looking at. I lift him up, sit him down on the edge of the table, and he starts humming to himself and swinging his legs.

'Isaac seems happy,' Layla says.

'It's because I haven't stopped him singing,' I say, and I smile at him and take his cheek in my hand. He smiles back. 'Elias lives in a wood, about twenty miles outside of the city,' I say. 'I'd remember the name of it if I saw it. We took a train to a town, then walked south.'

I see the station and follow a footpath downwards.

'There. Colet Woods. It's in there somewhere.'

'That train line doesn't work anymore. We'll have to walk from here.'

'Where's your house?'

'Here.'

She points at a village a few miles south of the woods.

'How long will it take us?' I ask.

'We could do it in one day, but it might be better to split it. I can get to my house in a night, but I walk fast, and we have Isaac. Two is better.'

For the next hour, we gather things for our journey – three sleeping bags, some mats, dry food, and water. I put as many of the supplies as I can fit in my bag and Layla takes the rest in a large rucksack. She needs to collect something before we leave, so Isaac and I wait on the bottom floor, surrounded by the abandoned shops. The moon shines cold light into the vast well, projecting hazy, distorted versions of the ceiling's geometric patterns onto the floor. Isaac is sitting in the centre of one of the shapes, looking at his reflection in the polished concrete, and I'm in the one next to him. Separated by degrees, not kind.

I go to Isaac, crossing the line between our worlds.

'Are you okay?' I sign.

'I'm okay. Where are we going?' he signs back.

'We're going to see someone very special. You'll like him.'

'When are we going home?'

'We can't go home. Not now. I'm sorry.'

'I like it here.'

'I know.'

I hear Mum's voice in my head.

'This is my home,' she said after I told her I had found a flat not far from mine. 'This is where you grew up. Why would you want me to leave? This is my home,' she repeated, stronger the second time. She started crying, and I hugged her. I didn't want her to leave either, but there was no choice. Home is where the people you love stay so long that they change the smell of a place. *Home doesn't have to be here*, I should have said, or something like that.

I look at Isaac, who's gone back to staring at his reflection. 'I just need to do something,' I say. I take him up the broken escalator and I see Layla standing outside of the Hub talking to Pedro. He notices me, and their conversation stops.

'Wait here,' I say to Isaac. I let go of his hand and walk up to Layla.

'Everything okay?' she says.

'I need to do something before we go.'

'What do you mean?'

'I have to see my mum.'

'Hannah, no, we haven't got time . . .'

'She's not well.'

'I'm sorry. But it's too risky,' she says urgently.

'I know, but I can't leave her like this. Please, Layla?'

She looks away, into the store.

'How long will you be?'

'Two hours, maybe.'

She sighs then gives a small nod.

'Okay,' she says.

'If I don't come back straight away,' I pause before going on, 'will you look after Isaac?'

She looks confused. I think about saying more, but don't.

'Why wouldn't you come back?' she says quietly.

'If something happens to me, will you look after him?'

'I don't understand . . .'

'Please,' I cut her off, 'just say you'll help me.'

Layla frowns and is silent for a moment, thinking. 'Of course,' she says, and she smiles at me in way you might smile at someone who's just told you they're dying. Pity and love. I go back to Isaac, lead him to Layla, and pass his hand into hers. He looks back at me, lost.

'It's okay,' I sign. 'I won't be long.'

'I'll take him to the top floor,' Layla says. 'You'll need this for the entrance.' She passes me a small key.

'Thank you,' I say.

I head down the escalator, look up and catch Isaac's eye on the stairs above me. I lift my right hand, point my thumb, index finger, and little finger upwards and, with my palm facing towards Isaac, move my hand from left to right, back and forth.

'I love you,' I sign, across the air.

I'm alone again.

On the ground floor, I put my coat on and pull the hood up – like someone who's just come off a day shift – and walk to the exit. But I stop at the door. I don't turn the handle or look back. I'm stuck again, like I was with Isaac in our flat. I see the man on the floor, the blood dripping from his ear. I know they'll be looking for me. I know they won't stop. And when it's over, they'll make an example of me. Maybe they'll even televise my death? What would I do at the end? Would I call out, tell the truth, or would I say nothing? *Tell the truth, but tell it slant.*

I leave the department store through the dark corridor, re-trace the path I had taken two days earlier with Isaac and Layla, and catch the train to the station nearest to Mum's flat. The carriage is busy enough for me to disappear. I sit down in a row of blank faces, keep my head low and my hood up. Outside the station, I cross the street and hear someone shouting behind me. I glance back. It wasn't for me, but I see something. On the other side of the road, attached to a red-brick wall, is an electronic billboard. On the screen is a blurry image of two people: one is a woman in her thirties, the report says, and the other is a child, aged six or seven. They are fugitives and possible members of the Babylon terrorist group. Text scrolls slowly across the bottom. *WANTED*, it says, *FOR CRIMES AGAINST THE STATE*. My stomach drops. I've seen and heard those words so many times – *crimes against the state* – but they've never been for me, always for someone else. In the image, I'm holding Isaac's hand. I'm looking down to the ground so you can't see my face clearly. But Isaac is staring up, as if at the camera. He looks like he's been crying. This must be from just after we left the flat, just after he'd seen his CD player shattered into pieces.

Someone knocks into me and I'm brought back to the world. I'm surrounded by people walking in every direction. Most are going towards the station, some are passing under the billboard, no one is looking at the screen. It's starting to rain and the sounds of water tapping gently on my hood masks my tears.

I run through the streets and the rain, keeping my head low and my face covered, and I see Mum's building towering above me. It looks different from this approach, and I slow down for a moment. Some people have their lights on, with their blinds open, and I can see into their lives: a family in their living room; a man sitting alone, gazing out of the window; an elderly couple eating together at a small table. The man looks in my direction and I drop my head.

There's no one outside the block. I go inside, run quickly up the stairs and unlock Mum's door. I push it open, but not fully. There's a sweet, warm smell coming through the gap, and I wonder if I have the strength to do this. I close my eyes and try to remember that holiday on the beach. I think of playing with Theo in the warm sand, Mum laughing and taking pictures with a disposable camera. A version of a memory. Once I'm inside, I close the door swiftly and catch my breath. I'm in the dark again.

I drop my bag to the floor, but don't call out this time. Something's stopping me. I walk slowly to the sitting room and look at Mum. She's sitting in her chair, unmoving. The blinds are open, and a shaft of cool moonlight cuts into the room, framing Mum in her chair. I drop down to her and squeeze her right arm. 'Mum?' Her skin is cold. 'Mum?' I squeeze again, but nothing. 'Mum, please.' I put my hand on her cheek and raise her head towards me. Her eyes are closed. Nothing. I rest her head back down and grab my chest. It feels like it's caving in on itself. I can't breathe. I let out a small noise. It hurts to speak. I collapse onto the floor next to Mum and grab her left hand tight. I bury my face into the chair like it might bruise my eyes. I breathe out and a wail comes with the air. I cry and cough. I wait there in the silence, I don't know for how long. The moonlight dims, as if some-one's siphoning off the light, and then everything turns black.

'I'm sorry, Mum,' I say.

I'm on the beach at night, and I see the shoreline stretching out in front of me. Theo is here too, lying on the sand next to me, looking up at the sky, and I think about staying in the cold air and salt water with him forever.

> *'On the beach at night alone,*
> *As the old mother sways her to and fro singing her*
> *   husky song,*
> *As I watch the bright stars shining, I think a thought*
> *   of the clef of the universes and of the future.'*

'That's beautiful,' I remember saying to Elias. We were in the garden of my childhood house; Mum was lying in a deck chair at the other end of the lawn, asleep in the warm night air.

'Shall we wake her?' Elias said.

'No, let her sleep,' I replied.

*

'I'm lost, Mum,' I whisper, my eyes still closed, my face wet and cold. 'Do you remember when I left for university, you said something to me. You said I should stay with you because everyone had left you. I'm sorry I left. I shouldn't have left.'

I force myself up and breathe in heavily. I try to look at her. I can't look at her. There's a blanket on the floor next to the chair. I pick it up, then turn to face Mum. I breathe out. Her head is leaning away from me and for a moment, I half expect her to turn towards me, to speak to me, to ask me where Isaac is, to tell me about Theo. I place the blanket gently over Mum's body, covering everything but her head. I stroke her cheek and wipe my eyes. I go to the kitchen and write a note on one of Isaac's pieces of paper in the blue light from the oven. I cross out the last line, write something new underneath, and put *Tess* at the top. Is this enough? Am I enough?

I go back into the hall and place the note on the floor. But before I leave, I make Mum's bed, close the blinds in the living room, kiss my mum on her forehead, and say goodbye.

As I close the door to the flat, I think of something. Mum is holding me. I'm wrapped in her coat and I'm singing. Theo is standing a few feet away, shivering like me. We're waiting for the ambulance. She told me once that I couldn't stop singing after I fell in the ice. I believed her, but I could never work out why I'd started. When people fall into freezing water, their body goes into shock. They gasp for air, blood rushes away from the hands and feet to the vital organs, they shiver violently, their heart races. They might scream, or curl into a ball, or bite their lip by accident, but they don't sing. But I remember why I did it now. Mum had sung first. A song that she used to sing to me when I couldn't sleep. Then I sang back, a call and response. I can still see my breath forming clouds in the icy air. I can still hear Mum's warm voice.

CHAPTER TWENTY-SIX

At the bottom of the stairs, I put my coat back on and pull up the hood. I try to slow my breathing, counting the air in and out. I look at the clock on the wall. It's nearly eleven. I need to get back. I need to be with Isaac.

The rain has stopped, but it smells damp, and the ground is wet. I take two streets quickly, then a third, but run around a corner too fast. I slip and fall. I look up slowly and catch the eye of a woman standing still on the pavement. She's frowning, and glancing at something behind my shoulder. I look back. The billboard outside the station still shows the vast image of me and Isaac. I'm wearing the same shorts as I am now, carrying the same bag, I have the same look of fear and exhaustion. The woman says something to the man next to her. I get up and walk away, to the station. 'Stop,' she calls out. I walk faster, then break into a run. 'Stop her!' the woman shouts. I throw myself down the stairs, nearly falling over again and find the platform. There's a northbound train about to leave and I jump through the doors as they're closing.

'Fuck, fuck,' I whisper. A young boy looks up. His father turns him away from me. I wipe the sweat from my head and look down. I can feel a hundred eyes on me. I don't look up for the rest of the journey. I wait for my stop and try not to move.

When I arrive back at the department store, the high street at the front is heaving. Groups clustered around a line of food stalls, people queuing outside a market selling clothes, children chasing each other around a slalom of wooden benches. I walk quickly past them, enter the alleyway at the side of the store and stop after the ramp. I look around. There's no one at either end of the street. I'm alone.

On the top floor I find Isaac lying upside down on a beanbag, holding a book on space a few inches from his nose. There's a cartoon rocket on the front cover, blasting past the moon, with flames being thrown from its thrusters.

'Isaac,' I say.

He jumps up, skips over, and throws his arms around my waist, pressing his book into the small of my back. I drop down and squeeze him. I inhale his smell. I start to cry small tears, small enough to hide.

'I'm back,' I say. 'I'm back.'

He lets go of the hug to sign.

'Why did you take so long?'

'I'm sorry,' I say. 'I won't go again, I promise.'

He looks at me and nods gently.

'I have something to show you,' he signs.

'Okay,' I say as he takes my hand. He leads me enthusiastically back to the beanbag and jumps over to the other side. He searches for something then picks up a piece of paper.

'What is it?' I say, taking it from him.

'It's for the safe place,' he signs.

'The safe place? Do you mean the Sanctuary?'

He nods again. 'For when we come back,' he signs and looks at me in that way that only children can. A sort-of naive hope. *For when we come back.* Can we ever come back? I look at the picture. In the middle of the page is a large flower with semi-circular petals around a pink circle, all set inside a bigger pink circle. I glance at the pin fastened to Isaac's shirt and smile.

'Sasha helped me,' he signs.

'It's beautiful,' I say. 'Where is she?'

Isaac shrugs.

'What about Layla?'

I take Isaac's hand and lead him to Layla's room. She's not there, so we go down to the Hub and see a group of people gathered around the screens. Layla and Pedro are with them. There's a dull wall of voices but I can't make out anything they're saying. Layla sees me and walks quickly to the front of the store.

'Everything okay?' I ask.

'No,' she replies. She takes me by the arm and leads me to the side.

'There are officers outside. Were you followed? You're the only person who's been out of the store tonight.'

'No,' I say. 'I thought . . .' I look over at the screens. On the largest display in the centre is footage from the security camera in the side street. There are two men in the image, both wearing body armour and helmets. One of them is shining a torch into the underground car park.

'I wasn't followed,' I say. 'Someone saw me near my mum's flat, but they can't have known where I was going . . .'

Pedro notices us talking and storms over, but Layla holds him back.

'Why are they here?' he half-shouts. 'Did you lead them here?'

'Pedro,' Layla says, her voice only slightly raised. 'Not like this.' Layla turns back to me. 'Hannah, where is your mum's place?'

'Just north of the river. I took one train.'

'Did you see any officers? Anyone in a UV suit?'

'No . . . I don't think so.'

'They might have not been obvious. They could have been dressed like us. Can you think of any reason you would be followed?'

'I . . .'

'Hannah?'

I know I need to tell them the truth.

'When you found me, on the train . . .' I say, 'someone had just tried to take Isaac – an Atavism Representative – but I stopped him. I attacked him. They could have found out where my mum lived and followed me. Or the woman who saw me . . .' Jarvis knew. Would he have told them?

'*Mierda.*' Pedro mutters. 'You shouldn't have brought her here, Layla. This is on you.' He looks at me. 'Are you working for them?'

'No,' I say desperately. 'I didn't know they were following me.'

'Then why are you here?' he says, walking closer to me. 'God didn't bring you. *Fue el Diablo.* Layla – why is she here?'

'I told you,' she says calmly, still looking at me. 'We need her.'

'*We*? This is Samir all over again.'

Layla snaps her head to Pedro.

'Don't you fucking dare,' she says. 'He took your shift, remember? He took *your* shift.'

'Pedro?' The voice comes from one of the people gathered around the screens.

'What is it?' Pedro asks impatiently.

'Come look at this.'

He turns back. Layla stares at me.

'Why didn't you tell me?' she says softly.

'I'm so sorry,' I say.

Pedro is gazing at the largest monitor. 'No . . .' he says under his breath.

'What is it?' Layla says.

'No, no . . .' Pedro takes out a handgun from his back pocket and runs past Layla out of the store.

'Pedro?' she calls. She turns around to look at the screen.

'Is that . . . ?' She glances out into the corridor. 'Pedro!' A shout this time. She picks up another gun and runs after him. 'Stay there,' she calls back to me. I take Isaac's hand. Even standing this far back, I can tell who it is in the black-and-white image. The way she's holding herself. Sasha. The two officers are standing in front of the ramp to the underground car park. They're pointing their weapons at her.

'Turn the microphones on,' a man calls out. 'Hector, Muhammad, you go down to the corner of Fifteenth, but stay out of sight,' he says. 'Petra, you go to the window of Store Seventeen. Cyrus, you stay with me. The rest of you, go into the corridor and wait.'

A switch is flicked. Static. Distorted voices.

'*Stop,*' one of the officers shouts at Sasha. Isaac squeezes my hand tight but I can't look away.

'*You need to leave,*' Sasha says, still holding her stomach. '*This is God's place.*'

The officer in front points his gun in the air and shoots. The audio clips.

'*Calm!*' the other officer behind calls out. He puts his hands up. '*It's okay,*' he says. '*We're not going to hurt you . . . Can you tell us what this is? Why are you here?*'

'*This is God's place,*' she repeats, trying to sound strong.

The officers point their weapons at something off-screen. Pedro appears from behind Sasha holding his gun out in front of him.

'Sasha,' he says quietly. '*Come to me, now.*'

She looks at her father. '*God will protect us,*' she says.

'*No, not now,*' he says. '*Come to me. Please.*'

'*It's what you've said. God will lift us up. You believe that, don't you?*'

'*Of course,*' he says. '*But you're not strong enough for this. Come to me, please.*'

'*This is our place,*' she says. '*They shouldn't be here.*'

'*I know, but you don't need to do this. Not now.*'

One of the officers turns around quickly.

'*Stay back, Layla,*' Pedro shouts. '*I've got this.*'

The officer closest to Sasha reaches for something on his belt. A radio.

'*Don't,*' Pedro says quietly.

He lifts the radio to his mouth and starts to speak. Pedro fires, so does the officer. Two more shots. A scream. I blink and when I open my eyes both officers have fallen to the floor; so has Sasha.

'*Sasha,*' Pedro screams.

He runs to her, dropping his gun. He clutches her chest. He lifts her head.

'*Sasha, no. No, no, no . . .*'

The audio crackles. Black blood stains the floor around them. I pull Isaac into my body, turning him away from the screen. 'Don't look. Close your eyes.' He tries to move away from me to sign, but I don't let him.

'*Sasha, come to me. Come to me. Mi bebé, mi hermosa bebé.*'

The last two people in the Hub run out, leaving just me and Isaac and the screen. The side door in the image opens and more people flood the scene. '*Inside, quickly,*' someone shouts, *'take the bodies, and their guns.'* The man directs the crowd like this has been rehearsed. The officers' limp corpses are dragged through the small door, their weapons thrown in behind them. Someone comes out with a bucket and throws water onto the trail of blood left by the bodies.

'Come to me,' Pedro says under his voice. *'Mi bebé. Mi bebé.'* He's holding his daughter in his arms, cradling her.

Layla touches his shoulder, but he swats her away.

'We have to take her inside, Pedro,' the man in charge says. His voice is quiet.

Pedro looks up at him and nods. He lays Sasha gently onto the ground. Two people lift her body up high and carry her into the dark corridor. Pedro is kneeling in the water, in his daughter's blood, his head bowed. Layla is standing a few feet away, staring at him. She walks slowly forward, gently touches his shoulder again, and leads him inside.

For what feels like a lifetime, I stare at the screen. The empty street. The black marks. The water running down the ramp into the car park. I look at the car stuck on the ramp. The security light reflected in its windshield flickers for a moment then disappears.

PART THREE

PART THREE

CHAPTER TWENTY-SEVEN

Mum used to tell me about a flat she lived in just after she got married. It had one bedroom, and the kitchen was so small only one person could be in there at any time. She told me that she and Dad used to imagine the sort of house they would own in the future – something in the countryside, with a large garden, and rooms for each of their children. Three. They planned to have three, but they stopped at two.

Now, the world has fewer places to live in but more people than ever to live in them. Stretching to the left and right of the road we're walking along, for as far as I can see in the night, are refugee villages. Fields full of cabins locked together by bolts, some stacked four storeys high with metal stairs clinging onto to their sides. Toilet blocks are shared by hundreds of residents. Floodlights wash the cabins in light, as if the people inside don't deserve to hide in the dark. Some villages have high fences and gates, some are open, some are overfull, some have cabins with holes in their walls. I remember them being built fifteen years ago, back when things were being shared with us. The news footage showed diggers moving tonnes of earth and cabins being flown in and stacked by helicopters. I was at home. Mum was sitting next to me, not watching. They were a temporary solution, the reporter said, but everything temporary is permanent to people who don't care.

'Can we stop?' I ask Layla. Isaac is walking slowly, heavily.

She looks at me and nods. She hasn't spoken to me since we left the store a few hours ago.

We head off the road and down into a flattened area that looks like it used to be a wood. In front of me, I see nothing but the night, but behind me, the refugee village closest to us glows white. Layla finds a tree stump and sits down. I get some crackers and water out of my bag and take them to Isaac who's now sitting cross-legged on the ground. He starts eating. Crumbs fall all over his lap and onto the dry earth around his feet.

Layla looks at me, then past me. 'They're building a new one,' she says. It's comforting to hear her voice again.

I look at the brown emptiness, then at the village a few hundred metres away. I can see someone in a third-storey cabin. It's a girl, maybe ten years old, leaning out of her window, looking down to the ground. Isaac sees her too, and he waves, but she doesn't wave back. She goes into her cabin, disappearing for a few seconds, and returns with an object in her hand. I can't see what it is from here. She stretches out her arm and lets go. Down below is another child, who catches the object and runs off. The girl goes inside again, brings out something new, and a second child appears below to catch it.

'We used to do things like that.' Layla is looking too. 'Little games. They're probably trading toys or playing hide and seek with them.'

'How many kids were in your camp?'

'Forty or so. I remember we used to play this game called *manhunt*. A group of us would be the *catchers*, and another group the *finders*. It was like hide and seek, but if you were caught, you became a finder, a hunter. Mama didn't like it. I don't think she liked the name, but it was fun, and there were lots of places to hide. Samir and I would always hide together. He was good at finding somewhere secret, somewhere no one had been before.'

She takes some bread out of her bag and takes a bite.

'We should go,' she says through her food.

'I'm sorry about Sasha,' I say, trying to find some way to talk about what happened.

'You don't need to apologise,' she replies. I can feel my guilt like a mass. It's a physical thing now.

'If I hadn't have gone to see my mum . . .'

'Don't,' she snaps and she looks away from me. 'Please, don't,' she says in a softer voice. 'I took you there. It's not your fault.'

'You could have stayed,' I say.

'I know, but there are others who can help. Pedro doesn't need me . . . You do.'

Isaac takes a glug of water and droplets splash onto his cheek. I gently wipe them off.

'Ready?' I say to him, and I look at Sasha's pin, still attached to his shirt. A flower trapped in a circle. I'll tell him when he's older. He can't know now.

Isaac hands the bottle back to me.

'Ready,' he signs.

We continue along the road for a while, heading away from the villages, and I hold Isaac's hand. His energy has come back a little, but every time I try to let go of him, he grabs tighter. There's sweat building up between us. We reach a turning off the road and stop.

'It's quicker this way,' Layla says, looking towards a field in the distance.

She takes us down the smaller of the two roads, and we head left though a metal gate into an open field. The gate sings as she opens it, and Isaac sings the tune back. Layla laughs.

'He's good at that,' she says.

As we enter the field, the wind picks up the Soundfield's Hum and throws it past us. Isaac lets go of my hand and jumps up as if trying to catch the sound, but lands awkwardly and falls to the ground. 'Are you okay?' I say as I pick him up and he brushes the grass from his shorts. There's dry mud on his knees and I imagine a life where he comes home from playing with his friends at the weekend and I have to wipe the mud off his cheek. Layla is a few feet in front of us, up a slight incline, and is staring at Isaac. She looks sad, alone. I catch her eye and she's taken out of her daydream.

'Come on,' she says, sounding a little frustrated that I'd seen her.

We move through the field towards a wooden gate in the far corner. The air is warm and restless, and carries a sweet smell with it. The gate is locked with a heavy chain, so we climb over one by one. Layla goes first, then I lift Isaac over, with Layla helping on the other side, and I go last. The field ahead is overgrown, and the moonlight catches the edges of the wildflowers blowing in the wind. The night is different this far from the city, away from the orange and yellow of the artificial lights. It's monochrome, almost. Deep black shadows and shining whites.

There's a noise in the distance. Isaac turns to me.

'Layla?' I say.

Layla walks towards the sound. I see something moving. I make out a head, and a large, heavy body.

'It's okay,' she says. 'He won't hurt you.'

Behind a water trough in the centre of the field, an animal is eating, its head nodding up and down as it pulls at the grass.

'What is it?' Isaac signs.

'It's a horse,' I sign by putting my thumb to my right temple and bending and unbending my first two fingers.

'What's this?' Isaac says, repeating the *horse* sign back to me. He's never seen that action before; I've never taught it to him.

'It's an animal,' I say. 'Like a cow, but we don't eat these. We used to ride them, and they used to help us farm our land.'

Layla moves closer to the horse.

'Hello,' she says. 'It's alright. This one's gentle.'

Isaac looks at me and runs to the other side of the trough.

'You can stroke him if you'd like,' Layla says. Isaac reaches his hand forward and stretches out to touch the horse's nose as it dips down to eat. It breathes out and Isaac pulls his hand back.

'It's okay,' Layla says. 'You have to move slowly, but they're usually very calm.'

She lifts Isaac up and he pats the horse's head awkwardly.

'That's it,' she says. 'Like that.'

She's smiling, and so is Isaac, and I see how much she needs this.

'I used to have a horse, back home,' she says, talking to me. 'Sam and I would ride them when we could. Mine was white – Nala, I called her. I had to look after Sam's, though. He didn't like cleaning out the muck.'

'What happened to them?'

'We had to leave them behind, like everything else.'

The horse breathes out again, heavily this time, and Isaac giggles. Layla drops him down, and he pulls some grass out of the ground.

'Flatten your hand,' she says, 'like this.' Isaac imitates her action, like he imitated my sign, and cautiously brings his hand to the animal's mouth. It laps up the grass with its shining tongue, and Isaac laughs again, wiping his wet hand on his shirt.

After a small pause, he runs back to me, and I tell him he's done a good job, and we leave the field through a small opening in the hedgerow.

'I would have liked to have known Samir,' I say as I push some brambles back for Isaac to get through, but Layla doesn't reply.

For a while, we walk in silence, locked in by a fence on one side and a tall hedgerow on the other. The hedge looks like it hasn't been cut in years, and there are nettles growing out from its base. Isaac tries to touch one, but I stop him before he can.

'They can sting, they can hurt you, if they touch your skin.' He looks at them with childish fascination.

'So, it's bad for you?' He signs to me whilst walking, a skill that he's never really mastered.

'Some things in nature are bad for you, yes, but a lot of things are good for you.'

'Isaac has never been in the countryside before, has he?' Layla says.

'No,' I reply. 'I've thought about taking him to the woods or the sea, but I've never had the time, with Mum and work.' I once dreamt that Elias was living with me and Isaac in Mum's house. I saw them playing by the lake – throwing stones into the water, swimming out to the island, lying on the beach wrapped in their towels. That's the only dream I've had where they're together. They're always separate in my dreams, like they don't exist in the same part of my mind.

'Does Yara come with you on this trip much?' I say.

She doesn't say anything for a few seconds.

'Sometimes,' she says. 'She likes the horses. I'd like to teach her to ride one day, when she's older. She stays with her dad most of the time. It's better that way.'

'Is he Babylon?'

'No, but he believes in what they do, like me. I met him at a shelter in the city. He's one of the good ones.'

Isaac picks up a small stick and starts running it through the leaves and branches sticking out of the hedgerow.

'Sam would have liked you,' Layla says quietly. 'He didn't talk much about how he felt, but I know he was lonely.' She looks at me. 'He wasn't even meant to be on duty that day. Pedro had to look after Sasha. So, Sam went instead of him.'

'What were they doing?' I ask.

'I don't know. In that part of the city, probably surveillance. I don't get involved in that sort of thing. Sam would tell me about things when he could, but he was vague about the details. He wanted to protect me, I think.'

I see Samir stretching out his hand towards me.

'I thought about leaving Babylon when Yara was born,' Layla says. 'I talked to Sam about it, but he wanted to stay. I understood why. Babylon was everything to him. But things change when you have a child.'

Isaac turns back to me and signs something.

'What did he say?' Layla asks.

'He's hungry. Is there anywhere to stop?'

'There's a place Babylon looks after about a kilometre ahead. It's for refugees, but they'll give us some food.'

Layla stops walking, and I stop too. She looks straight at me, and her eyes catch the moonlight. They're black now, not brown. A warm wind blows past us.

'Was it quick?' she says. 'Samir?'

'Yes,' I say, but I don't know for sure.

Isaac goes back to playing with his stick and starts singing, improvising on top of the Soundfield's Hum. It's another melody I haven't heard before, so all I can do is listen. In the stillness of the night, Isaac's small voice mixed with the drone from above sounds like a prayer to a distant god. I wonder if he's trying to say something to that god, speaking in a language that neither I nor Layla can understand.

CHAPTER TWENTY-EIGHT

It was in the last year of our research on the Soundfield that Pedro took one of Elias's team hostage. Her name was Jun. She was a specialist in astrophysics. Before she was taken there weren't that many guards in the lab – one at the entrance, a few posted on each floor – but afterwards, there were dozens. I wondered what good all the extra bodies and guns would do when they had no idea where she was or what Babylon wanted, what Pedro wanted.

'It's a hatchet job,' I heard one of the guards say.

'No note?' someone else said.

'No,' the other one replied.

Jun didn't stay long after Pedro let her go. There were bruises on her face, burns on her arms from the ropes. I hated Babylon for what they did to her, so I never thought about what it was like to be on the other side of the concrete wall between us and them. But I'm thinking about it now. I'm walking under thick cloud in the pitch-black night with Layla. I'm looking down to check my footing but also so she can't see my thoughts.

The dirt path we're on turns into a tarmacked driveway, and in the distance, I see flickering lights, suspended in the air. There are trees lining the drive.

'What is this place?' I ask.

'An estate. It was abandoned after the Soundfield arrived,' she says. 'It's been used for a lot of things since, but it's still farmed. By us, mainly.'

The tarmac turns into gravel, closing into a circle at the front of the house, with a smaller circle of dead grass at its centre. On the front of the house, tall windows are stacked in three neat rows around a wide entrance. Either side of the house are outbuildings – sheds, a garage with no car, a wooden roof covering an empty swimming pool. And beyond, fields for as far as I can see in the dark.

Layla moves into the shadowed porch and pushes the heavy door open. There are voices, lots of them, coming from a room on the left.

'Claire?' she calls out.

After a few seconds, a woman appears. She's about my age.

'Layla? Hey. I wasn't expecting you.'

'This isn't planned,' she says. 'Just dropping in. This is Hannah and Isaac.'

Claire nods her head towards me, and I nod back.

'Refugees?' she says to Layla.

'No, friends.'

She looks back at me, then to Isaac.

'Fine,' she says. 'There's soup if you want it.'

Layla follows Claire into the room, and we walk behind her. It takes a while for my eyes to adjust to the new, uneven light. It's coming from a fireplace on the right-hand wall. A heavy, concrete hearth and a roaring fire. A wide pot is sitting in the flames, like something from a history book.

'Take whatever you need,' Claire says.

Isaac has stopped and is gazing at the fire. I see the flames reflected in his eyes. He tugs at my hand then lets go.

'What is it?' he signs.

'It's a fireplace,' I sign back. 'We used to use them to heat our houses or cook things.'

'It's hot,' he signs.

'I know,' I say. 'We're here to get something to eat. We won't be long.'

Layla looks back at us.

'Take a seat,' she says, pointing towards an empty corner of the room. 'I'll get some food.'

We sit down on two wooden chairs, like the ones we had at school, the ones that dig into your skin. I look around. The room is lined with dark panels and I wonder if this was a dining room before the Field. Something is hanging from the ceiling. It's not a light – more like a sculpture. A thing to look pretty, not to serve any function. It's made of glass and metal, and it spins with the hot air from the fire, catching the light and throwing it onto the ceiling. Isaac is looking up at the pattern, trying to make sense of it. There aren't as many people in the room as I'd guessed from the noise. Fifteen, maybe fewer. They're sitting in small huddles, their chairs turned towards each other. I do the same with ours, creating a small circle of three.

'Here,' Layla says.

She gives me two bowls of soup and Isaac jumps off his chair and holds his hand out to take the spoons.

'Thank you,' Isaac signs to Layla.

'What's the sign for "you're welcome"?' she asks me.

'You usually just use the sign for "thank you",' I say. I flatten my hand with my thumb sticking out and touch my chin with the tips of my fingers, then bring my whole hand forward. Layla copies me and repeats the sign to Isaac. He smiles and jumps back up on the chair and hands me a spoon. Layla goes to get another bowl and when she returns, we sit in our group of three and eat together. Leek and potato. Mum used to make this, with soft potatoes and big bits of leek.

The conversations die away to a whisper as we all eat. I can hear the fire, but also a faint hum. Not from the Soundfield this time, but from inside the room. Isaac has noticed it too – an old man sitting by himself in the far corner is humming as he eats. His song is interrupted every time he takes a bite of bread so it's difficult to make out the melody, but I get it eventually. So does Isaac. It's CP1. The first melody.

'Who is that?' I say to Layla, looking at the man.

Layla glances back. 'He lives here. He's been here for as long as I've known about the place.'

Isaac jumps to the ground, spilling a bit of soup on his top, and puts the bowl on his chair. Before I can stop him, he starts walking over to the old man.

'Isaac?'

I put my food down and follow him. Isaac is with the man now, and he's started humming along with him. I walk quickly past the chairs and people.

'Sorry,' I say when I reach Isaac.

'Don't be,' the man says, coughing on his food, 'he wasn't bothering me.'

'Come on, Isaac.' I put my arm round his shoulder, but he pushes back.

'What's your name?' the man says, putting his bowl down beside him and leaning forwards in his chair. Isaac signs his name – I-S-A-A-C – pausing before the second A as if he was trying to remember how many there were. The man looks at me.

'Isaac,' I say.

'Well, my name is Radek. It's very good to meet you.' He smiles widely and coughs again. It's nice not to have to explain why Isaac can't talk.

'What are you doing here?' Radek asks kindly, again to Isaac.

'Eating,' Isaac signs by touching his thumb to his fingers of his right hand and bringing it to his mouth.

'Don't worry,' Radek says, putting his hand up to me. 'I understood that one.'

'Layla says you've been here a while?' I say.

'Oh, Layla. You're with her? Such a lovely girl,' he says, showing his age. 'Yes, I've been here for years. Five, or thereabouts. Time goes so quickly, don't you think? Now, you can't have been much older than a sprout when I came here,' he says to Isaac. 'How old are you?'

He opens one hand out fully and sticks up the thumb of his other hand.

'Six!' Radek says. 'Well, that's a very special age.'

He picks up his soup and starts eating.

'Please, sit, if you'd like,' he says, glancing at two empty chairs. I look at Layla and I think about taking Isaac back to her. But then I see Radek's face – the hope – and I sit down. So does Isaac. Radek looks grateful that we're here. Happy, almost.

'You heard me singing, didn't you?' Radek says to him. Isaac nods. 'Sorry about that,' he says to me, smiling. 'Not something you hear people humming much. You know, however hard I've tried, I can't seem to get that melody out of my head.' He laughs and it makes him cough again.

'What do you do here?' I ask.

'Oh, what I can. I'm too old for farming, so I help with the cleaning, organising the books in the library, that sort of thing. Mostly inside. It's too hot for me outside. Now, you don't look like the sorts of people who come here.'

I don't know what he means by this. We've lost our home, but we're not refugees, not like Layla.

'No, well, we're just passing through,' I say, and Radek smiles. 'What brought you here?'

'My children, in a way. Yes, you could say that. I came here because of them, but they're not around anymore. You see, I know more than you think about this world. You've heard of the *Atavism Programme*?'

I nod and smile politely.

'Well,' he continues, 'my granddaughter was a very special girl. Very special. She was one of the first children to be invited into the Programme. Her parents, my son and his wife, put her forward, right at the beginning. You remember all those adverts? *Future* this, *promise* that. Sounded exciting, didn't it? Well, my son and his wife sent Lilly for the tests, and she passed, or they said she'd passed. Of course, they found out what it was like eventually, and they asked to take her out of the Programme. They demanded, but they wouldn't let them have her. Told me all about it after. So, one day, when they were visiting, they decided to take her. They ran out of the building with her, and across the street, and, well, that was that. They shot them, whilst they were running. In the back. They didn't even tell me straight away. I came here a few weeks later. Come to think of it, I only started singing that song after that . . .' He trails off. 'Oh, I shouldn't be telling you all of this.'

'It's okay,' I say quietly.

'Don't be sorry for me,' he says. 'You've got your own worries. They did it because they had to.' He coughs from his chest and looks at Isaac.

'What's your favourite food, son?'

Isaac looks at me, then back at Radek.

'Raisins,' he signs.

'Raisins,' I say. 'How do you keep going?' I ask.

'Raisins!' Radek says, ignoring my question. 'Well, mine is roast beef. I used to love roast beef.'

Isaac looks at me.

'We should finish eating,' I say. 'It was nice meeting you. Say goodbye, Isaac.'

'Goodbye,' he signs, and Radek waves back.

As we leave the estate, heading back down the long drive towards the main road, I think about when EK's parents would visit the lab. They would come in and spend a few hours or the whole day with EK. We'd let them control the schedule – if they wanted, they could take them out for a week or a month, we wouldn't stop them. We made that clear from the beginning: they were doing us a favour, not the other way round. But I wonder what the visits were like after the Programme began. Why bother letting the parents in if they were going to kill them for trying to take their child away? Was it a test? Did they want them to fail? I wonder if they used the same room for visits, the one with the toys on the floor and the crayon drawings on the walls. I hope they didn't.

'We need to find somewhere to sleep,' Layla says, interrupting my thoughts. 'There's a barn about an hour away. It should be empty.'

The air is beginning to brighten. Black turning into blue.

'That's fine,' I say, answering a question she didn't really ask.

'What did Radek say to you?' Layla says.

'Nothing,' I lie. I can't face it yet.

CHAPTER TWENTY-NINE

Out here, this far from any towns, there are only a few cars scattered on the road. People didn't want their vehicles cluttering their homes, but there was little sense in leaving them out here, in the middle of nowhere. These people would have run out of fuel when they weren't expecting it, and they would have had to walk to the nearest town or village to find their way home. When Elias and I went back for Theo's funeral in Elias's car, we had to manoeuvre around these abandoned vehicles, or drive through fields and side roads when the main road was blocked. At one point, when Elias was forcing the car through a gap between a truck and a stone wall, I saw a man standing in a field by the road, looking in our direction. I thought he was going to run at us, and I told Elias to move faster. He scraped the edge of the car on the wall and drove off, and I looked back at the man, who hadn't moved, but was still staring at the car. We had fuel, and people would kill for it, but I wasn't willing to die for it.

'How much further?' I ask.

'Not long. You see that building up there?' Layla points towards a small structure up a hill in the distance, just off the road we're walking on. 'That's the barn. That's where we're going.'

We travel in silence, watching the air change colour. I learnt enough from Elias about atmospheric physics. In the morning when the sun rises the light passes through more layers of air than at midday, scattering the shorter wavelength blue light, leaving just reds and oranges behind. It's orange now. No, darker: auburn. Elias always called the atmosphere the *giant* and spoke about it like it had a life of its own. But I didn't like calling it that. I didn't like the thought of this invisible thing crushing us from above and not being able to do anything about it.

There's a lorry on its side in front of us, blocking most of the road.

'Through here,' Layla says. She walks off the road and to a gap between the cab of the lorry and the hedgerow. She stops, halfway through.

'Layla?' I say.

'Move back,' she says.

'What?'

'Down.'

She pushes Isaac and me to the ground. I bring Isaac close to me.

'What is it?' I ask.

'Lights. In the distance.'

'Where?'

'Be quiet.'

I hold my breath and cover Isaac's mouth with my hand. I see the lights now. They're getting stronger, and so is the noise. An engine. The truck slows as it approaches the upturned lorry. It moves into the ditch on the other side of the road, then back towards us. It passes by and I let go of Isaac. My hand is moist from his breath.

'Keep still,' Layla says. 'Not yet.'

The truck stops. I look back. There's noise, shouting. The rear door is thrown open and a figure emerges. They look around and run into the field opposite us, fast. More shouting, doors opening. Silence, a breath. Then a shot, and the figure collapses. I make an involuntary sound, like an animal in pain.

'Quiet,' Layla says again.

Two men walk slowly out to the field. They stop and look at the body, prodding it with their weapons like hunters standing over their prey. They're talking and gesturing. I can't hear what they're saying. They return to the truck and move off, leaving the body for the sun to find.

'Claire said they'd seen patrols,' Layla says.

'Are they looking for us?'

'I don't know.'

'Why are they out here?'

'Moving people between camps, maybe.'

'Are you okay?' I sign to Isaac, and he nods but I think he's learnt to give this response whenever I ask.

Layla leads us along the road towards the barn and I look around for more lights, more trucks.

'Radek did tell me something,' I say, trying to get the body out of my mind. The way they fell. It was like a doll. Limp.

'He said his granddaughter was in the Programme. She was shot with her parents when they tried to take her out. Did you know?'

'Yes,' she says.

'Then how can you still want to help me?'

She waits to reply. I can't see her face.

'You didn't kill them.'

I look at her, but she doesn't look back. She's wrong. I did kill them.

We move off the road and onto a track which winds up a small hill, following the path of a stream. The water trickles slowly downwards, shining in the first of the morning light, and I splash my face in it. At the end of the track, I see the silhouette of a barn surrounded by trees.

'It's a little uneven,' Layla says. 'Watch your step.'

I take Isaac's hand. The rocks jut out of the path, and the ground is thick and wet, and I can feel him struggling.

'Are you okay?' Layla asks, looking back.

'We're okay,' I reply.

At the top of the hill, the ground hardens and flattens. I drop down to Isaac. He looks away from me and frowns.

'We'll be able to sleep soon,' I say.

'Why are we here?' he signs, still not looking at me.

'Just to stay the night,' I say.

The barn is a lot larger than I had guessed at the bottom of the track and sits alone in the landscape – there's no farmhouse, or cultivated land, or animals.

'Who owns this?' I say.

'I don't know,' Layla says. 'I found it a couple of years back and slept here a few times with Yara. I don't think it's used for anything.'

Layla heads to a small door at the front. She turns the handle then tries to force it open with her shoulder.

'This wasn't locked last time,' she says. 'I think there's another entrance at the side.'

We follow her round to the left of the building, and the light disappears as we enter the gap between the barn and the woods. I look into the trees and then behind me. It's light enough for me to see the road we've just walked along and the jack-knifed lorry next to where we hid. I half expect to see someone walking along the road towards us, following us. I make myself feel cold.

'Here,' Layla says, and she pushes open a sliding door. She moves inside and disappears into the shadow. 'Your eyes will adjust,' she says, from nowhere.

The air inside is damp and smells of hay. I look to my left and see blue light pushing through the ill-fitting slats, partially blocked by stacks of hay bales, piled five or six high at the back and reducing to one or two at the front. Isaac finds a bale that's detached from the rest and sits down. A few feet in front of me is a heavy wooden column, rising vertically from the ground into the rafters. I look up and see a mezzanine level tucked into the far-right corner, with a set of three windows and a wooden ladder leaning against its outer edge.

'There was a . . .' Layla says, but she's moved further inside before she can finish her thought. 'Here it is.' A dim orange light appears from her direction, which brightens slowly over the next few seconds. 'I'm surprised the batteries are still working.' She's holding a plastic light, which has been made to look like an oil lamp, like the ones used by miners and railway workers two centuries ago. The barn comes into focus, and the shadows are partly filled in. There's a wooden table with a few more lamps, a collection of rusting tools leaning chaotically against the wall – spades, pickaxes, a rake – and more hay bales piled into the far corner.

Layla takes the lamp to Isaac, puts it down on the bale next to him and asks me to get another. I go over to the table, take one and rotate the dial on the front, but it doesn't turn on. I pick up a second, one with a small solar panel on the top, flick a switch, and the wall in front of me lights up. It's covered in white drawings like the corridor in the department store, sketched in chalk onto the crumbling wood up to waist height, the level a child could reach. There are stick figures, crudely drawn animals, including one that looks like a horse, and a large drawing stretched across five panels of a house surrounded by trees.

'Yara did those when we stayed here,' Layla says. 'She was practicing for her space in the Sanctuary. She couldn't decide what to draw.'

Next to the house are two tall stick figures, holding hands.

'Is this you and her dad?'

Layla looks at the drawing.

'Yes.'

We eat our dinner in silence, turning the lamps down and then off as the warm light finds its way through the gaps in the barn walls. Layla has a stove, and a cylinder of gas. After eating, I unpack Isaac's thin sleeping bag, re-arrange some of the bales, and lay the bag down for him. He gets in, then signs something, forgetting that his hands are hidden. I ask him to say it again. He brings his hands out into the warm air, and signs *goodnight*. I squeeze him and say *goodnight* back. He's never known a world where he's slept in the night and been awake in the day, but it's like this idea has found a way into his language, through things he's seen or things I've said. Maybe it's just that he can't escape the feeling that he shouldn't be sleeping in the day.

Layla closes the shutters on the windows in the rafters using a large wooden pole and the light in the barn dims. All that's left are thick vertical shadows cast by the beams. Layla sits down on a bale a few feet away from Isaac and gets something out of her bag.

She holds a bar of chocolate towards me.

'Do you want some? It's a little old, but it still tastes fine.'

I had assumed I would never have chocolate again. You can get it in Holland market, but it was always too expensive.

'Thank you,' I say, and I snap a piece off the end. It's crumbly, but sweet. 'Can Isaac have some tomorrow?'

Layla nods, and we both gaze at him. He's already asleep.

'He's doing well,' she says.

'I sometimes think he's more resilient than me.'

'Hmm,' Layla replies knowingly. 'Where's his father?'

I don't answer immediately.

'He's never been a part of Isaac's life. He doesn't live near us.'

Layla stares at me but doesn't say anything. The silence grows and becomes uncomfortable.

'Does Elias know?'

I look at Isaac, and I wonder if Layla is trying to judge my reaction. Does she know what question she's asking?

'No,' I reply quietly.

'Doesn't he have a right to know?'

'Maybe. But it's too late now.'

'So why are you going to him?'

'Because I don't have a choice,' I say.

'You always have a choice,' Layla replies.

I continue to look at Isaac, who is breathing lightly, tucked into his sleeping bag, and I wonder if there is another path. I try to imagine going back to the city, or moving to another country, or going north. But no path remains fixed in my mind.

Choice is an illusion created by people who want to believe they are in control, but no one is in control, not really. In most situations, only one thing plays out because there is only one thing that makes sense. I went to university because I wanted to escape home. I worked on the Soundfield because I couldn't imagine anything more exciting. I stopped talking to Theo because I hated who he'd become. I slept with Elias during our research because I loved him. I'm going to Elias now because I think I still love him.

'Maybe I only have one choice, but can't you still think it's the right thing to do?'

Layla takes her eyes away from Isaac and looks at me.

'I don't know,' she says. 'Only you can decide that.'

CHAPTER THIRTY

I'm walking through pine trees, Isaac next to me. It's quiet, and I can hear the water lapping against the shore in the distance. There's someone else with us. I can't see their face, but I can hear their breath. A filtered sound, metallic. They're holding Isaac's other hand. The sand is warm on my feet, and I'm blinking against the brightness of the sun.

I'm woken by a noise and turn over to check on Isaac. He's still asleep, and so is Layla. I push myself out of my sleeping bag and walk towards the front of the barn. There's a wide gap between two planks and I look through. The sun is on the other side of the building, lighting up the stretch of road that leads back to Radek and the farm. The body is still there. In the field next to the lorry. A small black dot in a sea of yellow grass and bright sun. I notice a truck in the far distance moving in our direction. Is it the one from earlier? Maybe. I follow its path down the road, to the stream and track that leads up to the barn. There's someone there. Another figure, this one alive, standing next to the gate at the bottom of the track. They're in a black UV suit with something covering their face, like a gas mask or a respirator. I hold my breath and glance back at Isaac. They're looking up the hill towards the barn. Are they looking at me? I can't move or do anything. I wait for them to move first. The truck reaches the gate and stops. The front door opens, and the figure in the mask gets in. I stare at the bottom of the hill for a while, even after the vehicle is out of sight, waiting for the sound of the truck to fade into the Hum.

I lie back down on top of my sleeping bag, re-find a comfortable position, and make myself fall asleep again.

When I wake for the final time, Layla is already up, eating. Isaac is sitting beside her.

'What time is it?' I ask.

'Sorry, did I wake you?' Layla says.

'No.'

'It's just past seven,' she says, looking at her watch. 'The sun hasn't set yet. Want something?' She points with a fork towards the unopened cans, and I push myself up. My muscles ache. I go over to Isaac and kiss the top of his head.

'You move a lot in your sleep,' Layla says.

'Bad dreams,' I say, and I hope she doesn't ask more. I sit down on the bale next to Isaac. My feet touch the floor, but his dangle carelessly off the side.

'I've been thinking about our route,' she says, looking at the map laid out in front of her. 'The one I normally take to my town would bring us up here.' I follow her finger along a footpath, then onto a main road. 'But I think we should go this way.' Layla's hand moves to the left, through a few fields and a wood. 'Some of it is a little wild, but we should be okay.'

'That's fine,' I say. 'Layla – did you hear anything last night?'

'What do you mean?' she says.

'Nothing,' I reply.

I eat the pieces of beef Isaac has left at the bottom of his can whilst he reads his book on dinosaurs. 'We should go,' Layla says after I've finished. She's standing with her rucksack on, and in one swift motion, she moves the gun from the side pocket of her bag into her back pocket. She sees me looking at it but doesn't say anything.

'Isaac,' I say, and he looks up at me. 'We have to go.' I take the book from him, and his face crumples like he is about to cry. 'I'm sorry. You can read it later, okay?' He nods and holds back his tears, and we follow Layla out of the barn.

As she opens the sliding door, I'm hit by a warm wind and the Soundfield's Hum. In front, the trees block out most of the setting sun, but through the gaps between trunks, I can see a sharp band of red that turns orange at the horizon. I'm with Mum and Theo in the garden, lying under a blanket. We're watching the sun set. It's summer. I'm six, maybe seven, and Mum's letting us stay up, maybe for the first time. When it's finally dark, she sings to us.

> *'Star light, star bright,*
> *First star I see tonight;*
> *I wish I may, I wish I might*
> *Have the wish I wish tonight.'*

'Hannah?' Layla has moved to the back of the barn and is waiting for us.

'Coming,' I say, and I take Isaac's hand, glancing back one final time to check we're alone.

The Soundfield's Hum is loud in the starlight, like the shell encasing the Earth has crusted over. I sometimes go days or weeks without noticing it, but it always finds me again on a night like this. I can feel it inside me as we walk along the dry earth. Isaac has noticed a change too. He's looking upwards, towards the stars and the Field, ears wide to the noise. When we first signed up participants to study the Soundfield, we would ask them to describe what they felt when listening to the Hum, and the Calls. There was one person, a woman in her thirties, who said something that I haven't been able to shake from my mind. She was listening to a Hum and she said *it hurts*. Just those two words, and nothing else. When Freya asked her to elaborate, she couldn't. She couldn't explain where it hurt, or what the pain was like, or if the pain was physical or psychological. She just said that it hurt. Mahesh thought she was making it up, but from the way Freya told us about the woman's comment, I knew she wasn't. We didn't speak about it afterwards, but two years after the woman had left the study, after EK had arrived, Freya brought it up again.

'You remember that woman in the first round of participants?'

I nodded; she didn't need to explain further.

'Do you ever think about what she said?'

I did think about it, but as I walk through the night and feel the Hum from the Soundfield, I can't help but wonder if she was wrong. It doesn't *hurt*, not in the way it hurts when you break your arm or when someone shouts at you, it just makes you feel so strongly that it's like you're hurting. In the right context, surrounded by the right people, it can feel like love.

We make our way through two more fields, following the left-hand edge of the first and cutting through the middle of the second, and walk towards a wooded area. The path through the wood follows a river, and we travel for several minutes in silence and almost complete darkness. Dappled moonlight falls on Isaac's face, and I catch glimpses of his calm expression. He looks up occasionally, trying to hear the Soundfield through the thick trees. We never listened to the Field in a context like this. It was always sterile – in a lab, via speakers, or headphones, played through machines, processed – but it sounds different out here. It's alive. A few minutes into the wood, the Hum changes pitch. It slides upwards, settling somewhere between an A and a B-flat. Isaac stops in a small clearing and sings the small melody back to the Field, exactly imitating the glissando between the starting and ending pitches as he stares at the sky. I keep looking forwards, but in the calm of the woods, and with the sound of the river and the wonder on my son's face, I nearly join him in looking up at the Field and the stars.

At the end of the wood, the river bends to the right, and the path disappears. In front of us is a field that banks upwards, covered in wheat. Layla takes out the map and angles it to catch the moonlight.

'We have to cut through here,' she says, looking ahead. 'There should be a road on the other side.'

Isaac lets go of my hand, and moves into the field, pushing himself into the tall wheat. He stretches out his arms and splays his hands, letting it pass through his fingers. He starts walking faster, then runs, and I can hear him laughing. At the top of the hill, about fifty metres away from Layla and me, he stops and looks straight up.

'Isaac?' I call out, but he doesn't move, or look at me. I start walking towards him, fast, and am about to say his name again but I don't. The Hum has gone, it's dropped away, and for a few seconds, the world is calm and still. Out of the silence, a piercing note appears, suspended in the air, and Isaac sings it back. The note slides into another, then one more, and Isaac sings every note in time, still staring at the sky. The Call shifts into a rhythmical sequence of seven pitches which start slowly and then accelerate towards the end. Isaac runs, trying to chase the sound, his movements matching the music. He sings the seven pitches back, but alters them slightly – a response to the Call. The melody lands on a high note, then rises again, higher still, and Isaac stops singing. He stands still and reaches both hands to the sky as the melody slides upwards and dissolves. The last note echoes around the valley, reverberating in the stillness, and Isaac holds the sound in his hands. He lowers his arms, and at the same moment, the Hum returns, like he's conducting the sky.

Layla and I walk slowly to Isaac. His head is bowed, his eyes closed. When we reach him, he glances up at me. I smile, but he doesn't smile back. He almost looks upset. Is he sad that the Call is over or is he sad that he can't talk to me about it? I want to talk to him, more than anything. I want to ask him what it's like, but maybe I'll never know how. Without saying anything, I put an arm round his shoulder and hold him close. I nod towards Layla and in a comforting silence, we set off together, making our way down to the road at the bottom of the hill.

CHAPTER THIRTY-ONE

I'm by Layla's side as we walk past the cars and debris, Isaac a few feet in front of us. Old road signs come and go, ransacked trucks, overgrown verges, animal carcases, half-open gates to empty fields, farmhouses with smashed windows. Layla is waiting for me to speak. I can feel it. So, after a while, I begin, and I can see the final parts of my story in front of me, like paper pulled from a fire before it burns.

'What we saw in the lab,' I say, softly, so Isaac doesn't hear, 'with the responses to the Field by EK and the other children, that was nothing compared with the things I've seen Isaac do since. Maybe it would have been different if we'd changed the conditions – let them experience the Field outside, rather than in a clinical setting, I don't know – but it's like Isaac is speaking a more advanced version of the language, or one that's more free.'

I breathe in deeply. The warm air fills my lungs and I think about the blackened text in my paper, and I see myself writing alone in my office. Not through my eyes, but from behind, like an observer, in third person, not first.

'That last part of the paper, the redacted section . . . it was just conjecture at the time. I had no evidence for what I was saying; that's why it was at the end. It came after the data and the analysis because it was just an idea. I thought I'd made that clear, but . . . After the paper was finished, I gave copies of those last paragraphs to everyone in the group, and we sat in my office, Elias too, and talked through them. Mahesh and Freya didn't have any comments, but Elias argued that we shouldn't put them in. We talked about it for a few hours but, in the end, agreed that it was wrong not to include them. Looking back on it now, I think I pressured Mahesh and Freya into it, and maybe I knew it at the time. They were young. They respected me . . . I wrote a note at the end of the paper to say that that last section was written by me, and that they were my thoughts only. People don't do that in scientific papers. Everyone takes collective responsibility for the whole work, even if some data was gathered by one researcher, or a particular section was written by one person. But I felt I had to take responsibility for that part.'

Layla is silent, walking beside me. We're both looking ahead, and she's listening to my final lecture.

'Our DNA is a time capsule. The genome of a species does change – through mutation or genetic recombination – but these changes are often so small and so gradual, happening over millions of years, that you can easily trace the history of a species by looking at its genes. We know that chimps and bonobos are our closest ancestors, for example, because we share almost ninety-nine per cent of our DNA.'

I see Dad sitting beside me, telling me about Watson and Crick and how the structure of DNA was discovered. It doesn't matter if this memory isn't real. It's real to me, and that's enough.

'DNA is made up of sequences of four nucleotide bases – A, C, G and T – which combine to make genes, which, in turn, code for different proteins. There are tens of thousands of genes encoding tens of thousands of proteins, but many of these proteins are involved in the workings of other genes. So, when a mutation occurs, instead of leading directly to the development of a novel characteristic, the protein formed might *indirectly* affect an individual's phenotype by repressing or activating another gene. And if this can be done in one direction, it can also be done in the other direction – it can be reversed. Our DNA is a time capsule not only because we can use it to trace our ancestry, but also because genes that may have been suppressed for thousands or even millions of years of evolution have the potential to be reactivated.

'And the *FOXP2* gene, the one that was altered in EK and the other children, is an example of this type of gene – one that controls the behaviour of other parts of the genome. My conclusion was that they had all undergone a change which had led to the activation of a *separate* gene which, for two hundred thousand years, had been repressed. A gene which had once allowed our hominin ancestors to communicate via

a musical protolanguage. Or, in other words, they had undergone what's called an *atavism*.'

This was a normal word once, but it isn't now. It stains the
air as I say it.

'Atavisms have appeared in many different species, humans
included. It's the reason people have colour blindness, why
some horses and guinea pigs have extra toes, or why some
infants are born with vestigial tails. But like all mutations,
atavisms are random. If the trait that they confer turns out
to be advantageous for the individual, given the right conditions, the mutation will be naturally selected for and fixed
within a species even if it's been lost in the past. But humans
have escaped nature – we're not evolving, or competing for
survival – so there was no chance of this language naturally
re-appearing. All we could do was wait. Wait for random
mutations to happen in one of the most protected genes in
the human genome and hope that the people with this mutation came forward.

'I understand Elias's reaction now. I understand why he
didn't want me to put that section in the paper, but . . . I'm
not trying to justify it, but a thought had stuck in my mind
that I couldn't get rid of. It's what I said to my team, and Elias,
in my office that night. It's how I convinced them and myself.
My thinking was that maybe there could be a person in the
future who could actually *speak* this protolanguage, not just
respond to it more strongly than others, but actually speak and
understand the Soundfield's language. That person could be
the answer to everything. They could find out why it was here,

what it was for, why it was speaking a dead language, and maybe how to get rid of it, or at least how to live with it . . .'

I'm still looking away from Layla. Isaac is ahead of us, not listening. I'm saying all this before I can take it back.

'In the final lines of the paper, I suggested that the atavism, the mutation which EK and the others had, could be controlled. Not by nature, but by *us*.

'Elias told me that I hadn't thought through the implications of what I had written, but that wasn't true. I had thought about it, almost every day. I dreamt about it sometimes. But I never imagined it would happen . . . I thought we'd be in control.'

I see an image of Elias standing in my office with a look of pity on his face. Layla makes a noise as if she's about to say something but doesn't. I gaze at her, and she looks down at the ground until she's ready to talk again.

'Why did the government shut down your research?' she says.

'What do you mean?' I ask.

'If it was just your idea, why did they get rid of everyone else?'

I think about my answer carefully.

'Maybe they were trying to work out what to do. They might have wanted us back at one stage, but it never happened. I only heard about one other scientist working on the Atavism Programme: a geneticist, Lucas Philipps, a professor from TEU Four. They needed people, but just not us. Maybe they didn't think we'd be able to do what they wanted.'

Neither of us speaks for a few minutes, until Layla breaks the silence with two words.

'Artificial selection?'

'Yes,' I say.

We keep walking and my mind wanders. I think about the hour before my final lecture, two hours before our research ended, when Elias came to see me in my office. I was pacing around the room, my paper in my hand, mouthing the words to myself. I wanted it memorised, not just learnt.

'Got a minute?' Elias said.

I stopped pacing.

'Yes, sure.'

There was an awkwardness, hanging over us from when we'd argued about the final part of the paper. He came a few feet into the room and stood still, his hands in his pockets, his head slightly tilted to one side.

'I'm sorry about the other day,' he said. 'Things got a little heated.'

'It's okay.'

'I'm nervous about this, and I said things I didn't mean.'

'I'm nervous too,' I said.

He didn't reply straight away, letting the tension re-build.

'But are you?'

'What do you mean?'

'You have no idea what I've had to do, not really. I've told you some of it, but . . . Did you not think it's strange that you've not had to speak to anyone about your work?'

'No,' I said. 'That's what research is. It takes a long time. It's lonely.'

'But someone is paying for it. Wouldn't you expect them to talk to you?'

I didn't answer.

'Well, they haven't because I've been holding them back,' he said. 'This is government work; it's not private. We're accountable to people. People far more powerful than us. And they have wanted to know *exactly* what you've been working on. But I told them not to approach you, that I would relay everything. I knew you were doing things that no one else could have done, and that you shouldn't be interrupted, but I also knew that you wouldn't have coped if you were even *slightly* aware of the pressure we've been under. There have been periods of weeks, months sometimes, where we've barely spoken, but every week I have had to sit in a room full of politicians and explain what you've been doing. They have no idea about the science, so I can confuse them, send them off track, say that this is all part of the process. But there are only so many times I can do that, Hannah. They're not stupid; they can see through the lies. Did you not *once* think what your single-mindedness was doing to the people around you?'

'Why are you saying this?' I was trying and failing not to show my anger. 'You know how much work I've had to do. I've given everything to it.'

'We've all had to make sacrifices,' Elias said. 'I have no life other than this job. I can't sleep because I worry about what I'm going to say to the people paying for our research. I have no relationships other than with you, but at times, it hurts to be near you.'

'I . . .'

'And now, you want to put *this* in.' He pointed at the paper angrily. 'This section about *atavism*, without even thinking about what it could mean.'

'I have thought about it.'

'No, you haven't.'

'Elias . . .'

'Do you know what race suicide is?'

'What?' I said impatiently.

'Race suicide?' Elias said. 'At the beginning of the twentieth century, thanks in part to the industrial revolution, there was a huge amount of immigration to America. New industries needed workers, and they came in their hundreds of thousands. Mainly Catholics from Europe, but also people of other races and cultures. And this worried the people in charge. They believed their blood – mainly Protestant and white – was more pure than the immigrants' blood – Hispanic, black, Catholic – and they were concerned that these other races would breed so much that it would overwhelm and destroy the wealthy Protestant communities. Race suicide, they called it. "The greatest problem of the twentieth century", according to Teddy Roosevelt. So, how could they control it? Stop them breeding. Indiana was the first state to pass a compulsory sterilisation law, but other states followed. Of course, the fear was baseless, but that didn't stop one of the most powerful countries in the world from instigating a policy that aimed to stop the most marginalised groups in society from having children. Poor people, racial minorities, the disabled.'

'I know this story,' I said. 'Why are you telling me?'

'America invented a problem and tried to fix it with genetic control on a national scale. We have an actual problem, and what you're suggesting is that we can only fix it by finding people who have the right genes, people who can speak the Soundfield's language. And how do you ensure someone has the *right* genes? You select for them. You only let certain people breed. Eugenics, Hannah. That's what will happen.'

'I'm not suggesting that,' I said firmly.

'Then what are you suggesting?'

'I'm saying we wait. We wait for the atavism to appear in more children, and then we work it out from there.'

'That relies upon the people in charge having patience,' Elias said.

'But if what I'm saying is correct, then won't someone else work it out?'

'Yes,' he said, more calmly than before, 'but it would be them saying it, not us.'

CHAPTER THIRTY-TWO

After my final lecture, it didn't take long for the government to remove us from the building. I was sitting in my office when a guard came in. He didn't have a gun, but he grabbed my arm and pulled me out of the room. I objected and tried to call out for Freya, who I thought was in the lab next to my office. She didn't appear. The man took me down to the entrance and left me there with two others. One of them was a technician, and the other a junior member of Elias's team. I didn't know their names. I could see Elias through the glass in the front door. He said he would leave the research if I put in that last section, but he was waiting for me. I'd never been more grateful to see him. Someone came and escorted out the technician and the junior researcher leaving just me and two guards. They had guns now. I asked what was happening and where EK was, but they didn't speak to me. They weren't violent, but their silence was enough to make me feel ill. I don't know why they kept me there for so long, but they let me go eventually. They walked me out of the building, and I went to Elias and hugged him. For days afterwards I wondered if he would say something to me about our conversation and about the paper, but he never did.

We walk along the road for another two miles until we reach a small village with six houses, three on either side of the tarmac road. Isaac is walking next to me, Layla ahead of us. At one end of the village, there's a V-shaped patch of dead grass, and, at the other, a high stone wall. The houses all look empty. There are no lights on, no movement. Layla walks ahead and looks in through the window of the first house on the left, cupping her hands over her eyes to block out the moonlight. She moves away from the window and tries the front door. It swings open. Without saying anything, or looking back at us, she goes inside.

'Layla?' I walk to the door, push it open and see a dark hall leading to a kitchen at the back and doors coming off either side. I call out Layla's name again.

'In here,' she says. I follow her voice into a room on the right, Isaac following behind me, and see her sitting in an armchair in the corner, like the one Mum is sitting in right now. There's a sofa under the window and a wooden table in the centre, littered with dusty magazines.

'It looks like they just left, doesn't it?' Layla says. There are photos on the walls, but it's too dark to make out any details. I see the outlines of people, bodies but no faces. 'There aren't enough houses in the city for half the people, but these are empty,' she says. 'People are living in shipping containers, and this house could fit two families easily.'

'They must have been forced to move,' I say, looking through the dirty window. 'There's nothing here by the looks of it. They won't have survived without a train station.'

'When Sam and I were on the barge, playing our version of the house game, we'd sometimes look out over the sea and imagine the kinds of places we might live in when we got here. One of us would describe the hallway, then the other person would describe the living room, then the kitchen, and our bedrooms. In my room, I imagined a big double bed with a thick duvet and posters on the wall, my own TV, that sort of thing. We'd draw our little house and show it to Mama and Baba and we'd tell them where we'd all sleep. This isn't far off what we imagined,' she says, looking around the room.

'You can still have all this. You and Yara,' I say. Layla looks at me and laughs softly.

'Maybe. . . but I'm not sure I want it anymore.' She gets up, puts her bag over her shoulder and wipes her eyes. She walks past me.

'You have to make it work,' I say, and she stops. 'What I've told you, it has to mean something . . .'

'I know,' she says. 'It'll help us, I promise. I understand now.'

Isaac pulls at my top.

'Can I see?' he signs.

'He wants to look around the house, I think.'

'We're close now,' Layla says, 'we should go.'

We walk in darkness as we leave the village – first in the shadow of the stone wall, then under the cover of tall trees lining the road. Layla is on my right, Isaac on my left, holding my hand. At the end of the road, we move onto a footpath, which takes us up a steep incline, and I can feel the last of my energy being taken from me.

'We should get a good view from up here,' Layla says, breathing heavily. 'We'll be able to see Elias's woods, I hope.'

Isaac is slowing. He looks at me as though he wants to be carried, but I can't do it now.

'Not long,' I say.

The path is flanked by low-lying walls, separating us from steep, muddy fields on the other side. I stop to catch my breath and Isaac stops with me, but Layla moves on ahead. She reaches the top of the hill, and stands with her hands on her sides, looking out in the opposite direction.

'Come on,' she shouts.

'Ready to go?' I sign to Isaac. He nods, and we climb up the last of the path and join Layla at the top. The landscape opens out in front of us. A vast patchwork of fields, hills, woods and streams, stamped into the ground. Some fields have been let go, gone wild, and overtaken by nature, but others are being worked, growing the food that will survive the heat of the day. Wheat, mainly. The air is blowing gently through the valley, passing the Soundfield's music through the fields, water, and earth below, creating a chamber of sound, waves resonating and interfering and combining to create new music, not just reflecting the sound, but changing it, like light diffracted.

'There,' Layla says. She points towards a thick forest at the bottom of the valley. 'It's in there. You'll have arrived from the north when you came.' About a mile above the woods is a small town with a few houses, a church and hall, and a station. There are lights on in some of the windows; people are still clinging on.

'Do you remember where it is?' Layla asks.

'Yeah,' I say. I see Elias and I walking through the woods at night, holding hands. I see his timber house, nestled in the trees. I see myself lying on my back, picking at some wood that was rotting from the inside. Elias was next to me, asleep. His bed was too small for both of us, so my left shoulder was pushed up against the wall. I remember leaving the room to get a glass of water. I couldn't sleep in the heat. I remember standing, naked, looking out of the living room window onto the huge clearing in the wood, bathed in sunlight.

'I'll go with you, to make sure your safe,' Layla says.

'Thank you,' I say, 'for everything . . . I'd like to see you again if I can. I'd like to meet Yara, too. So would Isaac.'

She looks at me with sad eyes, smiles and takes my hand. We wait for a few minutes more, looking at the view, breathing the air, listening to the Hum.

'You lead the way,' Layla says.

*

Layla and I walk down into the valley as a pair, with Isaac running ahead of us. He skips down the steeper parts, jumping over rocks in the path, hiding behind bushes as he waits for us to catch up. At the bottom of the hill, he reaches a gate. We're twenty feet behind and I tell him to stay where he is. The gate sits in the middle of a long stone wall that runs along the southern edge of the woods. Beyond the wall, there's almost no light. The trees have taken it. Isaac gets bored and starts climbing up the gate, clumsily, but stops before jumping off. He's at the top, one leg on either side. He's looking straight up.

'Isaac?' I say. He doesn't move. Twice in one night?

The Hum drops out again, and another Call appears. A shorter one than before, made up of just three pitches: one long, sliding cry then two staccato notes. But Isaac doesn't sing this time. Instead, he silently moves his hands. His left hand is pressed against his chest, curled into a fist with his thumb pointing towards his chin. He's also made a fist with his right hand, and is sliding it up against his left hand in a repeated motion, from his belly to his head. Even after the Call has gone, he repeats the sign over and over, first to the sky, then to me.

'What's he saying?' Layla asks.

'Danger. It means danger.' I run to Isaac and look beyond the gate to see if anyone, or anything, is there. 'What do you mean, danger?' I ask him. 'Where's the danger?'

'I don't know,' he signs back.

'We have to go,' Layla says, her voice urgent.

'What?'

She runs in our direction and climbs over the gate.

'We have to leave now. Follow me.'

I clamber over the gate and lift Isaac onto the dry grass. Layla starts walking, fast.

'Layla?' I take Isaac's hand. 'Layla?' She doesn't look back and her walk turns into a run.

'Follow me,' she calls out.

I see her take the gun out of her back pocket. Isaac and I run into the woods after her, and the light reduces almost to nothing. She stops, glances back, and starts running again. She's twenty metres ahead of us, more. We try to keep up, but Isaac's small strides hold us back. I feel the leaves and branches hitting my bare skin as I run. Running is easy as a child. Isaac makes a noise, as if he wants to say something, but I'm holding his hand, so he can't sign.

'Keep going,' I say to Isaac. 'Layla!' I shout.

'Quiet and keep moving,' she replies. Layla moves out of sight, and I lose myself for a second, but I keep pushing on. I reach the top of small mound. I look left and I see something through the trees. People, maybe. Black marks beyond the woods. I think of the man who tried to take Isaac from our flat. I think of the officials who took Ellie and David's son. I think of the figure in the black UV suit and respirator who was staring up at the barn. I search for Layla. She's stopped at a clearing. She's holding the gun in front of her. 'How does she . . . ?' I say, under my breath. We move down into a ditch and up the other side. Layla runs across the clearing to a small house. We reach the edge of the wood and Layla waves us forward. 'Come on,' I say to Isaac. We run across the gap and Layla knocks on the back door. We're on the porch, catching our breath. I drop down to check on Isaac and ask if he's okay. He nods back at me.

'Layla . . .' I say. 'What was that? What's going on?'

The door opens, and out of the corner of my eye, I see her embrace the man in the doorway. I stand and turn. Layla drops her arms but doesn't look back at me. She walks into the house.

The man gazes at me, and smiles.

'Hello, Hannah.'

CHAPTER THIRTY-THREE

I take Isaac's hand and lead him slowly into the cabin. Elias shuts the door behind us. Layla goes to the kitchen and puts the gun down on the side. She has her back to me still. She won't look at me.

'What's going on?' I ask her again.

'Hannah. It's good to see you,' Elias says, and he goes to hug me, but I don't hug him back, nor do I let go of Isaac. I'm holding him as tight as my hand will let me.

Elias steps back and looks at Isaac. He smiles.

'Is this your son?'

I don't answer, and Elias crouches down. He furrows his brow slightly as he looks into Isaac's eyes.

'What's happening?' I say.

He continues to stare at Isaac.

'EK?' he says. 'You're EK, aren't you?'

'He doesn't remember that name,' I say coldly. 'He's called Isaac now.'

'Why is he with you, Hannah?'

'No. Not now. Tell me what's happening.'

Elias gets up and walks towards Layla. 'It's okay. Why don't you sit down?'

'I don't want to,' I say, trying to sound strong. 'Tell me.'

Layla goes over to Elias and rests her head on his shoulder. Reaching up on her toes, she kisses his cheek. She whispers something into his ear, and he squeezes her arm. Elias looks at me.

'Layla is my wife, Hannah.'

My skin is cold, like I'm deep in icy water, but Theo isn't here to pull me out this time. I look from Elias to his wife, but she doesn't look back. I want to catch her eye so she can see how I'm feeling but she won't look at me. I'm dead to her.

'Layla?'

'We met through Babylon,' Elias says.

'Layla. Is this true? You . . . you saw me on the train. How can . . . ?'

It wasn't an accident. It was planned. She found me. She was waiting for me.

'I'll explain, Hannah,' Elias says.

'No, let her explain. Let Layla explain why she's been lying to me.'

Layla is behind the counter in the kitchen, her back to me, not moving, not speaking.

'So, what is this?' I say. 'Layla, what is this?'

Isaac pulls at my top with his free hand, and I look at him.

'It's okay,' I say, trying to stay calm but failing.

'I'm sorry,' Layla says. 'Elias, I can't do this. I thought I could, but I can't.'

'Do what?' I ask her. I'm losing control now. I need to know. Without looking back, Layla goes into the bedroom and shuts the door.

'Hannah, please sit,' Elias says. 'There's a lot to explain.'

'No, we're leaving. This was a mistake. I shouldn't have come here.'

I turn around and take Isaac to the door.

'You can't leave, Hannah. They'll arrest you and they'll take Isaac.'

I stop. Did Isaac know? *Danger*, he had signed.

'They're here because of you,' Elias says. 'Police officers, Atavism officials, I don't know how many. They've been here for weeks, only two or three of them to begin with, but more have arrived recently.'

I don't say anything. I'm trying to line everything up in my head, but it's falling apart. Pieces are breaking off. I try to catch them, but they turn to sand when they touch my skin and flow through my fingers.

'They won't come for you, not whilst you're in the house. I'll explain, but you can't leave, not yet.'

There's a bookshelf on my right running the full length of the wall. I see the book I read the night I came here, a novel about a pandemic that killed most of the world's population. I remember putting it back and looking at the shelves. The image is different now; there's something new. Photos, six or seven of them sitting in front of the books. I pick up the one closest to me. It's a picture of Elias holding a little girl, no older than two.

'You have no idea how difficult it was to get that printed,' he says.

'This is Yara?' I say.

'Yes.'

'She's four now. She was born when we were still together?'

'Yes,' Elias says softly. 'I'm sorry.'

Yara has her mother's eyes, and her uncle's. Deep brown.

'Where is she, Elias?'

Elias starts a reply, then stops.

'She's been taken,' he says. 'She's been taken by the Programme.'

I put the photo down.

'Okay,' I say quietly. 'I'll listen.'

At the far end of the living room is a large window, made from a single pane. I remember thinking how out of place it was in this log cabin – modern design forced into old walls. When I was waiting for the sun to set last time I was here, I imagined smashing through the glass, and seeing it splinter around me: bursting into the light, shards flying outwards. I read somewhere that your brain sometimes imagines the worst scenario in any situation to stop it from happening, like when people used to drive, they would see their car veering off the road, or steering into oncoming traffic. But at that moment standing in front of the window, the thought of jumping through the glass didn't make me scared – it made me want to do it more than anything. To feel the light on my naked body, I thought, it would be worth the pain.

I'm looking out of that same window now, sitting on the sofa, Elias in the chair opposite me, and I still feel the same as I did all those years ago.

'Would you like some coffee?' Elias asks, pointing towards the pot on the table.

'No, thank you.'

Isaac is sitting cross-legged on the floor with his two books out in front of him, one on dinosaurs, one on space. He can't decide which to read. Elias and I are both looking at him.

'Does he want something else?' he says, looking at me.

'He can understand you.'

'Of course. It's been a while. Isaac, I have other books,' he says, gesturing towards the shelves behind him. 'You're welcome to take a look.' Isaac gets up and stares at me.

'Go on,' I sign, 'it's okay.' He skips to the bookcase and starts tapping the tops of the books on the bottom shelf with his fingers, tilting his head to read the spines. Elias looks at him with fascination.

'How old is he now?' Elias asks.

'Six.'

'He's grown,' he says with a smile. 'I don't suppose he remembers me . . .'

'Actually, I will have some coffee,' I say.

Elias pours me a cup, and I take a sip. He leans forward in his chair and clasps his hands together as if in prayer.

'You remember what it was like, Hannah. The pressure. Our government were murdering refugees, executing innocent people, and we were working for them. I wanted our research to continue but it wasn't enough. Even before we found EK – Isaac – I started going to meetings, helping at shelters. Refugee support groups, small gatherings, that sort of thing. Nothing public. I was always careful not to be seen. I met Layla at a shelter.'

'So, what was your plan?'

'What do you mean?'

'Were you just going to keep Yara away from me?'

'You make it sound as though it's all my fault,' he says, losing his temper slightly. 'We never spent any time together, Hannah. You were obsessed with your work . . . That was all you cared about. I understood that, I did, but I needed someone who understood *me*. I'm sorry I didn't tell you, I should have ended things between us . . .'

Elias stops and looks down at the table.

'We didn't plan on having Yara, if that's what you mean . . .' he says, 'but she was so beautiful.' He looks at Isaac. 'I always wanted children.'

'You never told me that,' I say.

'Well, we always talked about work,' he says softly, looking back at me. 'That's all we had.'

'Has she passed the tests?' I ask.

'She will,' he says. 'She was musical, even as a baby. I would sit on that sofa and put on records from the old days and her face would light up.' He smiles widely. 'By the time she was two, she was already playing the piano, making up little songs. You were always a better judge of the children than me, Hannah. I thought that Yara was like Layla and her family: musical, but not like Isaac. Layla's father played the harp, I think, and her mother sang. But it wasn't just that. Yara had it . . . she had the mutation in her *FOXP2* gene. She *has* the mutation. I never had her tested, but I think I always knew. I should have kept her safe, kept her here for longer . . .'

He trails off and looks at Isaac, who has taken a book off the shelf – a photographic journal of the Artemis missions.

'It happened near Babylon's place,' Elias says. 'Layla sometimes takes Yara there. They have a whole floor for children – books, toys, everything. They were out on the street one night – Layla was distracted doing something, buying food I think – and Yara wandered off and started singing. By the time Layla got to her, she was already being processed by Atavism Officials. Layla came back to me, she ran back, and she was . . . I've never seen her like that, Hannah. You've known her for a few days, but I've known her for years. She's strong, far stronger than me, but she had nothing in her that night. She couldn't even keep her body upright. Her screams were so loud. I keep trying to erase it from my mind, trying to get it out of my dreams, but it's stuck there, like a virus.'

He breathes in deeply, steeling himself to carry on.

'I thought I could do something, with my connections. I thought I would be listened to. So, I went back.'

In my mind, I can see the entrance to the lab. The prefab building, the rows of single-glazed windows, the squared-off roof, my office, my desk, my work, my home.

'They had put more guards in place, a fence, barbed wire. It was like a prison camp. I went to the entrance and told them who I was, and that I wanted to speak to someone. I waited there for four hours, but no one came. Maybe they were hoping I'd just leave, but I wasn't going anywhere. My daughter was in there. Someone came out eventually, and they took me into an office just off the main corridor. I'd never been there before. It had no windows. Another person joined them. I didn't recognise either of them. I tried to be as rational and calm as I could, but seeing Layla like that changed me. I said I'd teach, or try to recruit some of my old colleagues, or come and work at the Programme again. I would have done anything to get her back . . .'

He stops and looks directly at me.

'Hannah, being a parent. It changes you. Everything becomes about them, not about you. You feel that, don't you? I can see it in the way you are with Isaac, I can see it in your face, and your eyes. You have it. That drive to keep them alive, that thing burnt into you that will make you do anything to protect your child . . .'

'What did they want?'

'They wanted you, Hannah.'

'And if I go back,' I say, 'they'll give you Yara.'

'Yes,' he says in a broken voice.

CHAPTER THIRTY-FOUR

We sit in silence for a while, like the silence we used to share. Isaac turns a page in his book, and I see a wide picture of the lunar surface. Orange bands of light radiate outwards from the grey rock. I imagine what it's like up there now, above the Field, above the world, suspended in the cold.

'What did they say?' I ask.

'They wouldn't tell me much,' Elias says, pouring himself more coffee. 'All I know is they've hit a wall. They're desperate. You've seen all the adverts, Representatives everywhere, spot inspections. Philipps is in charge now. He was always too self-serving to be a good scientist.'

'You know him?'

'From my undergraduate days.'

'Why do they want me?'

He looks at me and laughs kindly.

'You were the only one who achieved anything.'

'Anyone could have done what I did . . .'

'You know that's not true.'

I stare at Elias and we hold each other's gaze for a while. Isaac turns another page in his book. I glance over at him. I can't see what he's looking at.

'Do they know about him?' I ask softly.

Elias puts down his cup. He looks at Isaac with me.

'I don't know,' he says. 'All they said was that they wanted you.'

Isaac turns onto his back and holds the book above his head, his legs hanging over the armrest.

'I did a day shift with him once,' Elias says.

'I don't remember that.'

'Freya had to be somewhere, so I stepped in. It was before the other children came. I remember trying to get him to brush his teeth, but he refused. Freya told me the next day that you had a special tune which you sang together before he could do it?'

'Sorry. I should have told you about that,' I say.

'In the end, I just gave up,' he says, laughing. 'I wasn't exactly a natural. But I'm learning now.'

I see Isaac standing on an upturned bin, reaching for the sink, brushing his teeth with bright blue toothpaste, foam all around his mouth.

'What happened?' Elias asks. 'Where are his parents?'

I breathe in deeply, memories turning in my mind. This is a story that I've spent years rehearsing in my head. I've already worked out the things to include and the things I have to leave out. But I never imagined I'd be saying any of it to Elias. I thought I'd be reciting it to a row of faceless officials, minutes before being told I was going to die.

'Do you remember the night our research ended, when I was being held inside?' I say. 'I saw you through the front door?'

'Yes,' he says. 'I thought they were never going to let you out.'

I look away from Elias.

'I know I should have been thinking about us, or about our research, but all I could think about was Isaac. I'd seen him just before my lecture. He was reading a book – something about tigers. All I could think about was what was happening to him. I asked one of the guards, but he wouldn't tell me. I thought about running upstairs to his room and carrying him outside, but they would have shot me. His parents had trusted us, they'd trusted me . . . Before I joined your team, I thought my life was going to be about work, and nothing else, and I was okay with that. I wanted that. But then I met Isaac. When he first arrived, he couldn't sit still, even for a minute . . . I remember that so vividly, the way his head would dart around when we tried to put the cap on for the EEG. Then he'd start dancing when we played the Calls, flinging his legs around. Freya had to hold him still. He had this way of making me laugh. He still does . . . Isaac wasn't my son, but it sometimes felt like he was.'

I can feel Elias staring at me. But I can't look at him, not yet.

'After things ended, I kept going back to the lab. There's a small street near the entrance that looks onto the front of the building. I would go there and wait for an hour or two, staring at the window to the playroom. For weeks, I looked and no one appeared. I don't know what I was expecting. But then, one night, the light went on in the room, and Isaac was at the window. It was a miracle he saw me. It was raining and there was only one light in the street, above a door, and so I stood in the doorway and waved at him. When he saw me, he signed *hello*. You know the way that he does it, like he's saluting you . . . I moved closer, and we spoke. Our sign language wasn't as good as it is now, but it was enough. I hadn't exactly worked out what I was going to do, but . . . you remember the liquid nitrogen storage? How the lock on the door was always broken?'

Elias nods.

'There's a window at the back of the room that leads onto an alleyway. I told Isaac to look for the door on the ground floor with the big yellow sign on it, to go in there and find the window. I said I'd be waiting outside. I didn't know if he'd be caught, or if he even knew where he was going. For two hours, I waited in the pouring rain. Then I heard a noise and Isaac was there. I couldn't believe it. He unlocked the window from the inside, and I lifted him out.'

I can't help but smile thinking of that moment. The way he threw his arms around my neck. The way he pushed his cheek into mine. He made a noise like a laugh, or a whimper, like he was trying to speak to me. I closed my eyes tightly and listened for a word.

'My plan was to take him home, and to tell his parents to

leave the city,' I say. 'I'd taken him home a few times, so I knew the way. It didn't take long to get there. We moved quickly, and I carried him when he got sleepy. He was so light back then I could almost hold him with one arm.'

Isaac turns another page. He lands on a picture of the command module. A close-up of one panel shows it covered in lunar soil. He looks at me.

'What's this?' he signs, pointing at the picture.

'The buttons?' I sign.

'No, around them,' he signs.

'That's dust,' I say.

'From the moon?' he signs.

'Yes,' I say.

Isaac nods and looks around the room. He picks up his book and takes it to an armchair in the corner. He sits down, opens the book into his lap, and I look back at Elias. I lower my voice for this next part.

'As soon as we arrived at his parent's house, I felt something was wrong. It was like there was no one inside. Not that they had left, but that something had happened . . . I knocked on the front door, and it swayed open. There was a smell. I told Isaac to wait in the hall and I closed the door behind him. I called out, but there was no answer. I went upstairs, into the bedroom, and turned the light on. I was nearly sick. They were lying in bed. Their throats had been cut.'

I remember seeing the outlines of their bodies under the soiled sheet. They were holding hands.

'What did you do?' Elias asks.

'I went downstairs, took Isaac's hand and walked away.' I wipe my eyes. Isaac looks at me.

'Are you okay?' he signs.

'I'm okay,' I sign back.

'That's when EK became Isaac,' I say to Elias.

'Did anyone know what you were doing?' he asks.

'No,' I say. 'Not even Mum. And I don't think anyone saw me.'

'Have you told him about his parents?'

'No. How can I? It's all so . . . We brought him there, Elias. His parents are dead because . . .'

'They chose to send Isaac to us.'

'I know, but he's too young to understand. And it's too late now.'

'Weren't you worried he'd be found?'

'Every day,' I say, looking back at Isaac. 'But I had no choice. He's my son.'

Isaac is running his fingers along some text. He looks at me, picks the book up and props it against his knee.

'What does the first word mean?' he signs.

The page has a diagram showing the flight path of a rocket. The text reads *Artemis III: Humanity's Return to the Moon*.

'Artemis,' I say. 'It was the name of the mission.'

'But what does it mean?' he signs.

'I don't know.'

'Artemis was a Greek goddess,' Elias says. 'The goddess of the wild and care of children.'

Elias looks at me and smiles.

'It's nearly sunrise. We should get some sleep,' he says, pushing himself up. 'You and Isaac can have the spare room.'

He gestures towards a door coming off the kitchen and walks to the window, looking out over the flattened earth. The air is brightening.

'Do you ever think about the lecture you gave me?' he asks without turning back to me.

'Sometimes,' I say.

'You remember that poem I quoted?'

'The Whitman?'

'*When I heard the learn'd astronomer*. It's my favourite.'

I call Isaac towards me. He closes his book, leaving it on the armchair, and climbs up onto my lap. I wrap my arms around him. He nestles into my chest.

> '*When the proofs, the figures, were ranged in columns*
>   *before me,*
> *When I was shown the charts and diagrams, to add,*
>   *divide, and measure them,*
> *When I sitting heard the astronomer where he*
>   *lectured with much applause in the lecture-room,*
> *How soon unaccountable I became tired and sick,*
> *Till rising and gliding out I wander'd off by myself,*
> *In the mystical moist night-air, and from time to*
>   *time,*
> *Look'd up in perfect silence at the stars.*'

He stops and waits for the words to dissolve.

'I could only do so much, Hannah. When you're looking at a thing from a particular point of view, you only see what your mind wants you to see. I was thinking about the Soundfield as something physical – particles, molecules, air – something observable, knowable. I thought that if we could just get more data, we could understand it. But you, Hannah. You saw it as something metaphysical, something beyond what we could understand from an empirical perspective.'

'I saw what I wanted to see, too. We all did.'

'No. You weren't like everyone else. You had an instinct. You remember that night at the lake?' I see us lying on the beach in the darkness. 'You thought it was what I had said, about the Field sounding like us, sounding *human*, that led you to your conclusion. But you were already there. I was just a catalyst. I'm the lecturer, obsessed with figures, and data, and facts. But you, Hannah, you're the poet, the dreamer, looking at the stars.'

I send Isaac to our room and pick up my bag. Elias watches Isaac until he disappears behind the door.

'Sleep well, Elias,' I say.

'Sleep well,' he replies with a warm smile. He knows that this is the last time we'll be together.

Isaac is sitting on a small single bed in the corner. Facing the bed is a sofa, where I'll sleep if I need to. I sit down next to Isaac and put my bag on the floor by my feet. I get out some raisins and crackers, Isaac's other book, a piece of paper and the blue crayon. Isaac takes the crayon and starts drawing a blue arc from the left edge of the paper to the right, adding to the drawing he started in the small room in the station where I first learnt Layla's name. Isaac colours in the space underneath the arc, moving up and down with his crayon, vibrating, resonating.

'The Soundfield?' I sign.

'The Soundfield,' he signs back.

'Isaac . . .' I stop. I've never asked him this before, not because I've been scared to talk to him about it, but because I've always thought I'd have the chance when he was older. I've imagined a scene twenty years in the future. Isaac is visiting me, and he's telling me about his life, his relationships, his job, if he has one. In a quiet moment, I ask him about the Soundfield. He looks at me knowingly, as if he's been waiting for this conversation, and starts signing. When I first met Isaac he was so young. I tried to ask him what it was like for him to listen to the Soundfield, but he could never really tell me the truth. Not because he would lie, but because he only had language for the childish parts of his experience, taken from the words that we'd learnt together. All language fails in some way. How can you say what it feels like to love someone? How can you say what it's like to feel guilty? It's all messy, distorted, memories played over and over in your mind, burnt out like a video tape replayed too many times. But maybe as an adult, Isaac could finally tell me what it was like, not what the phonemes, or Hums, or Calls actually meant – that didn't matter anymore – but what it really *felt* like to hear them.

'Isaac, you remember earlier, when you signed after hearing the Call?' He nods. 'Why did you say *danger*?'

'What do you mean?' he signs, going straight back to drawing once he's finished the action.

'Why that word?'

'That's what I wanted to say,' he signs with the crayon still in his hand.

'Is that because that's what the Soundfield said?'

'No, it's what I said.'

He makes a small noise, like he's trying to say something, but no words come out. Instead, he just looks at me, his eyes wide, checking to see if he's given the right answer. I smile and hold his cheek in my hand and kiss his head.

'It's okay,' I say. He scatters a few raisins across the paper, picks one up and starts chewing as he finishes a shape in the bottom right-hand corner of the drawing.

I'm colourblind asking what it's like to see the world in colour. I'm in the shadows asking my son what it's like to live in the light.

CHAPTER THIRTY-FIVE

Isaac is asleep, the completed picture at his legs, moving with him whenever he shuffles in his dreams. I pick the drawing up and sit back against the wall next to the bed, tucking my knees into my chest. The outer edges of the blind are glowing a warm orange and light spills into the room. I look at the picture in my hand. There's a box-shaped house in the bottom-right corner, an arc of blue above, and a ring of stick-trees encircling the box, rings in rings, joining outside the frame. Inside the box are four stick people. Around the people are what look like random marks, scribbles. Isaac stirs and moves onto his side, clasping his hands together under his cheek, his knees tucked into his chest like mine. I look at the sheets rising and falling with his breath, and I imagine him on the day he was born – crying, reaching for his mother, blind.

*

I sit there for what feels like hours, watching him sleep. When the sun is brightest in the sky, the outline around the blind becomes so strong that it burns, and I wait for flames to engulf the room.

On my right is a circular mat covered with interlocking shapes that look like they were once filled with colour – blues, pinks and greens – but have now faded. On top is a small plastic chair, a few books, a toy car, a bear with one missing eye. One missing child.

I can hear Layla and Elias arguing in the next room. Only Isaac is asleep in the house. He turns over. I notice Sasha's pin is still attached to his shirt.

The sun has cooled and the room with it. More hours have passed. I stroke Isaac's hair. He makes a small noise and half opens his eyes. He looks at me, sleepy, confused.

'Hello,' I say in a whisper.

He blinks and lifts his hands out from under the sheet.

'Is it evening?' he signs, then stretches out his arms.

'No,' I sign. 'Not yet.'

'Why are you awake?' he signs. His hands fall back down on the bed with a small thud.

'To see you,' I sign.

He opens his eyes fully. I look directly into them and stroke his cheek.

'Do you remember the first time I met you?' I whisper.

He shakes his head and the sheets rustle.

'Well, I was nervous to meet you. You were so young, and I wanted to get it right. I remember your parents brought you into my room and introduced me to you. They were either side of you, holding your hands, and do you know what you did?'

He shakes his head again.

'You ran up to me and gave me a hug.'

'I hugged you?'

'Yes,' I say. I wipe my cheek. 'You hugged me, and I said hello for the first time.'

'Where are they?' he signs.

I look down and bite my lip.

'I don't know,' I say.

Isaac holds his left hand out towards me and spreads his fingers. I put my fingers in between his and we lock hands. He's still so small. What we will he be like when he's older? I lean in, pressing my forehead against his. I smell him. Sweet, musty. We stay like this for a while until Isaac pulls his head away and stares into my eyes. He lifts his left hand, points his thumb, index finger and little finger upwards and, with his palm facing towards me, moves his hand from left to right, back and forth.

'I love you,' he signs.

He's asleep. I'm standing at the door to the bedroom, looking at his picture in the dim evening light. On each of the faces of the four stick people are two circles for eyes, three small lines

for the nose and eyebrows, and one semi-circle for the smile.
Around each of the figures are marks. But they're not random.
They're musical notes, wrapping each person in song. I lift my
eyes from the picture and look at my son for the last time.

In the kitchen, I turn the drawing over and write my message
to Elias and Layla. I put my name at the bottom and place
it down in the silence.

I'm at the back door. I glance right at the rows of books. I
remember the dream I once had where Elias and Isaac were
playing together by the lake. They skipped stones across the
surface of the water and waved at me from the island. I used
to think that scene could never be real. A lie or a half-truth.
But I can see it now. I see Elias and Isaac reading space books
together before bed. I see Isaac learning to swim in the night
air. I see him arguing with his sister over who gets to use the
crayons. I see him hugging his new mother when he's upset.
That life can be real. I can make it real.

I hear footsteps behind me.
    'Hannah?'
I don't look back.
    'Where are you going?' Layla says calmly. I let go of the
door handle.
    'It doesn't matter,' I say.
    'I know you're angry.'
    'You lied to me.'

'It wasn't like that,' she says.

I turn around.

'I didn't go to your lecture all those years ago. And before we met, I knew about your research and about Atavism, but that doesn't mean I didn't want to hear it from you. The way you speak about what you've done – you shouldn't be ashamed of it. You're not responsible for what happened.'

'You have no right to tell me how to feel.'

'No, I don't. But it wasn't all a lie. Babylon, my parents, Samir, Yara. All of that was true. I never lied about my daughter; I just couldn't talk about her.'

'You manipulated me.'

'You would have done the same. You *did* the same.'

'That was different.'

'How?'

'I didn't hurt anyone getting Isaac out. It was just him and me. I would have found another way to help Yara.'

'There was no other way. Elias tried.'

'It's my fault. I shouldn't have trusted you.'

'You have to trust me.'

'Why?' I say.

'Because I couldn't do it. I was going to hand you over to the Programme when we arrived here. That was my plan, to give you up without you seeing Elias. They're waiting there now, at the edge of the wood, that's what we agreed with them. Elias knew you, but I didn't, so I thought I could exchange you for Yara. He tried to stop me, but I had to get her back.'

She pauses. Her face is half in shadow, half in light.

'But then I met you, and I met Isaac. I spent three days with you, and I couldn't do it. I couldn't save my daughter.' She inhales sharply and her breath stutters. 'You have to trust me because I thought there was nothing I wouldn't do to bring her back. But I was wrong.'

I don't say anything because I can't.

'I hope I'll see you again, someday,' she says.

The room begins to darken, and the Hum reduces to nothing, carried away by the evening wind, like a deadening sound.

'Where are you going to go?' I say.

'North, I think. Elias has family up there.'

I look at the closed door to the room where my son is sleeping.

'Look after him,' I say, my voice thin and cracking.

'I will.'

I'm outside, my hood up, shielded from the setting sun. I look back at the house. The back door is closed, and the house seems to dissolve into the trees, like it's being reclaimed by nature, engulfed by earth.

I walk ahead, through the clearing, and see light filtering through the black trees. I put my hand against a trunk and feel the bark, and I hear my brother's laughter as he runs across the sand. I walk on and footsteps appear beside me. Rough outlines in the dry ground. Small steps. I put my left hand down to my side and let the leaves brush against my skin. I breathe in the air. It's rich and sweet, made electric by the dying light. In front of me is another clearing, smaller than the one I just left. I walk towards it and put my bag down at its edge. The woods towards the West are thinner and I see the last of the sun disappearing into the horizon. I uncover my face, put my hood down, and let the warmth hit me. All the blue has gone from the light, lost in the space between me and our star, dispersed by the air. All that's left is a rich orange. I remember holidays when I was young when I could let the sun beat down on me. I'm seven, swimming in the ocean, my body cold and my face warm, trapped inside an endless summer.

In the distance, hiding in the white-hot edges of the sun's glow, are trucks, men, weapons.

The sun disappears into the Earth, and darkness grows out from the world, covering the sky.

'I'm ready,' I say to myself, and I take a step forward to the place I have to go to. As I leave the clearing, the air seems to thin. Then, as if turned off in the sky, the Soundfield's Hum fades to nothing. It's quiet. I hear the wind pushing through the trees. I hear birds around me. I hear the sound of water breaking on the shore and I see footsteps in the sand following me on either side. When I reach the edge of the wood, the door to a black vehicle is opened for me. My hands are bound, and I'm pushed towards the car. But before I get in, I stop, and in the moist night air, look up in perfect silence at the stars.

EPILOGUE

'So, this one is "how are you?"'

The girl walking next to Isaac pushes her fists together, with her thumbs pointing upwards, and then rolls her hands forward. She repeats the motion, and Isaac copies her, and nods.

'Teach me another one,' the girl says. 'What about "I'm hungry"?'

Isaac nods again and cups his hands into a C-shape with his palms facing his chest. Starting from his neck, he moves his hands downwards towards his stomach in one smooth motion. The girl imitates the action, repeating it three times.

'Like this?' she says. 'Mama, I learnt a new one!'

The woman, who's walking a few feet ahead of the girl with an older man, looks back.

'Well done, Yara, now leave Isaac be for a while.'

'Okay,' she says. Yara leans over to Isaac and whispers in his ear. 'You can teach me another one later. You promise?'

Isaac puts his right index finger to his lips, then stretches out his right hand and places it flat on top of the thumb-side of his clenched left fist.

'Is that another one?' Yara says quietly. 'Does it mean you *promise*?'

Isaac smiles.

'Thank you,' she whispers.

Layla looks back again, and Yara runs ahead to catch up with her mother. She waves for Isaac to follow her. He runs ahead too, his small rucksack rocking from side to side as he hurries, his strap hitting against the circular metal pin attached to his shirt.

They're now walking as one unit, in a line of four.

'Do you remember where we're going, Yara?' Elias says.

'To Uncle's house?' she replies.

'Yes, that's right. You've never met him before, but he'll look after us.'

The path opens in front of them into a wide, flat plain. It's as if the landscape has been pushed downwards, the trees pulled to one side, and the hills levelled. The grass is brown like burnt sugar.

'Not far now,' Elias says to the group.

Yara holds out her left hand, and Isaac accepts it. His hands are small, hers too, but they hold each other tight to avoid slipping away. The Hum is loud in this open world, skirting across the dry ground, and Isaac hums the pitch to himself, two octaves up. Yara notices and joins in, adding a major third above Isaac's pitch, and Layla finishes the chord by singing a minor third above Yara. Elias laughs.

'You know I can't sing, that's not fair,' he says.

Layla moves up a tone, then down again to her starting pitch. She repeats her small melody, and Yara matches her movement, creating translucent chords on top of Isaac's note. Isaac stops when he runs out of breath, and the chord fades, leaving only the Soundfield's music, and for a moment, he thinks he can hear an echo of their chord in the sky, but it might have been in his head. Elias and Layla pull out in front and Isaac lets go of Yara's hand. He stops and she stops too. She looks back at Isaac.

'Mama, Baba,' she says.

They turn around and see Isaac standing a few feet behind them, staring up at the sky. 'Isaac?' Layla says. Yara looks up with Isaac, and for a few seconds no one moves, nothing moves. But then, a song appears: a cascading, ancient melody which goes on for several minutes. Isaac wasn't there when this was first heard, when the Soundfield appeared out of the earth, but he's here now. He used to sing along to this melody – at dawn, just before sleep, when his mum would sometimes hold him – but he doesn't sing this time.

As the last note fades, Isaac lowers his head. He sees Elias, who has tears in his eyes.

'Come on,' Elias says warmly.

Isaac walks slowly towards Elias and Layla and takes his sister's hand on the way past. They reach their parents and continue on to the edge of the flat land, walking in the last of the shadow before the sun rises, heading towards a new home.